Terri,
Always Ke...
your hope ♡
Lindi B

Rich in Hope

Lindi Peterson

ISBN: 978-1-942419-00-6

Cover design: Lynnette Bonner
indiecoverdesign@blogspot.com
Cover images © Dreamstime.com: 32737301 10225327 8542973
Editor: Emily Sewell

DEDICATION

To Caleb Christopher. Our very own Christmas blessing.

"The Lord bless you and keep you; The Lord make His face shine upon you, and be gracious to you; The Lord lift up His countenance upon you, and give you peace." Numbers 6: 24-26 NKJV

Other Novels by Lindi Peterson

Her Best Catch

Summer's Song

Richness in Faith Trilogy
Rich in Love
Rich in Faith
(coming February 2015)

www.lindipeterson.com

Isaiah 61:3 To console those who mourn in Zion, To give them beauty for ashes, The oil of joy for mourning, The garment of praise for the spirit of heaviness; That they may be called trees of righteousness, The planting of the Lord that He may be glorified. NKJV

BEAUTIFUL

I MADE A LOT of money when I was beautiful.

But I'm not beautiful anymore.

So now I'm broke.

The cab door squeaks as I open it before the cab driver, Malcolm, his identification read, can come around. Patience is not a virtue that I possess at the moment.

Pointing toward the trunk, I indicate to Malcolm that I don't need his help exiting the cab, but I do need his help with my bags.

With a scowl, even though he's wearing a festive Santa hat, he complies.

My gaze travels to the unfamiliar million-dollar plus house I'll be inhabiting for the next few weeks. The sage green stucco one story sits in the center of the cul-de-sac, a silhouette against the dawn.

Quiet.

Alone.

Like me.

At least for a couple of days.

The trunk slams. Trying to breathe normally, I clench the cab fare in my hand, refusing Malcolm's offer to help take the luggage to the front door. As the early morning breeze kicks up, my blonde hair swirls around me.

I wish the long, luxurious locks would wind around my face and head, like a tall turban, and cover the hideous markings of a supposedly simple surgery gone very wrong.

As it begins to rise, the sunrise splashes orange and yellows across the gray sky. The December air is much warmer here in Florida, sharply contrasting the flat-out cold temperatures I left behind in New York City.

The city that never sleeps.

The city that doesn't forgive is more like it.

As I hand Malcolm his fare, one of the twenty-dollar bills becomes caught in the wind. It doesn't travel far, and Malcolm and I try to stomp on it at the same time. My boot wins.

In the rush to save the bill, I'm distracted. The auto-response of looking directly at him as I hand him the bill that tried to escape causes the reaction I've become familiar with, yet can't become used to.

His widening eyes, which quickly turn to pity, seep into my being.

My hand shakes as I give him the rest of the money then stand, my lack of control unfamiliar and irritating. A storm of uncertainty rages inside me as I grab my luggage with both hands and start pulling. The weight of the luggage forces a slow pace, while the sound of the luggage wheels thumping over the brick driveway drown out the cab's exit from the cul-de-sac.

But the sound doesn't drown out the mantra playing through my head.

It's not looking good, Jenny. I'm afraid there'll be scarring. Jenny, the cheek is very hard to reconstruct. Months to recover.

And then from my parents the ever faithful, *you'll always be beautiful to us, Jenny.* The same words they spoke to the overweight, lonely girl I was in school. I'm now almost thirty and am in danger of reliving my childhood. Not the overweight part, but the lonely part.

In fact, I think it's already started.

Tears I thought no longer existed, prick the corners of my eyes, blurring my walk to the front door. Sheer habit forces me to blink them away, refusing to focus on the hopelessness of my situation.

I pull the house key my best friend Katherine gave me out of my jean pocket as I reach the front door. The front door which, when I enter through it, will let me escape the festivities of Christmas. Will let me hide and be hidden from the world.

Having this avenue of escape has been one of the things that has kept me from totally losing it, totally curling into a heap on the floor, totally deciding my life is over.

But in reality, life as I know it *is* over. The hope I had for the future I always envisioned is gone.

All because I was a little too vain.

What I wouldn't give to see that tiny pimple on my cheek again.

It only takes seconds to unlock the door and let myself in.

The house is quiet, like it's asleep, and I'm sure the sound of me tugging my luggage inside would wake it if it were alive. My expensive luggage now sits on the expensive marble floor. Finding the house key a place in my purse, I realize I'm over-dressed, too warm and exhausted. Flying at night has never been something I've enjoyed, but it is much less populated. And since staying away from people for a few weeks is my goal, it's what I had to do.

As the door clicks shut, I breathe a thankful sigh.

Alone at last.

And I'm thankful there are no Christmas decorations. I'm not in a pretty bow, mistletoe kind of mood.

Only now can I truly relax.

This beautiful house will help. An elegant wrought-iron chandelier hangs overhead. The living room is straight in front of me, so I look down the hall to my right, deciding that's where the bedrooms must be. I grab my suitcases and head to the second door on the left. I stand outside the room Katherine told me I could use until she arrives in a couple of days.

Cautiously I step inside, my gaze sweeping the room.

Relief escapes in the form of a sigh as I see the walls and dresser tops void of mirrors. Perfect.

Katherine's memory of this room was spot-on.

Smiling, I think back almost ten years ago when Katherine and I met. We were both after the same modeling job. Turns out they hired us both and we became best friends.

With a sense of comfort, because thinking of best friends and being surrounded in luxury can do that to a girl, I bring in my suitcases from the hall. One holds my clothes, and the other holds the items that will launch my new career.

Or destroy it.

Catching my breath from the unfamiliar strain of actual manual labor and potential second-career failure, I notice the white furniture and king-size bed. The burgundy and tiny white polka-dotted bedspread is cute and feminine. Long, wide windows grace both outside walls of the corner room, which will let in plenty of light during the day. Wanting nothing more than to put on my pajamas and curl up into the comfy-looking bed, I reason I need to unpack.

After all, there's no one here to do it for me.

I try lifting one of my suitcases onto the bed, but the overloaded bag is extremely heavy. So, I climb up, boots meeting gorgeous bedspread, and use every ounce of strength I have to pull the flowery luggage onto the bed.

I'm now at the point of almost sweating, but I press on, shoving the over-sized, useless decorative pillows against the headboard. I yank my other suitcase onto the bed, the reality of my new, hopefully temporary, life sinking in as I sink into a sitting position against the useless decorative pillows.

No bellhops, no doormen.

No housekeepers or cooks.

Just the three of us—me, myself and I.

Welcome to Jenny's DIY.

Well, it can't be that bad. Leaning forward, as I put my finger on the zipper to open my luggage, I become aware of a scent in the room. A subtle scent that reminds me of outdoors. Woodsy outdoors, not beach-like or tropical.

Probably one of those air fresheners plugged into a wall somewhere. After all, the bathroom is right off the bedroom.

I unzip the suitcase that holds my clothes, then eye the dresser. I also see the doors to the closet. Looking back at my suitcase I realize this is going to be a project.

Might as well start.

As I slide off the bed I notice a photograph on the nightstand. Picking up the photo, I smile as I take in the image. A lion has both of its paws wrapped around a man. I can only see the man's profile, but the dynamics of the photo threaten to burst through the glass.

This lion loves this man.

And this man must be Stephen Day, Katherine's brother. According to Katherine, he's a renegade, rogue wildlife photographer who can't stay in one place for any length of time. And right now he's halfway across the world in some remote country she couldn't pronounce, taking pictures of four-legged creatures she'd never heard of.

Which is why we're borrowing his house.

The photo seems much too bold to be in this room, on this tame, plain white nightstand with its frilly, lacey lamp.

I return the photo to the nightstand before grabbing a stack of clothes out of my suitcase. Walking to the dresser, I set my clothes on top of it as I open the drawer.

A foreboding feeling comes over me at the sight of clothing in the drawer. Making sure my stack is straight and not ready to tumble, I walk out of the room and look around.

Second room on the left, Katherine said. So, yes, I'm in the right room. I step back into the room. Burgundy bed spread with white polka-dots, exactly like she described. No mirrors just like she remembered.

I have to be in the right room.

I pull out the top clothing item in the drawer.

Black boxer-briefs.

As I hold them, a freshly laundered scent mingles with that woodsy scent. My cheek may be scarred, but my brain isn't.

Somebody is staying in this room.

"Never seen briefs before?"

The black briefs slip from my hands at the sound of the oh-so masculine voice. I watch as the briefs miss the drawer and land silently on top of my brown boots.

My mind flies back to childhood and the story of the three bears. I can't help but laugh as the words "Who's been sleeping in my bed" try to block out the "never seen briefs before" question.

I look up, turning slightly. Immediately my laughter dies. I swallow the huge lump in my throat, now feeling like Malcolm the cabbie with *my* eyes widening. Only mine widen in surprise.

And as a woman who appreciates beauty, what a nice surprise.

A put-together-in-all-the-right-places man leans against the doorway, making the doorway appear much smaller than it had when I walked through it moments ago. His rich brown hair, hint of sideburns and gorgeously angled face are model-worthy. And it doesn't stop there.

Lips that any girl would love to kiss part slightly to reveal white, straight teeth.

Muscular arms, flat abs, no shirt, black running shorts, just-the-right-amount-of sexy legs and brand-new-looking running shoes root me to the

6

unfamiliar point of being unable to say a word.

Not even hello.

Oh, and did I mention the sheen of sweat that only enhances all the attributes I've run through my head?

At least I hope I haven't voiced any of my thoughts.

He's staring straight at me. He doesn't look away. His dark-eyed gaze evokes no pity.

Actually, it hardens the longer I stand here. Like I'm invading his space.

Looking down at the drawer, then across the room, I realize I am invading his space.

My suitcases are strewn across his bed. My hands are literally in the cookie jar of his stuff.

Personal stuff, too.

He pushes off the door frame in a smooth move. "The beautiful Jenny Harris has come to visit."

He knows my name?

He starts a slow, lazy walk toward me. "Even my underwear," he says as he bends down to pick up his black briefs, "are so enamored by her beauty, they literally fall at her feet."

His sweaty, heady scent slices through my "I'm not beautiful anymore" mantra that constantly buzzes through my mind.

I swear I can feel the heat off his body.

Except that it's probably only my face flushing at everything about him.

But he's so close.

I can reach out and touch him if I wanted to. And I want to, just to make sure he's real.

Because I think the photograph has come to life.

BENEFICIAL

HE SCRUNCHES HIS briefs in his fist. "I guess I'll need these in a minute when I take my shower." He nods toward the door leading into the bathroom.

"In *my* bathroom," he adds.

His emphasis on the word *my* sends my mental blocks tumbling. Yes, this amazingly beautiful man is Stephen Day. "Your sister said you were out of the country."

"I was. Now I'm back. So do all underwear models go looking through strange men's underwear drawers, or is that a task enjoyed only by you?"

Snatching my stack of clothing, I walk to the bed, dump it in my suitcase and start zipping my luggage shut. "I apologize for intruding, but I had no idea Katherine would offer your room to me, even if you were out of the country."

"This isn't my room. I've ordered new furniture for the master, but my early return and a back order issue has me staying in this guest room."

At least that explains the frilly décor. "Katherine will be here in a couple of days. She's going to model clothes I designed and her boyfriend is going to photograph the line. So is there another bedroom I can use?"

He closes his gorgeous eyes momentarily, then shakes his head. "That's what that message meant. I'm catching on now."

"What do you mean?"

"There was a message on the house phone from Katherine this morning. You might want to check your cell. I don't think she's coming."

Shock runs through my body. My best friend knows my future depends on this amazing opportunity I've been offered. "Please tell me you're kidding."

My purse is sprawled out on the bed next to my luggage. I rummage through it until I find my phone. There were no messages when I landed, but there are now, I see.

I push a couple of buttons, tapping my foot, anxious.

One message.

I press the button and hear Katherine apologizing. Joe surprised her with a Christmas Mediterranean cruise. Her voice squeals and whispers at the same time that she thinks this may be the proposal cruise, and it's the only reason she's ditching me. My heart sinks as she explains that she'll be returning January fourth and she'll call me. If I'm still talking to her.

I know she's been waiting on a proposal from Joe for a while now. I want to be happy for her, and I'll admit a part of me is excited, but honestly, I'm tired and overwhelmed and having a hard time coming around to what this means.

Thumb shaking, I hit the delete button before tossing my phone into my purse. "She thinks he's going to propose."

Stephen smiles. "That's good. He's a nice guy. So Katherine was going to model some clothes and Joe was going to take some pictures?"

"Those 'some clothes' are my designs that need to be photographed and in a certain gentleman's hands by the end of the year."

"Can't you just call up one of your other model friends?"

I shake my head at his ignorance. He has no idea how my world works. At the moment I have no idea how my world works, but I'm not letting him know that. I need to form a new game plan. "It's not that easy. Can you just tell me which room I can stay in?"

He sighs. "I'm not trying to be harsh or anything, but it's not real appropriate for us to be here together. Alone. I can refer you to a hotel."

"Hotel?" Whoever said chivalry is dead hasn't met Stephen Day.

"Yes. There's a great selection of nice hotels not far from here."

My tired brain is spinning fast to come up with an excuse as to why I can't leave. Excuse? I'll just tell him the truth. "I really don't have the money for a hotel." There. Done.

Surely he'll sympathize.

"A successful underwear model like you? Come on."

He has no idea. Between my elective surgery gone wrong and a poorly chosen business venture, I'm broke with a capital B. A fact which I can barely admit to myself, so I'm certainly not admitting it to this gorgeous guy. It appears I have no choice but to leave. "Okay. In ten minutes you won't even remember I was here."

"All right, Cheetah."

He did *not* just refer to me as animal. "Cheetah?"

"Cheetah. You're a fast mover."

He walks to the bathroom door, tosses his underwear on the counter, then makes his way back to the bed. "Let me be of assistance."

Still trying to take in what has happened and regretting that I acquiesced to his demand I leave, I tap the luggage now zipped shut. "Be my guest."

With his strength, my luggage slides easily off the bed, landing with a soft thud onto the stone-tiled floor. Then he grabs my bags, totally dispensing with the pull handles, and simply carries them the old-fashioned way.

With well-defined muscles.

Muscles I can't ignore due to his total lack of upper-body clothing.

Very few situations have the ability to leave me feeling out of control. My scar is one of them.

And Stephen Day, who didn't even blink at my now less-than-perfect face, is another one.

Yes, I consider Stephen a situation.

How else would you describe a man who hugs lions and calls a woman a cheetah?

My brown leather purse is a bag I can handle. I sling it over my shoulder and exit the bedroom in search of my luggage.

I find it in the foyer, sitting on the expensive marble floor.

Stephen is not with it.

The enormity of my now-gone-awry-carefully-made-plans hits me full force. I have nowhere to go.

Talk about irony.

The reality is, I do have friends in Miami, which isn't too far from this house in Hampton Cove. I could probably call one of them and in no time have a place to crash.

But there would be questions.

Explanations.

People.

Never mind Christmas. And I need seclusion. Katherine said she and Joe would be here long enough to do the shoot, then they were going to Key West for the rest of the holidays. She had offered me the use of this house until I had to be back in New York at the first of the year.

My foot taps out my nervous energy as I despair in this awkward moment. This awkward moment of feeling tears about to fall again.

I have one hope of setting my life right. And I can't blow it.

"Cheetah," his voice calls. "You're welcome to come into the kitchen or living room until your cab arrives."

Cab arrives? He must think I've already called for one. Well, I guess having stood here willy-nilly for the last few minutes does indicate I'm ready to leave.

And, he thinks I'm fast.

I walk past the comfy living area into a gorgeous kitchen. Oak cabinets, high-end appliances and beautiful granite countertops exude elegance. A bar stool invites me to sit at the end of the island.

"I've started some coffee." He nods toward the coffee pot. "And if you'll excuse me, Teresa will be here momentarily, so I'm going to put a shirt on."

Teresa? If she was a girlfriend, I doubt he'd be donning a shirt. Although, you never know. The coffee pot gurgles. To the left of the coffee pot, I see a laptop.

My leg, not quite touching the ground, swings back and forth. I slide my purse off my shoulder and set it on the tiled floor. I also shrug off my sweater in an attempt to relieve the too-warm feeling I've had since I entered this house.

I would love to kick off my boots, but that would surely give away the fact that I haven't called a cab yet.

And I need to stall as long as I can.

"Hello?"

The female voice almost startles me off the stool, but I grab the granite island counter top to steady myself. A woman, probably in her early thirties with dark brown hair, stands to my left. Her soft-soled shoes gave her the ability to arrive undetected.

Her gray uniform indicates she's not a girlfriend.

"Hi." I stand. "I'm Jenny Harris."

"Teresa." She holds her hand out. "Mr. Day's housekeeper."

Taking a step forward, I shake her hand. "Very nice to meet you."

Her hazel eyes linger too long before shifting away.

I release Teresa's hand and settle myself back on the stool. Heart hammering, I try to not think about how The Beautiful Agency didn't renew my contract. How I can't afford another elective surgery to fix this scar.

How if I'm doomed to life behind the camera, I need to go for this career opportunity while I can. While people still know my name.

These are the reasons I need to be alone. I don't need any distractions.

What I do need apparently is a model. And a photographer that photographs something besides wildlife.

My financial situation is precarious after being out of work for months on top of trusting my life savings to an old friend's new business venture, which failed miserably. Between that and the botched surgery, my life in no way resembles the life I had just a few short months ago.

"Can I pour you some coffee? It's the latest Christmas blend. A really nice flavor." Teresa pulls cups down from one of the cupboards.

"That sounds great."

DIY Jenny is on hiatus for the moment.

And vastly relieved.

Teresa sets the full cup of coffee in front of me. "Have you been here long?"

She obviously hasn't seen my luggage. "No. Just arrived, actually."

"You're a lucky lady." She winks. "So many women try to capture the attention of Mr. Day. I see you have succeeded. And just in time for the holidays."

The liquid burns my tongue as her words burn my heart. "No," I sputter. "Actually, I haven't succeeded in anything."

"I'm the housekeeper. You don't owe me any explanation. I'm just glad to finally see another woman around this house besides me. It's been far too long."

Before I can say anything, Stephen walks into the kitchen.

"Good morning, Teresa."

"Good morning, Mr. Day." She hands him his coffee.

His amazing torso is now covered with a black T. It's a snuggly fitting T which shows off his physique.

And Teresa thinks I'm his woman.

He nods at me as he turns on his laptop. "I see you've met Jenny."

Teresa's eyes take on a sparkle. "I have."

At least he didn't call me Cheetah. I can tell by the look on her face and in her eyes that Teresa thinks we have a relationship. But that relationship exists only in her mind.

He's under the impression I'm leaving momentarily.

"Today I launder all the bedding, so I need to start."

With those words, Teresa leaves as silently as she appeared.

The coffee is much stronger than I normally drink, but I find taking small sips keeps me focused on something besides Stephen messing around with his laptop.

Totally ignoring me.

"Cabs don't usually take this long. Which company did you call?" He doesn't even look away from his computer.

One of the first things I determine about Stephen Day, besides his physical attributes, is that the man doesn't know how to be still. Something that surprises me as I would think being still would be a necessary attribute for someone taking photographs.

Especially photographing wildlife.

The second thing I determine?

He's direct.

Do I really want to tell him that I haven't called a cab yet?

Not really.

He types for a few seconds, shifting his weight from one leg to the other, before focusing his attention on me. "Sorry. Had to send that email."

"Working?" Maybe my question will take his mind off the cab situation.

"Yes, I am." He looks at his watch.

I need to run interference. "As you can see," I point to my scar. "I've had somewhat of a career setback. I can't model right now."

At my words his shoulders square. He looks at me with a confused expression on his face. "I'm sure a doctor can fix that little scar right up."

Little scar?

Is he serious?

I don't even know how to address his lack of sympathy. Those hard angles may be great for his facial features but aren't so great regarding the heart. "There's a lot of trauma that comes from a facial injury. It isn't something that is dealt with lightly."

"I understand facial injuries can be tough. Not trying to make light of your situation, but I could manipulate that scar out of the picture. Is that seriously holding up your career?"

If I were a cat, my tail would be straight up and my claws would be out. Why is he talking like this is no big deal? He has no clue what the ramifications of this disastrous surgery have been.

Will continue to be.

"Even *if* they could brush over the scar for the photos, I still have live appearances. Shows. Our annual Christmas show was ten days ago, and I watched from backstage. Honestly, wearing a bag over my head would be the only way to *brush* the scar in those situations."

I'm not aware that I am crossing my arms until I realize I'm clenching them with a strength I didn't know I possessed. Can you say full defense mode?

Well, almost.

All I need to do now is cross my legs and narrow my eyes.

Although the ever-fidgety Mr. Wildlife Photographer probably wouldn't even notice.

"Somebody as pretty as you should never wear a bag over her head. You'd be robbing the world of viewing beauty. A crime in my opinion."

What is he seeing? "You don't get it. I'm not beautiful right now." I point to my face. "This ugly, protruding, huge, red scar messes up the look, you know?"

He bridges the distance between us in a couple of steps. He leans toward me until he's close enough that I can see his full, black eyelashes one by one.

"Jenny." I almost faint at the way my name falls off his lips. "With the stunning amber-colored eyes, which widen in amazement. Your seriously

Rapunzel-like hair is the envy of women. Makeup artists all over the world would kill to create a lipstick the color of your full, beautiful lips. Think about it. It's all in where you decide to focus."

I let out a breath, only realizing then that I had been unable to breathe during his slow-talking perusal of my features.

I watch wide-eyed, just like he said, as his hand moves toward my face. Instinctively, I guess, I close my eyes. Seconds later I feel one of his fingers gently touching the tips of my eyelashes.

"Long, thick, beautiful eyelashes." He moves his finger up tracing my eyebrow from just above my nose to my temple. "Your eyebrows arch in perfection."

His fingers gently brush the top of my ear, before inadvertently I'm sure, tickling my ear lobe. "Pretty ears, the perfect backdrop for dazzling diamonds."

I know I will melt if I open my eyes.

So I don't.

His fingers continue their tirade by sliding down my neck. When they stop momentarily, my flesh burns and I wonder if his fingerprints are embedded into my skin. "Smooth, silky, alabaster skin."

His fingertips trace the top of my shoulder, and it's only when I feel them leave me that I open my eyes.

He's still staring intently at me. I don't know what to say. Once again, I doubt my ability to speak.

One thing is certain. This man is good for the ego.

The other certainty?

I still have a scar dividing the upper half of my cheek from the lower half. Why doesn't he see that? Describe that?

For all his inability to stay still a few minutes ago, he is now staying too still, his gaze on me. Not in a weird way. But I feel the need to shift the focus off me.

"Katherine told me you were gone until after the first of the year. What happened to bring you home from the far-away country she couldn't pronounce?"

My question apparently stops his perusal of all my unmarred features. He backs up and picks up his coffee cup.

"I got kicked out."

He seems so serious, I can't help but chuckle. "Kicked out of a country?"

"Yes. It's not the first time. But this time Gary told me to take a break until the New Year. So I'm listening to the boss man. I'm staying put."

"So, what does one do to get kicked out of a country?"

"Finds himself in places he's not supposed to be. Restricted areas, you might say." He takes a sip of his coffee.

"Restricted by?"

"Daddy. The king. Seems he is very protective of his daughter, and dinner with an American isn't acceptable behavior."

This man's ability to render me speechless is unmatched. I'm trying to picture him among royalty. I visualize a lot of tension.

It defies reason.

So does his explanation. "Just dinner? That's radical."

"The king can be radical. It's his country."

"Wouldn't know. I've never met a king." This whole scenario seems suspect. I'm not sure I believe the gorgeous photographer even though Katherine said he was a Christian. A good guy.

Stephen Day is untamed, restless and too good looking.

A lethal combination for the female population.

A combination that a king would notice, would warn his daughter away from.

Even if Stephen wasn't an American.

He glances at his watch again. "You might want to call the cab company and see what the problem is."

A sound coming from his computer saves me from answering.

"Geez." He looks at the laptop. "You've got to be kidding me."

He clicks the computer mouse a couple of times. An older man appears on the screen. Stephen is Skyping.

With someone he's apparently not too happy to be Skyping with.

"Gary." Stephen looks at the screen as he speaks.

"Don't tell me you're surprised to be hearing from me."

Stephen leans over, elbows on the granite counter. I now see his face in the small box on the bottom. The image Gary is seeing. I'm sure Stephen's image doesn't evoke the same response from Gary as it does from me.

Gorgeous.

"Not surprised." Stephen shakes his head. "But there's really nothing to say, is there?"

Gary wipes his forehead. "Yes. Yes, Stephen, this time there is something to say."

This time? Is Stephen always in trouble with his boss?

I watch Stephen's amazing torso breathe in deeply.

Exhale deeply.

I think he's forgotten that I'm here.

"Say it, then." Stephen's voice is void of emotion.

Now Gary's expression looks pained. Like he's not thrilled with what he's about to say. "You know, Stephen, we're used to you pushing boundaries. It's one of the qualities we love about you because you know when it's time to stop pushing. But this time, it seems you've pushed too far."

Stephen shakes his head, palms firmly on the counter. "Come on, Gare. I can't explain fully, but trust me on this. It's going to be okay."

The older man chuckles sarcastically. "Not too sure about that. We're just now getting back to where we were before the economy hiccupped. *Your Life, Wild Life* relies on sales to generate income, and the last thing we need is bad publicity."

"What do you mean bad publicity?"

"It seems the royalty of Zaunesia have threatened to go to the western media."

Zaunesia? Never heard of it. Must be the hard-to-pronounce country where the king and his daughter live.

"Come on." Stephen taps the counter with his fingers. "Zaunesia is a little, unimportant country. Who pays them any attention, Gary?"

"More people than we thought, apparently. A couple of our investors for starters." Gary rubs his thumb and index finger together as people often do to symbolize money.

"This is insane and blown way out of proportion, I might add."

"Maybe. Unfortunately your reputation precedes you, and there's nothing in your future indicating change."

Stephen stands, his handsome face no longer viewable by Gary. "What do you mean change? What kind of change?"

Gary can't see Stephen's perplexed look, but I can. It in no way takes away from the handsome factor he exudes.

And neither does the intrigue surrounding him. His reputation. Pushing the boundaries. His touch on my face, neck, shoulders, eyelashes. Even lions want to hug him.

"Well, Stephen, because it's come down to it, I'll be blunt. The single status you parade around is starting to bite. King Jarvis might be willing to let this go if he thought his daughter wasn't in danger of your advances. After what happened with Leah, you're determined to remain a bachelor, aren't you?"

"Ah!" Stephen slams his hand down and pushes away from the counter. His hand slips slightly causing his palm to connect with the corner of the laptop. The laptop swivels as Stephen turns. The camera points directly at me sitting on the stool, and before I can duck or even think about moving off the stool, I find myself face to face with Gary. His eyes widen and his eyebrows rise seconds before a smile appears on his face.

"Well, hello. I wasn't aware Stephen had company."

The way he says the word "company" leads me to believe he's under the same false impression Teresa is under. Katherine told me several times that Stephen was a loner and had far too many things he wanted to accomplish before ever considering a relationship or marriage.

She never mentioned Leah.

It appears she didn't exaggerate the other issues though, considering my presence provokes so many remarks and assumptions.

"Hi." I don't know what else to say.

Stephen starts shaking his head and slashing his index finger across his throat. I'm interpreting his drama to mean I shouldn't say anything else. He quickly turns the computer and the camera focuses on him again.

"Who's the pretty lady, Stephen?" Gary asks.

Pretty? I guess I'm so far away he can't make out my scar. Oh, and the fact that half the time I don't stop my hair from falling onto that side of my face probably hides it, too.

"Not important." Stephen's tone is curt.

Cut! It's been a long time since someone has referred to me as unimportant. Who does he think he is?

"Are you sure?" Gary questions.

But you're determined to remain a bachelor, aren't you?

Gary's words replay through my mind. I need something. A place to crash and attempt to salvage my life. Stephen needs something. At least according to Gary, Stephen needs something.

To prove he's not the eternal bachelor.

A plan, one that seems extremely beneficial for both of us, forms in my mind. If I help him, maybe he'll help me.

"Hi, Gary. I'm Jenny. So nice to meet you. Well, you know what I mean, right?"

Stephen looks at me with wild brown eyes. He steps back out of the camera's view and mouths, *are you crazy?*

I smile, shaking my head left to right. *Go with me, here,* I mouth.

No, no, no.

Not being able to help myself, I burst out laughing.

"Jenny, huh? Do I know you? You look familiar." Gary's voice is loud. Like, since he can't see me, he feels the need to shout so I can hear him.

"No." Knowing me and seeing my picture in a magazine or on television are two different things.

"Oh, okay."

My heart can't beat any faster, so I hope my words don't come out sounding shaky. "But you probably will soon. I'm Stephen's fiancée."

BEGINNING

I CAN'T TELL who's choking louder, Gary or Stephen.

"Fiancée?" They both say the word at the same time, but I'm hoping Gary is too overwhelmed to hear Stephen's voice.

"Stephen." Gary sounds triumphant. "There you go again, trying to play it cool. Why didn't you say something? This certainly changes the situation."

I have no idea what the situation truly is, but it looks like I was helpful. Now, if I can only convince Stephen that having me around for a little while will be to his benefit, things should work out fine for both of us.

"I'm speechless, Gary. I don't know what to say."

Stephen may not know what to say, but if looks could kill, I'd be sprawled across the tiled floor, dead.

"Don't worry about it, son. You've held out for a long time, waiting on the right one, I assume."

It worked. He's happy. Stephen watches me mouth the words then shakes his head.

I thought my words would relieve some of his tension, but they appear to have the opposite effect.

"Gary," Stephen steps back into the camera's view. "The reality is—"

"It's fantastic is what it is." Gary's voice booms over the speaker. "Alice, honey, come here. Congratulate Stephen. He's engaged."

Sorry. I shrug my shoulders aware of how uncomfortable this exchange might be. Women always want to go on and on about engagements and weddings.

"What, honey?" Gary's voice continues. "Okay. I will. Alice is in the middle of something, but she says she'll congratulate you tomorrow when we see you."

I'm sure the color is now draining from my face. My face which moments ago was the recipient of Stephen's touch.

"See me?" Stephen stammers.

"Yes. Alice and I are headed north for Christmas. We were going to stop by on our way out of town. Now, with this bit of news, we'll have a celebration."

"You live on the Gulf. I live on the Atlantic. I'm not exactly on your way north."

"What's going a couple of hours out of the way between friends? Besides, we need to talk about the Zaunesia situation."

"Seriously, Gary, we aren't, um—"

"Aren't what? Expecting company? I'm sure you weren't. We won't stay long. We'll be there for lunch, then hit the road."

I absolutely don't cook. I'm sure my fear shows in my eyes as I mouth the words.

Stephen's expression is one of pure revenge. "Great. Jenny loves to cook. She'll be happy to make you guys lunch."

My mouth opens in disbelief.

Gary laughs. "This will give us the perfect opportunity to manage the Zaunesia situation and firm up your itinerary for next year. Now, Alice needs my help. We'll see you tomorrow, probably around noon. Jenny, take care of this guy. Looking forward to meeting you. Bye."

And with that, the funneling sound of Skype being disconnected fills the kitchen. Stephen clicks the mouse, and his screensaver, a beautiful tiger, fills the space Gary's face just left.

I start biting my fingernails wondering how much trouble I've just caused.

A lot according to Stephen's expression.

"You need to give me one very good reason why you lied to my boss."

Lied?

I did lie, but it didn't feel like lying at the time. It felt like helping somebody out of a bad situation. "I was trying to help."

21

Stephen crosses his arms as if his rigid stance doesn't exude enough irritation. "Help who?"

My bank account balance floats in my mind. Deflates is more like it. But Stephen can't deny he was in some sort of trouble with Gary.

Still might be.

"Help you. And it would have been fine except your boss is actually coming here. That was unexpected."

"You blurting out the words 'I'm his fiancée,' now that was unexpected. I can't believe this."

The warmness of the room is unbearable. My hand becomes a makeshift fan, but doesn't cool my face. The more I think about Stephen's touch, the warmer it becomes. "Your boss seemed to like it."

He shakes his head. "Gary's old-school. He's been married thirty-years and counting." He downs the rest of his coffee before placing the cup in the stainless-steel sink. "Follow me."

I follow him to the foyer, where he lifts my suitcases once again. One in each hand. Nice. Looking at his muscles will never become old.

I'm right behind him as he walks down the hall, then maneuvers my luggage through the doorway directly across from the room he's staying in.

I step into the room which is nicely decorated in a combination of white and earthy colors. I try not to focus on the huge mirror hanging above the dresser, and try to focus on the fact that it appears he's letting me stay.

"You never called a cab, did you?" He places my luggage on the bed.

I've already lied once today, so I shouldn't lie again.

"No. I didn't—"

"Skip it. It's really not important anymore, is it?"

I set my sweater and purse next to my luggage. "Maybe not to you. But for me, yes. Coming here was supposed to be the beginning of a new life."

Life in uncharted territory.

"You've started a new life, all right. You've started one for me as well. One I don't particularly want. But since Gary is coming here tomorrow, you can stay tonight."

"Thank you."

"And when he gets here you can tell him the truth."

I swallow hard, the full impact of my words hitting home. The flip side? I have a little over twenty-four hours to convince Stephen I need to stay until the first of the year.

"And this room is void of all men's underwear, I promise."

His attempt at humor almost makes me forget about the huge mirror on the wall. The piece of reflective glass that screams "you're not beautiful anymore."

I may be pushing my luck, but right now I don't care. "Can you take the mirror down, please?"

He turns, looks at the mirror, then turns back to me. "That mirror?"

"Yes."

"If you're trying to give me a workout, I've already run five miles and your suitcases weren't exactly light."

As much as I like looking at his well-muscled arms, I wish that's all my request had to do with. I point to my face. "I don't like mirrors right now. Okay?"

My hopelessness regarding my situation hasn't struck him yet. How can body-face beautiful relate to what I'm feeling? He has no idea what it took to climb where I was only to now have it taken away.

He closes his eyes for a moment. A strange expression comes over his face as a strange sensation runs through me. This moment is like nothing I have experienced before.

At the same time his eyes open, my sensation slowly flutters away. Stephen, not taking his eyes off me, steps backwards until he reaches the dresser. With a look of resignation he turns and lifts the mirror off the wall like I would lift a strand of hair off my shirt.

Effortlessly.

"Welcome to your new life, soon-to-be Mrs. Day." His words are whispered as he walks by me, leaving me standing in the wake of all his masculinity and the mess I've created.

ONE THING Stephen Day has done for me is given me something else to focus on. My thoughts haven't been away from my scarred cheek for this long since it all went down.

I'm not sure if this is a good or bad thing.

After Stephen left the room this morning, I slept for awhile. I feel much more rested this afternoon, and incredibly amazed at the stunt I pulled this morning. As fun and innocent as it seemed at the time, I, now the possessor of coherent thoughts, cringe at what might take place tomorrow when Gary and Alice arrive.

Dealing with that will take some thought, and I can't lose sight of why I came here.

Yet, my sight doesn't want to veer from the rogue photographer who managed to get booted from a foreign country, which made his boss unhappy, which caused me to try and make the situation better.

It's the middle of the afternoon, and I'm lying on a chaise lounge in shorts and a tank top. The lounge chair sits under the covered part of the terrace, which suits me just fine. No sun on this body. I'm really proud of my pearly-white complexion. Along with my amber-colored eyes, it's my trademark.

Or was, rather.

Now I have a whole new trademark.

Stephen is a few feet away from me, pulling stray leaves, apparently dead ones, off potted plants sitting on the terrace. The water from the lap pool ripples as a breeze kicks up, causing everything on the terrace to come to some sort of life.

I fight to keep my hair off my face.

Maybe I should further explain to him why I came here. I'm not sure it will diffuse the tension, but it might smooth things over a little.

Somehow I know if I try to be anything but honest, Stephen will know. He's not the kind of guy you blow smoke at. I won't be able to string clever words together to form an explanation simply to pacify him.

So I don't.

"My plan was to hide out here for Christmas." I look at him as I speak wondering what his reaction will be.

He stops pruning to look at me. "Hide out? From who? Family? Boyfriend?"

Talk about sore subjects. "Family is in Scotland for the holidays. Boyfriend is dumped."

There are more plants at the other end of the terrace surrounding a pergola, but he works his way toward me. "So you're basically hiding from yourself?"

24

"As much as I'd like to, I can't hide from myself." He's so focused, I can't help but watch him.

His intense gaze as he peruses the plants.

His gentle touch as he parts the stems.

His preciseness as he plucks the dead leaves.

He walks over to me, his fist full of the brittle, brown leaves. "See these?"

"Yes."

He points to the plant. "The plant is alive. Almost everything about it is healthy, able to withstand disease, full of life. Just a few pesky leaves weren't as hearty."

"And we're going over Biology 101 because?"

"Observing. Sometimes I feel the need to pluck unhealthy leaves from my life."

I wonder if one of his unhealthy leaves is a beautiful daughter of an unhappy king half way across the world. Or are his unhealthy leaves more internal.

I guess if they are internal they wouldn't be called leaves. They'd be called seeds.

At least his gaze is focused on the leaves in his hand and not on me. His intensity reminds me of work. When a photographer became that intense, it became extremely hard to please them. I need to stay away from intense right now. Besides, there's nothing wrong with glossing over the harsh truth of reality until you are fully ready to face the facts, is there?

The sound of a door opening causes me to look up. Teresa walks out.

"Can I get you anything to drink?"

Stephen shakes his head. "I'm good."

"Me, too. But thanks for asking."

She nods. "Okay. But let me know if you change your mind."

"Thank you."

I watch her walk away, her nurse white shoes not making a sound.

So formal for a man like Stephen Day.

Not that I'd expect his housekeeper to be running around in short cut-offs and spaghetti-strapped tops, but initially Stephen seemed much more laid back than mandating the standard housekeeping attire.

Now watching and listening to him I feel somewhat enlightened regarding the renegade photographer.

I have more insight into the brother of my best friend.

Former best friend.

Somehow I think my peaceful holiday getaway isn't going to be peaceful at all.

Of course, part of that is my doing.

"What are your interests?" Stephen asks. "What are you passionate about?"

"When I became laid up because of the scar fiasco, I started designing clothing. I've always had a passion for designing but have been too busy modeling over the last few years to pursue it."

"So, Jenny is a designer as well?"

"Not yet. I drew some sketches and had a friend make some samples."

"Nice." He sits on the chair next to me with a serious I'm-not-messing-around kind of look about him. His sandaled foot digs at a discolored spot on the pool deck. Like he can scuff it away with a few swipes of his sandal.

I have to stay in my lounging position. To sit up like Stephen would make for an awkward situation as our knees would be touching, or I'd have to maneuver the chaise a couple of feet, which I'm not doing. "It is nice, except now I have this line of clothing, SunKissed!, sitting in the suitcase. They're not helping me in there. I need my line photographed and my portfolio in the hands of Dominick Redding before the end of the year. Now that Katherine has ditched me, I need a new plan."

"I'm glad to hear you know you need a plan. A plan more aspiring than being my wife, as flattering as that is."

"My impulsive, now somewhat regrettable actions were not meant to flatter. They were meant to help."

His jaw is set like he means business, and I'm sure he does. He reaches toward a chair and grabs a camera. He places the strap around his neck and now the big, black professional-looking camera rests against his chest.

The camera.

My friend or foe?

"What else is there to know about the woman I'm supposed to have given up all other women for?"

"That I could use a break right now."

"I know the feeling." Stephen fiddles with a couple of buttons on the camera.

His tone sounds dejected. Maybe I *can* help him out. "We could just hang out, you know. I could tell Gary I jumped the gun on the engagement, but we can appear united."

"United?" His expression is doubtful.

"It might give you that break you need with Gary. And we won't be lying."

He cocks his head like he's considering my solution. "We are hanging out, I guess."

I look away and shrug my shoulders, like this isn't thrilling me. But it's thrilling me.

"Truce, Cheetah?"

I shiver at his use of the nickname. Somehow it doesn't irritate like it did a few hours ago. I close my eyes and smile. "Truce."

Click.

The familiar sound of a camera clicks. The sound that previously brought cash into the bank is now foreign.

Invasive.

Scary.

I'm praying that Stephen Day did not take my picture.

BLIND

DARE I ASK?

Every nerve in my body tenses. Chills run down my arms as I open my eyes.

I need to make a stand here and now. "Please tell me you didn't take a picture of me. I'm off limits as far as your camera is concerned. Understand?"

He looks at me, his expression bold. "I'm naturally attracted to beauty that can make some people uncomfortable. I see beyond the surface of an image. It's how I make my living."

Furious, I sit up, facing away from Stephen. I had started to think he was kind of cool, but now he's just plain cold. I look around for my flip-flops. I'd like to think I'm irritated because my lounging time is cut short, but I know Stephen's lack of compassion is the real reason for my irritation.

"I didn't take your picture."

I give up my search, my mind swirling in many directions. Am I so caught up in myself that I automatically jump to conclusions? "Thank you."

Now it's awkward. I'm sitting here, my back to him, half-ready to bolt. Bolt to nowhere, I might add.

And it appears I've lost my shoes.

"Want to see what captured my attention?"

Nudging away the part of me that wants to wonder but truly knows why *I* didn't capture his attention, the grateful part of me responds. "Sure."

In one fluid, graceful movement, he literally steps over the lounge chair to sit next to me.

Pulling the camera strap over his head, he pushes some buttons on the camera. When he finally shows me the screen, all I see is a long, green creature. My skin starts to feel prickly, and I look around, pulling my feet off the tiled terrace for a moment. "Where is that thing?" "That thing is an anole and it was climbing that tree on the other side of the pool."

"I don't like bugs."

"An anole is not a bug. It's a reptile."

His tone says I should know this. His wink says it's okay that I don't.

"Yeah. Those too. I'm not a fan. At all. It crawls, and it's ugly."

"Remember, beauty is in the eye of the beholder. Don't judge so quickly."

Easy for someone who looks like he does to say.

After the realization that the crawly thing is not a threat, I settle my feet back onto the patio.

I'm also extremely aware of Stephen's proximity.

His arm brushes mine briefly as he holds the camera up again for me to see the screen.

"Look." He zooms in on the green face. "Look at his eye. Fascinating, isn't it?"

"His? How do you know it's a guy nole?"

"*Anole*. The colors and the markings differ between males and females."

"Oh. There is nothing about a lizard that will ever be considered fascinating to me."

Stephen frowns. "There's a bigger picture here. It's more than a lizard."

More than a lizard?

A stirring inside compels me, almost against my will, to look at his camera screen once again. I find myself mesmerized by the intricate green scales. The five-toed webbed foot looks like it effortlessly holds its position on the limb.

I look closer. A green eyelid? Really?

I shiver as the eye seems to be staring straight back at me.

The little white light at the top of the eye, not quite a pupil, but probably a reflection, adds an interesting aspect to the creature.

"Boo."

I jump at Stephen's voice. "What did you do that for?"

Chuckling he answers, "Couldn't resist. You were trance-like."

"I was taking your advice. Trying to see the picture as 'more than a lizard.'"

He nods. "Cool. What do you see?"

I cautiously peer closer at the screen, the essence of Stephen Day engulfing the nonexistent space between us. I mean this guy is all male. Rugged yet classic. Manly yet sensitive.

Hot yet cool.

Really, how he can be all contrasts is hard to grasp. Contrasts that complement each other, no less.

I don't dare look at him, so I lean in even closer to the camera screen as if that will stop any wayward urges I have. "I like how his body color fades into that yellowish color. And those darker spots on his back are almost invisible. You can barely see them."

"Yeah. It's a decent shot."

I switch my attention to Stephen. "Decent? You said he was across the pool. You must have really zoomed in."

He shrugs. "That's what a good camera does."

I like how he doesn't give himself too much credit. Katherine is the same way. Humble. "I think whoever is behind the camera has a lot to do with it, too."

"I've been shooting so long it's like second nature to me."

"Do you ever take pictures of people?" I ask, trying to keep the hopeful tone out of my voice.

"Not professionally. Only wildlife."

I smile. "Ha. I know some people who would qualify as wildlife."

The sound of him chuckling soothes me.

"Me, too." He drapes the strap back around his neck.

He stands.

He's leaving.

I wish I could say I was glad, but I can't fully go there.

"I need to work for a little while. Make sure I still have a job when Gary finds out we're not engaged." He makes it a point to stare at me as he says the word "engaged."

He strides into the house leaving me in the wake of his essence and aura. I lie back down on the lounger and try to settle in. Relax.

But it's hard, knowing Stephen is right inside the door.

I've been around a lot of men in my life. I've been around a lot of photographers in my life.

But I've never been around anyone who's made me feel on edge like Stephen does.

Adjusting my body, I try to get comfortable. Even though the air is warm for December, lying here under cover, the breeze chills me from time to time.

I rub my arms forcing away the chill bumps.

At least I think they're caused by the air. I refuse to believe they are caused by anything else.

Namely Stephen.

Another chill. I rub my arms again, this time with more drama. Like I mean it.

To say my first day in seclusion isn't going as planned is an understatement. Peace and solitude have been shattered by the presence of Stephen and my attempt at helping him. My mind can't begin to process what I'm to make of my life because he keeps intruding.

Literally and figuratively.

I once again shift my weight. You'd think that chaises with cushions this thick and soft would be comfortable.

Especially surrounded by this setting.

This backyard is perfect for my intended purposes of hiding out. Tall, leafy trees and lush bushes create a safe haven, unable to be viewed from neighboring homes. Being located on a bay there is a nice breeze, which keeps the air moving.

The pool, the pergola and other furnishings only enhance the relaxing feeling.

Almost like a spa.

This would have been the perfect spot to launch my new venture.

"MY MOM asked me to bring these to you. The man just brought them."

My eyes snap open at the sound of a young voice. I look to my left to see a huge vase of red roses. White baby's breath and green sprigs of some sort mingle with the deep red hue of the buds that haven't opened all the way.

Small, chubby, tanned fingers, turning deep pink at the ends from the pressure of holding the vase, I guess, grip the clear vase. The nails are short, probably bitten off, but clean. I sit up from my lounging position. "Why, thank you." I take the vase from the child.

I hear the sliding door and look that way, catching a glimpse of Teresa walking into the house. Maybe this is her daughter?

As beautiful as the roses are, I can't take my gaze away from the little girl. Probably about seven years old, deep, shiny chestnut-colored hair frames her face. Thick bangs, cut severely even, hide her forehead. Her eyelashes are just as thick, framing brown eyes.

Her face is round, her body a little rounder and her smile, huge.

"Thank you." She wiggles her fingers. "They were heavy. But they smell good."

I gently sniff. They smell like a typical rose. Nothing special in my opinion. But then again, I'm not an impressionable young girl anymore.

"Oh, yeah. Here's the card." She pulls a small white envelope out of one of the pockets on the front of her red and white candy cane striped dress.

"Thank you." I know who the flowers are probably from, therefore I have no desire to read the card. At least not right now.

I keep staring at the girl who keeps staring at me. Kids are so honest I know any moment she's going to ask me what happened to my face. Especially since her gaze doesn't seem to move from it.

"I'm Jenny. What's your name?" Might as well give her segue.

"My name is Phoebe."

"Wow. A really grown-up name for a little girl. I know a girl in New York. Her name is Phoebe. Her friends call her Pheebes."

"I don't have any friends."

Sadness jolts through me, stirring unpleasant memories. Her confession mirrors my life as a little girl. I balance the vase on my thigh, wanting to reach out to Phoebe. But my hands continue to grasp the vase as

I realize I don't have a response. "Do you go to school?" is all I can come up with.

"Yes. Do you?"

I shake my head, wondering at her question. "No, silly. I'm too old for school."

She tucks her head down. "I'm sorry."

Steadying the vase with both hands, I want to tilt her chin up. Did my words cause that sadness? "There's nothing to be sorry for. Okay?"

She nods her head, still staring downward.

With an intake of breath, and a subtle approach, I look for tears. Relief waves through me as I don't see any on her face.

"Everything's okay, right?" I ask.

"Yes," she answers. "Your voice is pretty."

I guess since she can't say that about my face, saying it about my voice is the next best thing. "Thank you. I don't believe I've ever had anyone tell me that before."

"You sound," she tilts her head pensively, her gaze now focusing upward, as a smile tugs at the corners of her mouth. "Like you have blonde hair."

Puzzled at her obvious statement, I look at her. She's much too young to grasp the blonde joke thing, isn't she? What does she mean I sound blonde?

"I guess, since I sound blonde, it's a good thing I have blonde hair, isn't it?"

"Yes." She smiles, then reaches for me in a swift movement. Her unexpected gesture catches me off guard and I flinch. In that moment my grip on the vase loosens, and it tumbles to the patio. The unmistakable sound of glass hitting the tiled patio shatters the air.

Phoebe starts to cry, and I notice she is trembling.

"It's okay, Phoebe. It's not your fault. Are you hurt? Did the glass cut you?" I look down at her short legs, but they seem to be fine. She seems to be fine except for her crying.

Her shoulders tremble with her cries while her head shakes back and forth and she doesn't budge.

"Honey, really, there's nothing to cry about. It's just a vase. Replaceable. No damage done. If you can back up carefully, then you can go get your mom."

She continues to shake her head. Has the child never seen broken glass before? Or does she really think it's her fault and I'm mad?

I'll admit to not being around kids much, but little Phoebe and I are truly off to a rocky start.

And honestly, it's about to become a little rockier if she doesn't cooperate. It's now obvious no one heard the crash, and I'm stuck.

"Honey," I say again, because right now, at this moment, her name does seem too big for her, "You need to get your mom. Or Stephen, okay?"

"I can't," she manages between sobs. "I'm scared."

I take a deep breath, trying to control my impatience. "There's nothing to be scared about, Phoebe." I switch tactics and use her grown-up name. Maybe she'll act in a grown-up way. "But we need someone out here to help us. As you can see, I'm barefoot and there's too much broken glass for me to maneuver through."

Glancing down, I notice little red marks on my legs. Funny, I feel no pain, but the evidence is clear that little glass shards have embedded themselves in my legs. My perfectly white, unmarred legs.

"I can't." She continues to cry.

"Of course you can." My tone is stern. Sterner than I had intended. Resisting the urge to wipe my hand down my leg I'm sure has put me on edge.

"No." She swipes her hands across her eyes. "I can't see."

I close my eyes, before glancing upward. Like looking up will magically fix this situation. My frustration level creeps up as each moment passes. I guess I don't have the patience for kids right now. It's a good thing I don't have any. "If you calm down and quit crying, you'll be able to see. Now calm down."

She shakes her head back and forth. "It won't help me. I'm blind."

BREATHLESS

I'M BLIND.

Her words rush through my mind, and at first I don't think I hear her correctly. I want to think she's being overly dramatic, but her blindness settles on me like a perfectly fitted dress.

But it doesn't feel nearly as good.

They smell good.

Your voice is pretty.

You sound like you have blonde hair.

I lean over, pulling her shaking body into my arms, ashamed that it took her blindness to soften my heart.

The minute my arms wrap around her, she climbs onto the chaise, into my lap. I smooth her hair, rub her back, not knowing what else to do.

"Phoebe?"

At the sound of her mother's voice, I feel Phoebe stiffen.

"Phoebe, did you drop Ms. Harris's flowers?"

I look up at Teresa who stands surveying the scene. I know exactly what she is thinking. She doesn't appear angry, just sad.

"Teresa, Phoebe didn't drop the flowers. I did."

Teresa places her hands on her hips and gives me an I-know-you're-lying look. "The truth?" Her tone and expression say she'll accept nothing less.

Phoebe reaches out her arms toward her mother. "Mommy."

I let go of my grip on Phoebe. Teresa leans over and helps Phoebe down, steering her clear of the broken glass.

"The truth is Phoebe brought the flowers to me. I tried to balance them on my leg, and it didn't work out too well."

Teresa is holding Phoebe's hand but looks at me with a still unbelieving expression on her face.

"I swear that's the truth."

I don't mention that Phoebe's gesture startled me.

Was she trying to "see" me?

Teresa motions to the broken glass. "Okay, then. I'll be right back to clean up this mess."

Teresa and Phoebe start to leave. "Bye, Phoebe."

"Bye."

Her little voice is like cold fingers walking up my arms. I look around once again for my flip-flops. As I do I notice the card that still sits unopened on the chaise. Probably from Jeff.

Jeff.

I'm surprised I can remember his name after meeting Stephen. I slide my finger under the flap and pull out the white card edged in gold. Very fancy and elegant. So unlike Jeff.

If you ever need anything from us, Jenny, please let us know. Sandy and everyone at The Beautiful Agency.

Waves of relief and disappointment mingle along with a sense of foreboding like the blood-red roses lying on the sandstone-colored tile amidst the broken glass.

Being very careful not to move my feet, I reach down and grab a couple of the flowers which managed to escape the shards of the clear vase. I look them over, perusing the outer layer of softness. Beads of water cling to the petals as if that alone can help them survive.

"What happened?"

The flower loses its ability to hold my attention as the voice of Stephen reaches my ears. "There was an accident with my flowers."

"The dumped boyfriend trying to change your mind?"

I smile. "He dumped me. So, no."

The look on Stephen's face can only be described as surprised. I guess I'm surprised he's surprised. I mean, who could blame Jeff? Who wants to date a girl with a huge scar?

On her face.

"I just assumed you were the dumper, not the dumpee. Stupid guy."

One of the water drops slides down the petal of the flower bud, leaving a shimmering trail. The drop reaches the end and disappears, no longer existing.

At least not in the form it had been.

Am I like that drop of water? Is Stephen's house my shimmering trail?

And when I drop off, will I disappear?

Beautiful still feels bad for not renewing my contract. Like a dozen red roses will make up for ditching me in my time of need.

"Mr. Day." Teresa walks towards us loaded down with the paraphernalia to take care of the flower disaster. "I'll clean this up now."

"I'll help you in just a minute." Stephen leans over. "Jenny, grab my neck."

Before I can protest, I'm in his arms, nestled against his chest. My pearly skin appears almost translucent against his deeply-tanned skin. I spy my flip-flops under the far end of the lounge chair.

I don't mention them.

Instead I squeeze my fingers around the two roses I am holding, then wince as I feel a thorn prick through my skin.

Blood oozes across my index finger.

The pain of the thorn and the sight of blood pale in comparison to the feel of Stephen's arms as they carry me away from the broken glass.

Suitcases, mirrors.

Now me.

I wonder what other loads Stephen carries around?

The mysterious ones I can't see.

Leah?

He crosses from the patio into the kitchen. "I think I can walk now."

He stops, setting me down next to the barstool. "Have a seat. Let's take care of that blood on your legs."

With one hand still clutching the roses I place my other hand on the counter, steadying myself from the empty feeling of not being in his arms.

The air conditioning seems to be working overtime now. I settle onto the bar stool, the same one I started my morning on.

Stephen kneels down. His palm cups my heel as the fingers of his other hand slide up and down my leg, his hot touch a jolt to my nerve endings.

All of them.

"You could always be a foot model." His gaze never leaves my foot. "Your feet rock."

Since he's not looking at me, I'm not sure if he's serious or not. "Nobody's feet rock. Feet are ugly."

"I disagree. There's beauty in everything. I'll be right back. Don't move."

Chills replace his warm touch as Stephen leaves. I try not to cringe at the sight of the small, red marks, mostly around my ankles and lower-calf area.

Surely they won't scar.

That's what I said about my face.

I set the roses on the island. Maybe Stephen or Teresa can point me in the direction of a small vase. Why I want to hold onto the two reminders of an aspect of my life that will never be the same, I have no idea.

But I do.

Stephen returns with a cloth, a tube of something and a box of Band-Aids. He runs the cloth under water, and as he wrings it out, I can see steam rising from the white material.

"Here we go, Cheetah." Crouching down in front of me, he gently wipes each red mark with the cloth. I honestly don't know when I've been more aware of a man.

Men have been the center of my existence. Male photographers, male makeup artists and really manly guys who can work miracles with my hair. Guys who not only design my clothes but have helped me dress for shows.

Guys who have had their hands all over my body positioning me for just the right shot.

Move your body to the left, Jenny. More, Jenny, like this.

They thought nothing of ambling over, their hands helping to maneuver my body where they wanted it.

Stephen's touch is different. Nothing mechanical or clinical about it. It's caring, gentle.

"These little nicks aren't bad. You don't even need any Band-Aids. I'll just rub a little ointment on them for now." He grabs the salve and opens

38

the tube.

"Okay."

I now know how the potted plants felt on the terrace as he perused them for any and all signs of dead foliage. Meticulous could be his middle name. His touch leaves me breathless.

Anxious.

I have to focus somewhere else. The white cloth with its pinkish-toned smears sits on the island. I grab it and wipe the tip of my index finger.

"Red roses, the symbol of love, can be dangerous." Stephen caps the tube of salve.

My body tenses. "In this case it's no love lost."

"So if it wasn't the ex-boyfriend, who doesn't love you anymore?"

"My modeling agency. They're not renewing my contract."

"Because?"

"You have to ask?"

He stands. "The scar can be fixed. Can't it?"

"It's a bit more complicated than that."

Stephen gathers the Band-Aids and the washcloth. "Somehow I have no trouble believing that you are complicated."

The warm, satiny feeling of being in his arms fades as my face heats at his assumption. "You know nothing about me, Stephen Day. Nothing. And I'm tired of your flippant attitude regarding a very traumatic time in my life. Maybe I *should* leave."

Without a glance at him, because honestly it might dampen my resolve, I head toward my room.

When I reach it, I shove the door open and unzip my suitcase.

I refuse to give any credence to the part of me that keeps glancing at the doorway to see if Stephen is there. To see if he will try to stop me from leaving.

The realization he's not going to stop me fuels my reason to leave, so before I pack up the last couple of drawers, I trade my shorts for a pair of jeans, grab my phone and dial the cab company that brought me here this morning.

Was it just this morning?

It feels like a lifetime has gone by.

Hanging up, with the assurance that the cab will be here within twenty minutes, I zip my suitcase shut.

With shaky hands, I sit on the bed and activate my GPS on my phone. I need to find a hotel. An inexpensive hotel. I have no choice but to dip into the funds that I was going to use to have my portfolio made.

The portfolio that isn't happening anyway.

Why is it when you are in a hurry, your phone isn't? As much as I need to ask Stephen for that hotel recommendation, I don't want to ask. He hasn't even bothered to check on what I'm doing.

My heart saddens as I realize he's probably thrilled I'm leaving.

I glance at my watch. Less than ten minutes have gone by. I wonder if Malcolm with the Santa hat will be the cabbie. If so, I could end my day just like I started it.

I stand my suitcases up and drag them down the hall. As I'm walking I see Stephen in the foyer.

Even the side view of him is amazing. His physique is lean, angled and simply beautiful to look at. Is his intention to stop me?

"Mr. Day?" Teresa calls, running into the foyer, stopping short of running into Stephen. "Mr. Day, there's been an accident."

"An accident?" he asks as Phoebe walks into the foyer.

"Yes, my parents. In Mexico." The woman is sobbing, and Phoebe is edging closer and closer to Teresa.

"My mother and father were in a very serious car accident in Mexico. I have to leave right away. Phoebe doesn't have a passport, but I must go."

Stephen's stance reveals how uncomfortable he is.

I set my purse on my suitcase.

"Mr. Day, I have no one to watch Phoebe. I know it's an imposition, but could she please stay with you? You and Miss Harris?"

"I, uh…" he stammers, looking at me.

Teresa obviously hasn't noticed my suitcases.

"Have you booked a flight?" Stephen asks Teresa, and honestly, I think I can see sweat forming on his brow.

"Not yet." Teresa wrings her hands. "I knew I needed to talk to you first. I promise to stay only as long as I'm needed."

Phoebe may not be able to see, but I'm sure is very aware of the tension in the luxurious foyer with the fancy chandelier, marble floors and people who don't know what to do with her.

The doorbell chimes into the awkward silence. I step around Stephen and answer the door.

"Somebody called a cab." The rough voice startles me.

"I did. It's for me." I turn around to face Stephen and Teresa.

"Are you ready?" The cabbie, who is not Malcolm, seems put out to even be here.

"Just a minute." I try to keep my voice calm.

"Meter's running." The cabbie starts the walk back to his cab.

I awkwardly step around Stephen.

A questioning expression covers Teresa's face. She covers her heart with her hand before glancing at Stephen.

"Miss Jenny?" Phoebe's voice is soft.

"Yes?"

She slowly walks over to me and wraps her arms around my legs.

"Will you please stay, Miss Jenny?"

I look away from Stephen and blink my eyes. Who could say no to that voice?

"Yes, will you please stay, Miss Jenny?" Stephen tries to spin his tone with laughter, but I see the total you-need-to-stay panicked look on his face.

My heart hammers. I'm not giving myself any illusions. I know he wants me to stay because of Phoebe. Moments ago he was content to let me walk out that door.

Things have changed now.

But I'm not sure my mind is one of them.

BOUNDARIES

IF PHOEBE wasn't standing here, I would love to make him squirm. "Okay. I'll stay."

Phoebe squeezes my legs. "Miss Jenny with the pretty voice is staying."

Stephen takes a couple of steps toward the door. "I'll go take care of the cabbie. Teresa, make your plane reservations. And I'll pay your travel expenses. All of them, so leave as soon as you need to."

Calmer tears stream down Teresa's face. "Thank you," she manages to choke out.

"Do I need to help you pack some things for Phoebe? I'd be happy to go to your home and help." I imagine her mind is reeling.

"Phoebe and I live in the apartment above the garage. If you can stay with her now, while I make my arrangements and pack, that will be helpful."

"Sure," I answer. "Phoebe and I will have a great time."

"Thank you." Teresa quickly leaves.

I grab Phoebe's hand. "Let's go into the kitchen. Maybe there'll be something yummy to eat."

"Yes, ma'am."

"No, ma'ams. It's Jenny."

"Okay, Miss Jenny."

"I can handle Miss Jenny." I walk with her to the bar stool. "Why don't you sit here while I raid the fridge?"

She climbs onto the bar stool and sits, her hands folded on the island. The same place I sat in what seems like forever ago. Is it possible that only a few minutes have gone by?

I open the freezer. "How about some strawberry ice cream?"

"My mommy bought that for me."

"Good. Then I think you need to eat some."

I start opening cabinets, looking for a bowl.

"The bowls are in the corner cabinet to the right of the sink."

I suck in a quick breath. "How did you know what I was looking for?"

"Because you need a bowl to put the ice cream in, silly. The spoons are in the drawer beside the sink, and the ice cream scoop is in the third drawer down by the stove."

"Thank you." I grab a bowl and set it on the counter. Then I find the spoon and ice cream scoop. All right where she said they would be. I start scooping.

"Mr. Stephen's back."

I turn to find Stephen standing at the entrance to the kitchen, staring at me. Flustered, I drop the ice cream scoop full of ice cream on the floor.

He smiles and shakes his head, then grabs some paper towels. But he doesn't hand them to me. Instead, he bends over, hands me the scooper and starts wiping up the mess.

I step around him to the sink, and wash the scooper off.

"Did you drop something?" Phoebe asks.

"I did."

She laughs.

I manage to scoop more strawberry ice cream into the bowl. I set the bowl in front of Phoebe, along with the spoon and a napkin. "Here you go."

"Want some?" I ask Stephen, as I decide some ice cream might be just what I need.

"No. You two enjoy. I'm going to get the study ready for Phoebe to sleep in. There's a pull out couch in there."

"Why can't I stay with Phoebe in her apartment? I'm sure we'd be fine there." And I wouldn't have to put up with his lack of compassion he's been displaying toward me.

"I wanna stay here. It'll be like an adventure." Phoebe sounds excited.

"The apartment is small anyway," Stephen adds, his tone sounding the opposite of exciting.

"Okay." I realize I'm not going to win this battle.

"I'm sorry, Mr. Stephen. I know I'm a bother, but mommy said there wasn't anywhere else for me to go."

The pained expression that crosses his face pains me.

"You're not a bother, Phoebe. Don't think that," he says.

"Mommy said you liked being a batcher, but maybe Miss Jenny was going to cure you."

"Batcher?" Stephen asks.

"I think she means bachelor." I try not to laugh.

"Yeah. That's it. That's what mommy said. Bash a ler."

"No comment." Stephen tosses the paper towels before leaving the room.

I lean against the island next to Phoebe, both of us silent as we eat our ice cream. It's interesting to watch her fingers touch the edge of the bowl as her other hand uses her spoon.

We take so much for granted.

Yesterday at this time, I was sitting in a coffee shop in New York City, my life void of Stephen, Teresa, Phoebe and a cabbie named Malcolm.

It's amazing how a life can change in less than twenty-four hours.

"YOU DON'T need to hold my hand," Phoebe says.

It's almost eight o'clock, and we're headed to the study where Teresa had put Phoebe's suitcase. We had chips and sandwiches for dinner after listening to a show Phoebe likes. I'm surprised how fast the time has gone by.

"Oh, okay." I resist the urge to baby her.

"My mommy has worked here a long time. I know my way around."

"All right, then."

"I'm going to the bathroom," she says just as we arrive at it. "Mommy said she put my pajamas in there. And I need to brush my teeth."

"Okay. Let me know if you need anything. See you in the study."

She steps into the bathroom and shuts the door. I'm so amazed by her. She's very mature for a seven-year-old.

Teresa was able to book a flight and left about an hour ago with assurances from both Stephen and I that Phoebe would be fine. We know where all her important documents are, we are in possession of her insurance cards and the phone numbers where Teresa can be reached, as well as all of Phoebe's school information.

At the end of the hall, toward the back of the house, is the study. I walk in to find Stephen trying to put the sheets on the mattress. "Need some help?"

He looks up. "Sure."

He's standing on the far side of the pull-out maneuvering the less-than-perfect-fitting sheets around the corners of the mattress, so I stand on the other side.

Stephen tosses the top sheet to me, the freshly laundered scent tickling my nose, and together we manage to tuck it under the mattress.

"I found these two blankets. I think they'll be good enough, don't you?" He points to two dark blue blankets he's set on the bed.

"Yes. They'll be fine. Hand me one of those couch cushions, though. Let's put them back so there's not a gap." I nod toward the back of the couch.

"Good idea." He tosses one of the cushions to me.

I put my knee on the bed as I try to shove the cushion between the frame and the back of the couch. Stephen is doing the same, and it doesn't take me long to become preoccupied by his closeness.

Leaning over to give a final push to the cushion, I lose my balance and find myself leaning into him. "Whoa," he says, his warmth searing into me, as he steadies me with his grasp.

I'm surprised at the urge to settle into his arms, to rest against his chest.

"Jenny." His voice is a whisper. "We have to set some boundaries."

At his words I struggle out of his embrace and off the bed. Face flushed, pride stung, I clear my mind of Stephen's touch. "I agree. Boundaries are good."

"First, physical boundaries. A must." He looks flustered as he runs his hand through his hair.

"Agreed. Stay ten feet away from me."

"Why does Mr. Stephen need to stay ten feet away from you, Miss

Jenny?" Phoebe asks, obviously done in the bathroom.

"Yes, why *ten* feet?" Stephen asks.

"I didn't mean literally ten feet. And Phoebe, Stephen and I were kidding around."

"Oh. Okay."

"Phoebe," Stephen says. "We've pulled the couch out into a bed. I know you spend a lot of time in here after school while your mom is still working but wanted to let you know things are changed a bit."

"Thanks, Mr. Stephen. How far away is it?"

"About two feet straight in front of you."

Phoebe shuffles to the bed, then climbs in. "Miss Jenny, will you tell me a story?"

"A story?"

"Yes. My mommy always tells me a story before I go to bed."

"I'll leave the storytelling to you two ladies. Good night, Phoebe," Stephen says. "I'll see you in the morning."

"K. Goodnight, Mr. Stephen."

Stephen shrugs his shoulders, smiling at me as he leaves.

Phoebe pats the bed. "Will you sit with me? My mommy always does when she tells me the story."

I have no idea what kind of story she wants to hear. I can recall some fairy tales. Not sure I know whole stories, though. I climb on the bed, bringing one of the blue blankets with me. I spread the cover out then settle next to Phoebe. "Which story do you want to hear? Cinderella? Sleeping Beauty?"

She shakes her head. "No. I know those. I want to hear your story."

"My story?"

"Yes. A story you make up. You can make up a story, right? My mommy does."

Mommy has some big shoes. And I'm not sure how capable I am of filling them. "What kind of story do you want to hear?"

Her lips purse momentarily. Then she smiles. "*You* need to make up a story."

Right now the stories that are running through my mind involve a ruined life, an ugly face and heat from an amazingly attractive man. Those elements don't sound so good for storytelling to a seven-year-old. But I really need to try. Phoebe has been ripped from her mother's arms, and although I know she knows Stephen, she doesn't really know me.

"Okay," I start. "How about there's a little girl—"

"She'll be a teenager," Phoebe says.

"Okay. There's a teenage girl who lives in…where does she live?"

Her expression looks lost in thought for a few seconds. "How about a city called Mexico. That's where my mommy is."

"Sure. So, living in a city called Mexico, there's a girl—"

"A princess," Phoebe interrupts.

"Oh. A princess? Nice. I like it. So we have a princess—"

"She has to have a name." Phoebe's voice is matter of fact.

"Of course she has a name. And her name is…"

"Bea."

"Bea?"

"Princess Bea," Phoebe states.

"Princess Bea it is, then. Princess Bea lives in Mexico. She lives in a beautiful castle with her mom and dad."

"The king and the queen."

For a little girl who insisted I make up a story, she's extremely helpful in setting the scene. "Okay."

"And her father is very handsome." Her voice now sounds sleepy, and we've barely begun our story about Princess Bea who lives in Mexico with her mom and dad.

Phoebe slinks down further into the pillow and covers.

"Are we done with our story?" I ask, wondering about Phoebe's father and if he was handsome.

"For tonight. Mommy adds to it every night."

I pat her on the top of the head. "Okay. Goodnight."

"Night, Miss Jenny."

The sofa bed squeaks as I climb off, but Phoebe doesn't flinch.

The room plunges into darkness as I turn off the light. The same darkness Phoebe lives in all the time. Unsure as to whether I should shut the door or not, I decide to leave things as they are.

I walk back to the kitchen to find Stephen leaning against the counter, a piece of paper in his hand. He seems to be studying it hard.

The space on the other side of the island beckons me. Palms flat on the island top, I look at Stephen, who has turned his attention away from the paper and now is looking at me. "Boundaries," I say.

He smiles. "It's not quite ten feet, though."

"I could crawl into the refrigerator or go into another room, I guess."

Staring at people is usually considered rude, but staring at Stephen can't be helped. Not only has he been aesthetically put together, but there's an air about him that can't be ignored.

"I want to thank you for staying. Not sure what I would have done if you had left." His tone is filled with gratitude.

I don't know what I would have done if I had left. But I'm not letting him know this. "It's all good."

"I'm not used to being around kids. At all. This is way out of my comfort zone. Way out. So again, thank you."

My heart laughs. I have no idea why a guy who likes being hugged by a lion would be so scared of a little girl.

I wonder what else Stephen Day is afraid of?

BELIEVE

IT'S ABOUT eleven in the morning. Phoebe is sitting on the couch in the room off the kitchen, listening to music with her headphones, while Stephen and I attempt to make lunch for Gary and Alice.

"I remember baking cookies with my mom when I was little," I say to Stephen as we stand in the kitchen, staring at the items he's picked up at the grocery store.

We have one hour.

"This will be easy. We'll make some sandwiches, and I bought this coleslaw already made. And here"—he points to a bag,—"is soup. Just mix with water, and voila, baked potato soup."

"Seems simple enough," I say. "Why don't I make the sandwiches and you can make the soup." I also notice his camera sitting behind the computer. I don't think the man goes anywhere without it.

He pushes his hand through his hair. "No, Cheetah. I'll make the sandwiches. I'll even toast the bread. That way we'll both be cooking."

My heart hammers at the thought of using the stove. "I'll try. And really, how hard can it be?" I ask, picking up the bag.

"Exactly. You just add water and stir."

As I locate a pan, I watch as Stephen lays out the sandwich fare. Ham, cheese, lettuce, tomatoes, some grassy-looking stuff. There's thick, crusty bread that he's going to need to slice.

"Pheebes, where are the measuring cups?" I call to her. She has these really cool headphones that let her hear outside noises.

"The cupboard above the stove. Left side."

"Thanks."

I open the door and there they sit.

Measuring carefully I add the water to the pan, before dumping in the dried soup mixture. I turn on the burner.

Stephen is slicing the bread, and his light blue T-shirt does nothing to hide his muscular arms. I find it hard to look away from him. His movements are so graceful. Always. It doesn't matter what he's doing.

"We can eat on the terrace," Stephen says. "It's nice enough out. Not too hot."

"Sounds good. As long as we can get five around the table."

"Five?"

"Yes, five." I nod my head toward Phoebe. *Remember?* I mouth.

He nods. "I'll grab a chair from another table."

"I'm sorry to be a bother."

Phoebe's little-girl voice cuts through the air, causing my heart to drop. "You aren't a bother. Don't think that."

"Well, I'm not supposed to be here. Is my mommy going to be home by Christmas? Will Santa know I'm here instead of in my apartment?"

I walk over to where she sits on the couch and sit next to her. "Honey, Santa knows where to find you. I promise."

"Can you promise my mommy will be home?"

Hesitating, I look at Stephen who is shaking his head. "No," I say. "I guess I can't promise she'll be home, but I can promise Santa will find you."

"I miss my mommy."

Her voice is soft, like it's on the verge of tears. I can't blame her. Here she is, left in the care of the man who employs her mom, and a woman she met yesterday. "I know you do. I'm sure she'll call soon, and you can talk to her on the phone."

She doesn't respond. Her little feet keep kicking in time to the beat I barely hear through the headphones.

A sizzling sound interrupts my daydreaming.

"Ah, Cheetah, it's boiling over."

I see a flash of Stephen moving across the kitchen to the stove as I leap off the couch. Steam rises from the pan on the stove, while liquid runs down the side. Stephen turns off the burner, and I grab a towel.

"Rule number one," he says. "When stove is on, stay in kitchen."

My face heats in embarrassment. The towel quickly becomes soaked as I clean up the mess. Looking into the pan I see little white chunks bobbing in murky water. "I don't think this is done."

"Not hardly."

"What's burning?"

Phoebe's voice carries in from the keeping room.

"Burning?" I repeat, seriously wiping up the mess on the stove. "Nothing's burning."

"Smells like it."

Stephen laughs. "You're right, but it's okay."

I carry the sopping towel to the sink and wring it out. Stephen steps around me and pulls open a drawer.

"Here's a clean towel."

"Thanks." I take the towel from him, wipe the bottom of the pan with it, then set the pan back on the burner and turn it on low. "What do those directions, say again? How long do I cook this?"

The crinkle of the bag indicates Stephen is reading. "Twenty minutes."

"Fine. I'll stay right here for twenty minutes, then."

"And stir," he says.

"And stir."

I must admit it's much more fun watching Stephen make the sandwiches than it is watching the soup that won't boil. After he finishes he places the sandwiches, cut in half no less, on a big platter.

"This isn't boiling." I stare into the watery mess.

"You probably need to turn it up."

"And risk having it boil over again? I don't think so. But this is taking forever and I wanted to change before your boss gets here."

"Change?"

"My clothes. Freshen up a little, maybe?"

"I'm not taking over your lunch job."

The loud noise of the doorbell slices through any answer Stephen might have been about to say.

He looks at me. "They're early."

I look at the clock. "Thirty minutes."

"I'll answer the door." He walks out of the kitchen.

I stay beside the stove.

Sounds of greetings float in from the foyer area. I can imagine warm hugs being given. Maybe a stern look from Gary to Stephen, unless Gary's totally forgotten about the Zaunesia incident.

"Where's that fiancée of yours?" The female voice rings to me. I hope Phoebe doesn't pick up on all this talk.

"In the kitchen. Stirring the pot, so to speak."

The sound of Stephen's voice causes a quickening inside me, and his innuendo doesn't escape my notice. I still don't understand how a man can affect me so much in such a short span of time. A man who doesn't even want me here.

I hear the sounds of footsteps crossing the tile.

Stephen steps into the kitchen first, somewhat blocking their view of me. "Gary, Alice, I'd like you to meet Jenny."

He then walks over to stand by me. I watch the expressions on Gary and Alice's face carefully. Yes, both, at once. Their responses mirror each other. Smiles and curious gazes change with a quick intake of breath, my scar doing its job beautifully.

Alice is the first to speak. Her right hand quickly covers her heart as her lips slowly form the same smile she walked in here with. "Why, hello. It's nice to meet you, Jenny. I'm Alice. Alice Tatum."

She steps towards me holding out her hand. With my left hand still stirring the soup, which has yet to boil I might add, I shake her hand with my right hand.

Gary is right behind her, his face familiar from the Skyping incident. As Alice steps back I shake Gary's hand as well. He is bold in his perusal of my face.

My gaze locks with his. His brown eyes hold compassion, not pity. He's an older man, more handsome in person than on the computer screen. Brown hair boasting more than a few silver strands is neatly cut, unlike Stephen's wild, unruly hair.

Gary's face shows signs of time, weather, laughter. A good face to have at his age. A life well lived.

Alice, on the other hand, has a face that says I've had work done. Her impeccable skin, no wrinkles and perfectly applied makeup don't reveal any clues as to what she's really like.

What she's been through.

"I knew you looked familiar." Gary turns to Stephen. "This is one secret you shouldn't have kept."

"Gary, there's no secret." Stephen moves toward me.

"Not anymore," Gary says. "Why didn't you say she's the Simply Midnight Jenny Harris?"

I laugh. "Probably because I don't model for them anymore." My hand instinctively rises toward my face.

"Jenny." Stephen's rough, strong fingers clasp mine, pulling my hand down. "No more, okay? I'll hold your hand all day if that's what it takes."

He's now looking at me with an I'm-sorry look. I'm not sure if he's playing this out, or if he's really sorry. I am sure that his hand holding mine causes me to become nervous. Causes me to lose focus.

Causes me to wish that Stephen was mine.

Because I can tell he's a protector by the way he has embraced the Phoebe situation. When he loves something or somebody, it's important to him. He's a man of integrity and to be honest, I don't know too many of those.

The ones I thought had integrity have disappointed me one at a time, leaving the field void of players.

"I don't mean to delve anywhere I'm not supposed to, but Stephen, come on, your fiancée is not somebody you keep hidden." Gary's tone could be considered challenging if there were something to challenge.

And he used the f word. Fiancée.

A wrong I need to make right because Stephen's honesty and integrity won't let him lie to his boss, even if it will save his job, or whatever he's in danger of losing.

But I need a little time. And it's not helping that Gary is so enthused about the fake engagement.

The warmth of Stephen's touch spreads through my body. I'm auto-stirring with my other hand, but I'm surprised my body heat hasn't melted the plastic spoon I'm using to stir the soup.

"Smile." Gary holds up his phone like he's going to take a picture.

"No pictures, Gare," Stephen says.

"Come on. I just upgraded my phone and want to check out the camera." Gary drops his photographer stance, a puzzled expression crossing his face.

Phoebe walks around the island. "You can take my picture even though I can't see it."

The look on Gary's face can only be described as priceless. "Who are you?"

"This is Phoebe," Stephen says. "And she can't see the photo because she's blind."

"My mommy had to go to Mexico, so I'm staying with Mr. Stephen and Miss Jenny until she comes back. They said Santa will be able to find me."

Gary and Alice are shooting glances between me and Stephen.

Stephen speaks. "My housekeeper Teresa had to go to Mexico yesterday because her parents were in an auto accident. Phoebe doesn't have a passport, so she's staying here until Teresa can return."

"But Santa will find me."

"Of course Santa will find you." Alice's voice drips with the tone people use when speaking to small children. Phoebe's not that small. "He knows where all the children are."

"And he's going to bring me everything I asked for." Phoebe smiles widely after she speaks, and it dawns on me that I have no idea what she wants for Christmas and I doubt Stephen does either.

He's going to have to ask Teresa when she calls. Without warning, the whole Christmas thing becomes very real. I'm in a house with a child, who's expecting Santa Claus just like every other child.

"Cheetah, the soup." Stephen's voice calls out and for the second time in less than twenty minutes, the soup is boiling over.

WE ARE NOW sitting on the terrace, sandwiches, soup, coleslaw and lemonade in front of each of us.

Stephen's sandwiches look delicious, the lemonade looks refreshing as does the coleslaw. And my soup, well you can say it looks interesting.

"Stephen, I must say, it's so endearing the way you call Jenny, Cheetah."

Alice speaks, carefully, slowly. There is no way any of us will miss what she has to say.

Phoebe laughs. "Cheetah. That's funny. Isn't that an animal?"

"It is," Stephen answers.

I'm doing well to sit here amongst all these people I don't know. I also have the admitting that "I lied" issue hanging over me until I can get Alice and Gary out of Phoebe's earshot.

Stephen looks quite comfortable. Relaxed, at home. Well, he is at home. And he's been around Phoebe for a while. He also knows Gary and Alice.

And he didn't lie.

"Are the things in the soup supposed to be crunchy?" Phoebe asks.

"Things?" I ask.

"Yeah. The water part tastes good, but the things in there are crunchy."

"I'm sorry," I say. "You don't have to eat it."

I don't dare look at Gary, Alice, or Stephen, all witnesses of my great cooking failure.

"Stephen and Jenny. You two lean in together. I want to take that picture now, if you don't mind." Gary holds his phone up.

Stephen looks at me and raises his eyebrows before he focuses on Gary. "Jenny doesn't like having her picture taken right now, Gare. Sorry."

"Just let me take one picture of you two together, I'll forward it to the people who can forward it to King Jarvis. I think he'll see that he was mistaken when he accused you of, let's say, consorting with his daughter."

"Somehow," Stephen says, "I don't think a picture is going to do the trick."

"Nonsense. It may not do all the convincing, but it will start the ball rolling if nothing else."

Stephen looks really uncomfortable. And it's my fault. I have to speak up now. Phoebe or no Phoebe. "Um," I start. "There's something I need to tell you."

"Can it wait until after Gary takes the picture?" Alice asks. "It's going to be the only way I can convince my friends that Stephen is taken. They've been after me for a long time to fix him up with their daughters, nieces, you name it. If they know anyone single, they're asking."

I breathe deeply of the cool Florida night air. "That's the thing. He's not taken. So you don't need the photo." What a mess.

Gary sets his phone on the table, while Alice sits up straighter.

"Not taken?" she asks. "What do you mean, dear?"

I shake my head and avoid all eye contact. Even Phoebe who can't see. Trying to steady my nerves, I blurt out the words, "I lied to you. I'm sorry."

"You lied, Miss Jenny?" Phoebe asks. "Lying is not good."

"I know, honey. And I'm sorry and now I'm apologizing."

"That's good," she says. "I'm done with my lunch. May I be excused to go listen to my music now?"

Great. Why couldn't she have said that less than a minute ago? Then I wouldn't have had to admit to lying in front of her. Oh well, my timing is way off lately. Today is no different.

"Sure, honey. Do you need me to go with you?" Translated, can I put off the explanation for a few more minutes?

"I know my way around, remember?" she says as she pushes her chair away from the table and slowly makes her way to the doors that open into the keeping room.

My placement at the table gives me a view of Phoebe as she reaches the couch. She plugs in her ear phones and starts messing around with her tablet where her music is stored.

But I can only look so long before the silence indicates I need to finish explaining my lie. To strangers, no less. Might as well get it over with. "Gary, Alice, I have to confess to you that I lied about Stephen and me. We're not engaged."

Alice pats the corners of her mouth with her napkin. "There, darling. You don't have to create all this drama simply because you don't have a ring."

"A ring?" I have no idea what Alice is talking about.

"Yes. I will admit to noticing right off that you didn't have one, but that's not the important part."

Stephen places his napkin on the table. "Jenny's serious. We aren't engaged."

Alice and Gary exchange glances. Gary shakes his head. "Stephen, son, we're not buying it. I know we've only been around the two of you for a short time, but it's so obvious. Why are you trying to deny it?"

"Deny what? What is so obvious?"

"That you two are completely in love with each other, that's what. It's written all over your faces." Alice has an expression on her face that says "I'm not a fool."

I look at Stephen who is looking at me. Like he loves me, apparently. Or maybe that's how I'm looking at him.

Either way, one or both of us have totally confused the Tatums. And now they need to be unconfused. "Actually, we're not in love. If you want to know the truth, we met only yesterday."

Gary laughs and elbows Alice. "These kids today. Stephen, I know you don't want me sending any photos to Zaunesia, but you don't have to put Jenny up to a falsehood. Just say you don't want me to send any pictures."

Wow. This thing is spiraling out of control. Quickly.

"Listen. I'm friends with his sister, Katherine. I needed a place to hang out, hide out, for the holidays. She thought Stephen was going to be gone, so she gave me his house key so I could stay here. Then Stephen was here, and it has all been nothing but a mess from the beginning. Including me lying to you about our engagement."

"Why would you lie about an engagement if you just met him?" Gary asks.

"Well, I heard your Skype conversation, and I didn't want him to be in trouble."

"Even though you'd just met him."

I guess it would sound conceited for me to say I have a big heart, but in reality, I do have a big heart. "Yeah."

Gary shakes his head. "That little girl in there may be blind, but I'm not. No, sir. So have you set a date yet?"

I don't have to look at Stephen to know he's frustrated.

"Look," I say. "You have to believe me. Stephen and I barely know each other. We aren't engaged."

"We can appreciate you wanting to keep quiet about your relationship, but I'm afraid the cat is out of the bag now," Alice says. "Do you want to tell them, Gary? Or should I?"

"Tell us what?" Stephen asks.

"Go ahead, dear." Gary's expression clearly says they are sharing a secret.

"We wanted it to be a surprise but couldn't figure out how to do it, so we're going to tell you. When we heard the news yesterday, we were so excited we contacted people from *Your Life, Wild Life.*"

"You didn't." Stephen's tone clearly indicates a less than favorable situation is about to happen.

"Of course we did. We knew everyone at the magazine would be happy for you. So, the whole staff, except for a couple of them who already had firm plans, is coming to Hampton Cove for a New Year's Eve engagement celebration for you two. We were fortunate enough to have friends in key places, and we booked a room at the Extravaganza Club."

The little bit of lunch that I've managed to eat rolls in my stomach. "You've done what?"

Alice reaches over and pats my hand. "Honey, I know we've just met, and please don't think us forward, but Stephen is like a son to us and we want to celebrate with him. You can invite your family and any friends you'd like. Just make sure to let me know how many so I can inform the club."

Stephen's soft grasp catches my hand midair and gently steers my hand away from my face.

I feel like I'm in a stranger's body.

And this stranger loves Stephen Day's touch.

BACHELOR

THIS SITUATION with Stephen is out of control. Totally.

"Alice," I say, "You mentioned the fact that I have no ring. There's no ring because there's no engagement. I'm sorry about the club and the New Year's Eve plans. Really, I am. I hope you didn't put down a deposit."

"No, dear. They wouldn't take a deposit because it is so close to the day. We had to pay in full for twenty-five guests. Any additional guests will have to be paid for the day of the party."

"Cheetah." His voice slightly above a whisper as his fingertips rub the top of my hand he's still holding, "This is why we don't lie."

"Exactly." Gary nods. "Now fess up and tell us the wedding date."

"We haven't set one yet. And that's not a lie." Stephen's tone is matter-of-fact.

"I can live with that." Gary pushes his plate forward indicating he's done with his meal.

Alice's plate looks like it hasn't been touched, and I wonder what, if anything, she eats. She's super thin in an unhealthy way. Her leggings and oversized top are stylish but fuel her thinness.

Gary looks at his watch. "Stephen, we're leaving shortly, and we really need to talk about the Zaunesia scenario. I'm sure you've told Jenny all about it."

"Briefly. We've just met, remember?" Stephen releases my hand and pushes his chair back, folding his arms across his chest.

"And the party. Honestly, we can't accept." I cross my arms in an attempt to appear united in front of Gary and Alice.

"The engagement party is a done deal. Eight o'clock New Year's Eve," Alice states.

Maybe united isn't the best way to appear.

Maybe the key will be in dividing.

That's it.

I lean toward the table and start gathering the plates. "Stephen, it appears our dilemma as to how we will ring in the New Year has been solved. We need to thank Alice and Gary. I'm sure the party will be wonderful."

Before Stephen can say anything, I grab a couple of plates, stand and lean toward him giving the impression I'm kissing him on the cheek. "Trust me." I whisper my words.

And with no intention other than appearing like an authentic engaged couple, I place a small kiss on his cheek. My lips tingle at the unexpected sensation of his freshly shaven face. The tingling continues through my jaw and neck before it crescendos into the roots of my hair.

I start to move away from him, but he places his palm on the side of my face, guiding me so I'm looking directly at him. His thumb rubs my scar, and I can't ignore the mixed feelings of ugliness and caring. "Don't be long, Cheetah," he says softly but loud enough for Gary and Alice to hear.

His ability to catch on quick makes me smile.

My smile is cut short as his lips cover mine.

I'm startled and mesmerized all at the same time. The kiss lasts too long.

My knees to weaken.

The dishes I'm carrying start to rattle.

I barely feel his tongue lightly brush my upper lip, causing a new slew of sensations. His hands steady the dishes as he leans back in his chair. "Hurry back."

Hurry back?

I can't convince my legs to walk away.

As he releases the dishes, I gather what strength I have to move one foot in front of the other. With a still shaky hand, I slide open the glass door and walk into the kitchen.

My arms tremble as I place the dishes into the sink.

My lips burn with the passion that is Stephen Day.

My heart becomes larger, like his kisses are the water necessary for love to grow.

Love?

I'm not in love with a man I met yesterday. Just because he makes me feel, doesn't mean I'm in love.

It means I'm foolish.

Foolish to succumb to the first guy who shows me attention since my surgery.

My elective surgery.

I did not elect to feel this way.

"You okay, Miss Jenny?"

I turn around to find Phoebe standing at the island. I didn't even hear her approach.

"I'm fine."

"Gathering your thoughts?" she asks. "That's what my mommy says she's doing when she's standing around not moving."

This little girl has no idea how she brightens my mood. "Well, then yes, I guess I was gathering my thoughts." And my wits, my heart, my composure.

"Okay." She smiles before walking back to the couch.

I hear the sliding door open, and Alice walks in carrying a plate.

Just one.

And her hands shake slightly. Is the plate too heavy or did Gary just kiss her?

I'm betting on the plate.

"Those guys are talking about that Zaunesia situation. It's senseless to me. Especially since we see that Stephen is smitten with you. There's no way anyone will convince me he was interested in the king's daughter. No matter how young and beautiful she is."

"How young and how beautiful?" I ask.

"Put your claws away, honey. Too young to be taken seriously, and not beautiful enough to compete with you."

I shake my head. "I'm not beautiful anymore."

"I disagree. And apparently Stephen disagrees, too."

Gary and Stephen come in from the patio, each of them carrying a variety of plates and bowls which they set on the counter.

As soon as Stephen sets his dishes down, he slides over to where I'm standing. It's like I'm a magnet for his body. And when he is this close, I find it hard to think straight. It's like I can't think of anything but him.

"I think everything is settled then." Gary leans against the counter. "We'll be in touch. Make sure you keep Alice posted on the number of guests you'll be adding."

Stephen slowly, meticulously, caresses every inch of my shoulder as he places his arm possessively around me, drawing me close to his side. I must admit we do mesh together well.

"We will keep you posted." Stephen gives my shoulder a gentle squeeze. "Won't we?"

"Yes. We will."

Alice playfully slaps Gary on the arm. "Why don't you cuddle with me like that anymore?"

"I got your cuddle, tonight in the hotel room."

"Gare, seriously?" Stephen says.

Gary laughs. "Ease up, kid. I'm all talk and you know it."

"This gal needs a little more than talk." Alice is tapping her foot, indicating she doesn't find Gary's joke funny at all.

"You two, take it to the car. We've heard enough." Stephen starts to shoo them out of the kitchen.

"Oh, I almost forgot. Wait right here." Alice holds up her finger indicating she'll be right back.

She heads toward the foyer. An awkward silence ensues as we wait for her return. Moments later she's back, a big purse slung over her shoulder. She pulls out a package wrapped in red paper with a big green bow. "Here." she holds out the present toward Stephen and me.

"Guys, no presents. We've never done presents." Stephen's stance tenses.

"You've never had a fiancée before. Open it. It's a together gift." Alice pushes the gift even closer to us.

Her smile is huge. Gary looks excited, too.

Stephen's arm drifts from around my shoulder and he unwraps the gift. A medium-sized burgundy velvet box begs to be opened. As his masculine fingers open the velvet lid he pulls out a beautifully decorated

Christmas ornament. Its lavender background is dotted with white, glittery angels and the words "Stephen and Jenny—first Christmas" make their way around the ornament.

"It's beautiful." My words come out soft and comforting, like we are engaged and it is a gift for us.

"You shouldn't have." Stephen holds the ornament delicately, like it's going to burn him if he holds onto it too long.

"We hope you like it." Gary nudges Alice. "Can't return it."

He and Alice laugh like he's made a really funny joke, and it's all I can do to keep from crying at this point. "Definitely nonreturnable."

"You need a tree to hang it on. Shame on you guys for not having any decorations. Especially with a little girl around."

"Honey." Gary gives Alice what they probably call the look. "Quit the lectures. They're grown, and we need to go. Merry Christmas." He hugs Stephen, then me.

The minute all of us start walking to the front door, Stephen drapes his arm over my shoulder again, like he's stopping me from running out with them.

If it wasn't for Phoebe, I might.

After saying goodbye way too many times, Stephen finally shuts the door as Alice and Gary leave.

He leans against the door. "Trust me? I believe I've trusted you right into celebrating a false engagement on New Year's Eve."

Stepping back I create more space between us. "It does appear that way. But I have a plan."

"Can we buy a Christmas tree? Mommy and I didn't get one yet and Santa won't have anywhere to leave my presents."

Being in the presence of Stephen obviously causes my guard to drop. Of course Phoebe is an extra quiet girl, but I can't believe I didn't hear her walk in.

"As soon as Jenny and I have a talk, we'll go look at trees." Stephen locks the front door.

"All of us?" Phoebe asks. "Miss Jenny, too?"

He shakes his head and I swear his eyes roll slightly. "Yes."

"Okay. I'll listen to my music until you have your talk. I hope the talk doesn't take long."

"It shouldn't. Jenny and I will be out on the terrace."

With those words spoken, Stephen walks out of the foyer. I shadow Phoebe into the keeping room where she plops herself on her favorite couch, and I continue outside.

"We need to clean up lunch." I nod toward the few items still left on the table.

"When we're done."

The afternoon breeze is nice, but I'm glad I've worn long sleeves and jeans. Much tamer weather than in New York, but there's a storm brewing inside Stephen if I had to guess, and I think the air senses it.

"Would you like to sit?" He holds a chair for me.

"Sure."

He settles in the chair next to me. So close.

"Okay, tell me what this 'trust me' bit is all about."

I can only hope he sees this the way I see it. "I've decided since they wouldn't believe I lied about the engagement that we might as well stop trying to fight that battle and start a new one."

"What do you mean?"

"It's simple. They left here thinking we are totally in love and engaged, right?"

"Yes."

"So, in a couple of days, or whatever time frame you think is appropriate, you call them, tell them we got in a big fight, and the engagement is off."

"Are you serious?" he asks.

"Yes."

He rubs the back of his neck like my words make him tense. "That's your plan?"

"It is. People call off engagements all the time."

"If they didn't believe us telling them we weren't really engaged, what makes you think they'll believe we've called the wedding off?" His fingertips press against the table.

"Like I said, people do it all the time. You call them and tell them they need to stop by on their way back in town. That I've broken up with you and you're devastated."

"Why do I have to be devastated? You should be the one who is devastated." He stares hard at me, his lips forming a straight line. Flat lined, like his attitude toward me right now.

"But then you wouldn't need them to come by. They know and love you. When they *see* how torn up you are, they will believe you."

He raises his eyebrows and tilts his head. "Unfortunately I think you have a point."

Dare I relax a little? "Not what you expected?"

He huffs out a laugh. "Jenny, you are so not what I expected."

My heart doesn't know whether to flip or flop at that statement. I decide it's going to flip. "I'm going to take that as a compliment."

"Take it however you want. You're the one who got us into this disaster."

I hold my hands out, palms up. "So it's only fitting that I get us out."

Stephen leans closer, pushing the hair I willingly let fall across my face behind my ear. "Your hair feels soft." The wind lifts his hair a little as he gently rolls strands of my hair across his fingertips.

"A good shampoo will do that." I wonder how his hair feels? I wish I had the nerve to find out.

"I think it's more like good hair genes."

I think Stephen has a plan. And it's to slowly drive me crazy. Me and my lips remember how his lips stirred an unforgettable passion in me. Being this close to Stephen is not good for me. "We're not doing too well with the boundary thing." I cringe at how breathy my voice is.

"No, we're not."

His gaze mesmerizes me. "We'll work on it."

"Yes, we'll work on it." But instead of working on it and letting go of my hair, he pushes through my tresses until he's gently caressing the back of my head.

"Stephen." I whisper his name, not wanting to break this spell.

"I'm sorry, Cheetah. I seem to be having a bit of trouble with the boundary concept."

Stephen, we're used to you pushing boundaries. It's one of the qualities we love about you because you know when it's time to stop pushing. But this time, it seems you've pushed too far. Gary's words replay in my mind. "I can't say I wasn't warned." My heart starts racing. I can't take my gaze away from his amazing face, his lips. I don't realize I'm holding my breath.

Until his lips touch mine.

Again. For the second time in the span of an hour.

I barely close my eyes, ready to sink into all he is, when he ends our kiss. He scoots back his chair and stands, crossing his arms. "I don't even know what to say. I don't act like this. This is not who I am. There's something so, so…"

"So what?" I ask, curious.

He shoves his hands in his pockets and rocks back and forth on his feet. "As much as I hate to admit it, there is something captivating about you."

His tone and his words clash. "You don't have to make it sound so painful."

"Maybe I'm practicing for the moment you break my heart." His smile indicates he's

teasing me.

"Oh, you know you'll be back to normal in no time."

He shakes his head. "I don't think I know what normal is anymore."

IT'S REALLY different shopping for a Christmas tree in Florida than it is in New York. And it's really different shopping with a guy who's so hot he'd melt the snow if there was any and a little girl who can't see but has so much joy about everything that I can barely wrap my head around where she's coming from.

Steven hasn't been home for Christmas in the past few years, so there are no decorations in the Day house. Buying ornaments is on the agenda as well.

"Here we are ladies. The Christmas tree farm."

Stephen is such a gentleman, opening my door and Phoebe's door. His demeanor has a very protective nature to it. Protective in a good way, not in an overbearing, creepy way.

As we walk across the gravel parking lot, I pull my sweater around me as a breeze kicks up. Not complaining though. A sweater is so much better than the heavy coat, scarf and gloves I'd be wearing in New York. The scent of pine drifts past me, bringing with it a nostalgic sense of days gone by. Days when I'd go with my mom and dad to buy a tree.

"They smell so good," Phoebe says before I can voice my thoughts. "I love Christmas." She grabs tighter onto my hand. Stephen is on the other side of me, and it doesn't escape my notice how I'm surrounded today by people I didn't even know forty-eight hours ago.

And, I'm starting to feel comfortable around them.

The familiar tune of "Jingle Bells" is being piped in, blaring from speakers set up around the area. Phoebe starts to skip to the tune. I find myself skipping along with her.

"You ladies dance well."

I stop abruptly at the sound of Stephen's voice.

"Don't stop on my account."

"Are the trees close?" Phoebe pushes the nose of her glasses. The glasses she told me she wears only when she's outside.

"Right over here." We walk down an aisle, green pines to our left and right. The trees are already cut, waiting for somebody to take them home.

Phoebe stops walking and points to the left. "What about that one."

How she even knows there's one there is beyond me, but there is a nice tree right where she is pointing. "Let's look." I cringe as the words leave my mouth.

I have to be more mindful of the words I choose.

Trees of all shapes and sizes are leaning against a make-shift wall.

"Here, I'll hold it up and you ladies tell me what you think." Stephen picks out a medium-sized one and steadies it. The branches fall into place.

Still holding onto Phoebe's hand, I walk around the tree.

Phoebe wiggles her hand out of mine. Her arm juts out as she walks straight ahead. After taking a couple of steps her fingers brush the tip of one of the tree limbs. She takes a couple more steps before she starts running her fingertips across the branches. Then she runs them up and down as far as her little arms will reach. "I think it's beautiful."

I look at Stephen who is still holding the tree but looking in the opposite direction of me and Phoebe. He's not paying either one of us a bit of attention. I follow his gaze to see what could be holding his interest.

My heart drops as a very cute brunette comes into view.

He is such a bachelor.

The brunette appears to be alone. Petite. Stylish.

I try and shake off the unwanted jealousy.

"Stephen. Focus." I nod toward Phoebe.

"What?" He looks confused.

"Phoebe thinks this is a great tree. What do you think?"

"I'm on board with Phoebe."

Phoebe smiles. "Can we buy it?"

"I don't see why not." Stephen gives the tree a couple of good shakes.

"Thank you, Mr. Stephen." Phoebe grabs my hand. "I can't wait to decorate it."

Stephen carries the tree toward the check out, Phoebe and I following behind him. "It's Beginning To Look A Lot Like Christmas" now serenades us.

I wasn't sure what Christmas would look like this year, but I know one thing.

I surely didn't picture it looking like this.

BALANCE

"THIS ORNAMENT is shaped like a star." Phoebe hands me a silver, glittery ornament.

We are in the keeping room, the tree securely in its stand. Phoebe and I are decorating the tree. The ornament Gary and Alice gave us? On the bookshelf, still in the box.

Where it will stay. "Thank you." I hang the star-shaped ornament up high, filling in the places Phoebe can't reach.

"I bet it's shiny, isn't it?" she asks.

"Very," I reply.

"I knew it."

She reaches for the next box, her fingers moving deftly over the ornaments. She pulls them out of the slots and hands them to me one by one. Stephen is in the office working. Or at least that's what he says he is doing. I'm thinking if you get kicked out of a country, that assignment is over and until you get another one, you are considered off work. Especially since it's so close to Christmas.

You'd think he'd take a break.

But I see where he's coming from. I'm not working and I'm not taking a break either. I've got a suitcase full of items waiting to be photographed. And I have no model. Facts which stress me out.

But as far as tonight goes, I'm hanging with Phoebe, decorating the Christmas tree, and when that's done we're going to make cookies together.

"Our Princess Bea is still in Mexico City." Phoebe cocks her head as she speaks.

Princess Bea?

Oh, yes. Our made-up princess who is supposed to be our bedtime story. The princess has now moved into daytime conversation. Oh well, what could it hurt? "Yes, she's a teenage princess living in Mexico City."

"What can happen to her? How does our story start?"

Phoebe is careful to place the lids back on the boxes when she realizes they are empty. She has also stacked the boxes neatly next to the couch. I can tell this is one organized kid.

I take my time answering her question while looking for the perfect spot for the golden ornament with red snowflakes glittered on it. "There. Perfect."

"I think," Phoebe starts, "that the prince should come to the palace."

She says the word prince and Stephen's face zooms into my mind. Need to squelch that image. Fast. He's not a prince. If he was, he probably wouldn't have been kicked out of Zaunesia. "Okay. Is he invited or is he an enemy?"

Phoebe tilts her head, like that might help her decision making. "I'm not sure. I think he should be an enemy prince. That would make the story more exciting, don't you think?"

"It would. What is the prince's name?"

"Jonah," she says quickly.

"Jonah?" Interesting name.

"Yes. Mommy tells me stories from the Bible, and Jonah was in a whale's belly. So I think he could be a prince."

"I think so, too. So we have Princess Bea and Prince Jonah."

Phoebe walks to the tree and starts feeling the branches and the ornaments. Her touch is light and the ornaments jiggle back and forth, their tinkling sound comforting as her hand brushes by. The colored lights blink, making my heart sad that Phoebe can't see them.

The tree brings the Christmas season to life. It's more real now, more tangible. Like it's going to happen. I know Christmas is going to happen no matter what, but now I'm going to be a part of it, whether I like it or not.

And I think I'm starting to like it.

"So," I say to Phoebe, "If Jonah is an enemy prince, how do they meet?"

"It's your story," she says.

I laugh. "Okay. Well, the story of Princess Bea and Prince Jonah starts like this. Princess Bea is in her palace playing the harp. She is a very good harpist. Prince Jonah has a decree from his father, the king of the country next door, that says all the land is now in his possession and Princess Bea's father must give up his kingship."

"What's a degree and is there going to be a war?" Phoebe asks.

"A *decree*. It's like a law. If Princess Bea's father doesn't do what Prince Jonah's father wants, then there will be a war."

"Oh, okay."

"So, Prince Jonah walks into the palace and hears the most beautiful music he's ever heard. Instead of going straight to the king, he follows the sound of the music. He has to know who's making such beautiful music."

Phoebe backs away from the tree and sits on the couch. "I bet the halls in the palace are long, aren't they."

"I think they are. But that's all of the story for now. We'll add more at bedtime because we need to start making those cookies." That and I have no idea where this story is headed. At least now I have a couple of hours to figure it out before she goes to bed.

We spend the next hour baking cookies. Phoebe unearthed Christmas cookie cutters. With the help of some food coloring, we make green and red icing. So now our cookies have a Christmas spirit about them. As we put the last batch into the oven, Stephen walks into the kitchen.

"I couldn't resist anymore. It smells good in here."

"We made cookies, Mr. Stephen." Phoebe waves her hand over the island. "Would you like to try one? They are white chocolate chip."

"Sounds good."

Stephen walks over to the platter. "Should I take a wreath or a snowman?" His hand hovers over the plate.

"Try the wreath." Phoebe smiles.

After taking a bite, he nods his head. "Very good, ladies."

Phoebe laughs. "I'm not a lady. I'm a little girl."

"Very good lady *and* little girl." He stands over the sink and brushes the crumbs off his fingers.

Phoebe smiles. "Thank you."

"I didn't realize you were so domesticated." He winks at me. "Seems

71

like we should have made cookies for Gary and Alice, not soup."

"Actually, Phoebe did all the work. I really can't take credit for these delicious cookies at all." I'm only stating the truth. She is a whiz in the kitchen. She knew when the dough was the perfect consistency, and she knew the exact moment to take them out of the oven.

"Good job, Phoebe."

"Thanks, Mr. Stephen."

"Can we bring some of these to church in the morning? These would be great with coffee, and I bet the other kids would like them." Stephen takes another bite as he finishes talking.

"Church?" I ask.

"Yes. We have church here. I converted the third garage into a meeting room. My uncle, Roger Day, is the pastor."

I reach up to touch my scar, my reminder that God didn't see me favorably regarding this issue. Then I remember Stephen's touch. How his fingers caressed my face, how he didn't let my ugliness stop him from kissing me.

How my thoughts can turn from God to kissing in seconds is amazing. Of course, only

Stephen's kisses could warrant such directional changes.

"Yeah." Phoebe starts jumping up and down. "I love it when we come to church here.

Miss Jenny, you are coming, too, aren't you?"

How is it that I'm in a house with two people who I have no power to say no to? I'm not sure what wrecks me more; Phoebe's unseeing eyes or Stephen's amazing kisses.

Not only do both of those things erase the word no from my vocabulary, they both render me totally helpless.

It looks like I'll be going to church in the morning.

IT'S EIGHT O'CLOCK and Phoebe has climbed into her sofa bed. Between her body wash and shampoo, she smells like tangerines and strawberries. I have never felt so comfortable yet uncomfortable around a little person in my life. I have no brothers or sisters. I never babysat as a teen. Little kids and their ways aren't familiar to me at all.

"So, what's happening with Princess Bea?" she asks.

"Ah, yes. Story time." I will admit to thinking about the story while Phoebe was in the shower. I feel a sense of obligation in not wanting to let her down in any way. That includes trying hard not to tell a lame story. "Well, Prince Jonah has come into the palace with bad news for Princess Bea's father. But he hears the music, and he thinks it's beautiful. So he follows it."

"Then he sees Princess Bea, right?"

"Right. He walks into the room where Princess Bea is playing the harp. The room is beautiful with its furniture and wall hangings and carpets, but the prince doesn't see any of that. He only sees Princess Bea."

"And she's beautiful," Phoebe says.

"She is. She has the longest hair he's ever seen. It's brown and beautiful to match her eyes."

"Oh, I know. She's wearing a pretty dress and she's wearing Cinderella shoes. You know, the glass slippers."

"Of course she is. And he's mesmerized," I say.

"Mesmerized? What's that?"

I'm becoming so swept up in the story I'm forgetting Phoebe is only seven. I need to remember she is the focus. "It means he doesn't really notice anything going on around him because he is only looking at her."

"Oh, okay. Like Mr. Stephen is mesmerized when he comes around you."

My story world bubble pops at her words. "Um, I'm not sure that's the same thing."

Phoebe settles comfortably in the covers. "I can tell a difference when you are both in the room." She speaks matter of factly. "I think he's mesmerized."

I don't want to talk about Stephen. "Let's focus on our story."

"Okay." Phoebe pulls the covers around her. "Prince Jonah is mesmerized by Princess Bea."

"So, Princess Bea quits playing the harp and asks him his name. And he tells her it's Prince Jonah. She tells him her name is Princess Bea and he knows she's the king's daughter. He walks over to her, but realizes he has the scroll in his hand. The scroll he's supposed to give her father."

"And the scroll says there's going to be a war?" Her voice sounds anxious.

"Well, the scroll says all the land now belongs to Prince Jonah's father."

"Oh. So what does he do?" She squeezes the end of the covers.

"Princess Bea asks him why he has come to the castle. He's never visited before."

"And he says, 'I've come to take your father's lands.'" Phoebe laughs after she speaks.

"Silly goose." I touch the back of her hand. "No. I don't think he's going to tell her. Because now, maybe he's not sure about taking all the land. Maybe he's going to go back to his father and tell him about the beautiful princess. He might suggest that he marry the princess, then all the lands will belong to their family."

"That sounds good. Then there won't be a war." Her fingers relax.

"Except the king won't see it the same way. He won't want to wait for a wedding. He'll want the lands now."

Phoebe's eyes widen. "Then there will be a war."

"Maybe," I say. "Unless Prince Jonah can change his father's mind."

"Does he? Change his father's mind?"

I tap Phoebe's nose gently. "I guess you'll find out tomorrow night."

"Ah, Miss Jenny. Really?"

"Really. It's time for you to go to sleep." It warms my heart that she's enjoying my story.

"Okay. Can we call my mommy tomorrow?"

"Of course. Mr. Stephen will help you do that."

"Okay."

I brush her bangs out of her eyes. Not sure why, I just felt compelled.

"Goodnight," I whisper.

"Night." She scrunches her eyes shut.

I walk out of her room and into the kitchen. I must admit I've never met anyone like Phoebe.

"So, why did you break up with me?"

Stephen's voice catches me off guard. "What?"

"I need to call Gary in a couple of days to tell him you've broken up with me. He's going to ask why, don't you think?"

"Probably."

"What possible reason would you have for doing such a thing? Breaking my heart like that." His expression screams disbelief.

In thinking about everything I know about Stephen, I try to determine what would drive anyone to break up with him. I wonder if something drove Leah. Or maybe he broke up with her. My mind drifts back to earlier today when we saw the brunette at the Christmas tree place. "Your wandering eye?"

"Wandering eye?"

"Yes. Don't think I didn't notice you staring down the brunette at the Christmas tree farm."

"Uh, that was work."

"Like dinner with the king's daughter was work? You have an interesting job, Stephen."

"It's very interesting. And the king's daughter has a name. Arabella."

He reaches behind his laptop and pulls out his camera. He starts fiddling with the buttons.

"Perfect name for royalty. So I understand that you wouldn't want to tell Gary you have a wandering eye. How about you want me to stay home, birth babies and do your laundry for the rest of my life."

"That might work."

"Really? Well, that right there might be the problem. Our problem. Tell him I've traveled the world, love it and want to continue doing so."

He looks at me, one eyebrow raised. "Are you serious?"

"Will he believe it?"

He shakes his head. "Not sure. I guess it will depend on how broken hearted I sound."

"Break out the tears if you have to."

"Never. Come look at this."

I walk over to him. My stomach flutters being this close in proximity to Stephen. I wish it wouldn't, but there are some things that can't be helped.

I need to find a balance when it comes to Stephen. A balance for my mind and my body. I can't continue to become flustered whenever I'm around him.

"Look at this picture." Our shoulders touch as he shows me a photo.

A sleek, lean cheetah fills the screen. The cheetah's face is turned toward the camera, its eyes wide, searching. One paw is slightly in front of the other, as if the cheetah is ready to pounce at any given second.

"I'm assuming you took this." I can't draw my gaze away from the photo.

"I did. I see you in this picture."

I try to appreciate his words.

But I'm not used to being compared to a four-legged animal.

BEFUDDLED (YES, REALLY)

"GRACE AND BEAUTY exude from this animal."

I look away from the photo as Stephen speaks. His voice carries a passion whenever he talks about his job.

I used to have that same passion. So much passion, in fact, that I risked going under the knife to be the best. But striving to be the best turned out to be the worst thing I could have ever done.

"I see the same traits in you." He cocks his head. "And Lord, help me, I want you to see yourself the way I see you."

My cheek chooses this moment to ache with an abandonment unsurpassed. The scar starts to itch, and it takes everything in me to resist scratching it. The itch starts to tingle.

As long as the tingle stays on my face and away from the parts of my body that are touching Stephen.

"Stephen, I appreciate what you are trying to do. I'm good with who I am. A few months ago I lived to be photographed. Things are different now."

"Different doesn't have to be bad."

He starts stepping backwards, bringing his camera to his eye, like he's going to take my picture.

"What are you doing?" My instinct is to turn away from the camera.

From him.

"Smile." He keeps the camera aimed at me.

Now I do turn away. "No. Are you crazy? And I'm not turning around until you set that camera down."

"Then you won't be looking at me much because I take Millie everywhere."

"Millie?" I will admit that staring at the kitchen cabinets is not as nice as staring at Stephen.

"My camera. Her name's Millie. After my grandmother who taught me to love everything about photography."

"Well, Millie and I aren't friends, understand?"

"Millie loves you."

I don't need his whispered voice close to my ear to tell me Stephen is by my side. My body knows when that man is close. It's insane.

"I set Millie on the counter." He walks around in front of me, palms facing toward me. "See. No Millie."

"Thank you."

Now a silence hovers, mocking the nothingness that really exists between us. We only seem to do two things well. Argue and kiss.

My gaze locks with his.

Blue pools of glass remind me of calm waters fueling the rapid beating of my heart as I realize his eyes have the power to drown me. The fact that simply looking into his eyes can pull me down into who he is, the depths of him waiting to be explored, makes me rethink everything I have ever known about loving someone.

Because I firmly believe I'm not in love with Stephen Day, yet after knowing him for less than forty-eight hours, he's emotionally taken me to places I've never been before.

Ever.

I was with Jeff for over a year and I realize now how lukewarm my emotions were regarding him.

And I thought I loved him.

I now know how little I know about love.

In an attempt to rise to the surface of reality I take a deep breath. The problem?

I'm breathing in everything about Stephen.

His scent, his closeness, his masculinity which causes my feminine side to totally whack out.

And all he's doing is standing in front of me.

I take a step back. "I'm tired. I need sleep."

He smiles and I steady myself against the counter.

"Sleep is overrated." He takes a step closer.

"Sleep is necessary." With all my strength I back up.

He moves closer. "I know you're trying to ditch me."

"I guess I'm not very subtle. Boundaries, remember?" I continue stepping back until there is a fair distance between us.

"I remember." He points to the counter. "Millie may be sitting there, but I'm mentally taking pictures of you."

"Why?"

"Everything about you is elegant. You move your arms and legs with grace. You aren't clumsy or hesitant."

He wouldn't be saying those words if he could see into my jumbled mind. My crazy, mixed up thoughts regarding him would scare him away. I have to think about what's next for me. And that doesn't include Stephen. "I need to see if I can find a model. And a photographer. Unless you—"

"No. Wildlife only."

"It was worth a shot." I'm not sure whether I'm disappointed or relieved at his refusal.

"I guess Phoebe and I have caused a disturbance in your world."

"This is your house. I'm the one doing the disturbing. I'll just work around you." As if that will be easy.

Stephen grabs his camera. "I'll stay out of your way then, Cheetah."

With those words he saunters off, leaving me standing in the kitchen alone. It's only when I feel the urge to sink to the ground in an emotional heap do I realize how wound up I become when Stephen is around.

WATCHING THE SUN rise should be a beautiful experience. But since I haven't slept all night, it's kind of a foggy-state-of-mind experience. I left the confines of my bedroom about a half hour ago in search of something to drink, when the hues of brilliant orange and yellow making a perfect backdrop for the early morning clouds caught my attention.

Forgetting all about my thirst, I walked outside, entranced by the sunrise. Without thinking, I cushioned myself into a comfortable position on a love seat. For the last few minutes I've been looking at the sky, pushing myself out of the work mode I'd been in all night. Now I'm letting my mind wander at will.

Not worrying about my future, and not regretting my past, I rest in the moment. I'm not letting right now be scary. I'm not letting right now be uncertain and weird and unfamiliar.

I'm letting right now be good. All right. Steady.

But steady, all right and good shatter in one blink. As my eyelids open, in a sleep-deprived motion, my vision of the sunrise is replaced by Stephen.

"Morning, Cheetah."

I smile. "More like goodnight."

"Haven't slept?"

"No. Not really."

"Restless night?" His voice is husky like he might have just crawled out of bed.

And Stephen crawling out of bed is an image I can't stay focused on.

My mind would race back to the events of last night if it weren't so tired. Still, visions of the clothing items, the new designs I tried to create, flash through my mind. "It was."

"I didn't get a whole lot of sleep either. Do you mind?" He points to the small empty space next to me.

I swallow as I nod, my body bracing for his nearness.

In the same movement as he sits, he reaches over and pushes my hair away from the front of my face and tucks it behind my ear. "Beauty should never be hidden."

I'm not beautiful anymore.

Being around Stephen tones down the mantra, but it's still there.

He sets Millie on his lap.

I try not to envy Millie.

I can't believe that thought entered my mind. This is why it is dangerous to be around Stephen.

Much better to have a befuddled mind from no sleep than a befuddled mind from too much Stephen. And I'm quickly learning that any Stephen qualifies as too much Stephen.

"Amazing sunrise." Stephen puts Millie to his eye. I hear the clicking sound of the shutter as he snaps pictures.

As long as Millie is not focused on me, I'm good.

"Wanna learn?"

"Learn what?"

"How to capture beauty through a view finder."

My first inclination is to refuse. But from nowhere comes this thought that if both he and I are behind the camera, I won't be in front of the camera. And I do have to have those items of clothing photographed once I find someone who will wear them. It wouldn't hurt to practice on a sunrise. "Sure, I'll try."

He holds Millie out in front of me. "Go ahead."

As he hands over Millie, I can't help but think how he's handing over his heart.

His world.

To me.

Yes, I'm probably overdramatizing this exchange, but being awake almost twenty-four straight hours has its drawbacks.

I put the viewfinder to my eye. My left hand wraps around the lens, and I turn it left and then back a little right, trying to focus. Satisfied with the view, I click the button.

The familiar it's-how-I-make-my-living sound reverberates through my being.

But in a totally different vein.

It's like my insides have burst to life. Like the blood in my veins is no longer a small stream, trickling its way to the mouth of a lazy river. No, it's like waves surging to the shore, drenching the sand, soaking into every corner of life they can find, thriving on what they're meant to do. Shape the sand.

Change the shoreline.

Yeah, that's how I'm feeling inside.

My hands tremble at the intensity of this recognition.

"Did you get a good shot?"

"I'm not sure." The three words are all I can muster.

"Let me look."

As he takes the camera, his hand covers mine, his warmth only serving to fuel this raging storm within me. He has no idea what he has unleashed, and I'm not going to tell him.

"Wow." His voice holds a hint of excitement. "This is brilliant. I think you have a natural eye."

His compliment wants to embed itself into my being, but I brush it away with a note that it's flattery, plain and simple. "Thanks."

"Seriously. What stands out to you about this?"

He nestles close to me, shoulder to shoulder, thigh to thigh. His hair touches mine as he invades my space with the most casual air about him, oblivious to the tornado of feelings he stirs in me.

With shallow breathing, lest I breathe in too much Stephen, I look at the screen.

I see a sunrise. And since that's what I took a picture of I think it's a good thing. I see nothing brilliant about it except its own brilliance. Nothing I caused. "It's a sunrise. Um, that's all I see."

"I know the screen is small, but look close. Toward the top. The super-intensified golden color at the top of those clouds. It's gone now, but you captured that moment in time forever."

His tone has ramped up my excitement a notch, and I didn't think that was possible.

I peer closer, blinking rapidly to focus.

"Here." He pushes some buttons zooming in toward the top of the picture.

A small gasp escapes as I see what he's talking about. I lift my gaze and look to the sky and see clouds void of the golden icing I captured in the photo. "I think it was luck."

"Cheetah, I think I have severe control issues when I'm around you."

I turn my head to look at him and quickly realize what a mistake I've made. His lips are right there, magnets drawing me in. As his lips touch mine, it comes to my attention that I don't remember what life was like before his kisses.

Before I knew lips could be so soft, their touch so demanding yet gentle in a please-don't-break kind of way. Boldly, I run my hand through his hair. It feels silky, like I thought it would. I'm amazed at how right and unreal his kiss feels.

"Mr. Stephen, are you kissing Miss Jenny?"

BLESSED

AS STEPHEN abruptly ends our kiss, my mind registers Phoebe's voice. Her insight once again amazes me. That child sees more than anyone I know.

I ditch her question. "Would you like some breakfast?"

"Sure. Was Mr. Stephen kissing you?"

Might as well answer, although she already knows. But she's not going to let this go. "Yes. A short kiss and it's over now."

Stephen nods his head as he stands, taking Millie with him. "I need to get ready for church. Roger and Celine will be here shortly."

My insides groan. How likely is it that I'll be able to crawl in my bed and sleep while all the church people are here?

"Do you need to get ready too, Miss Jenny?"

Not likely.

But I knew that. Really I did. The minute Stephen mentioned the church here, deep in my gut I knew I would be attending. The deep in my gut feeling wasn't a bad feeling, it was a strong feeling.

And that feeling doesn't dissipate as I walk with Phoebe into the house to fix her breakfast. As in cereal. Stephen follows, but heads down the hall.

"You two really like each other, don't you, Miss Jenny?"

I know I have to answer her. "He's okay. Do you want Fruit Loops?"

"Yes. I'm glad you think he's okay. My mommy says he's really nice and he's thoughtful of others. I think Prince Jonah is thoughtful of others, too, don't you think?"

No sleep combined with Stephen's kisses equal a not-so-swift-thinking me. But after a couple of moments, our imaginary prince rears his head in my mind. "Yes. I'm sure of it."

"Good. Because I think he's going to be thoughtful toward Princess Bea."

"Yes, he will."

I slide the bowl of cereal in front of Phoebe who sits on the stool at the island. The stool I was sitting in when I blurted out the untruth about Stephen and I being engaged, which I have to admit has landed me in a mess.

A beautiful mess if I think on Stephen's kisses. But a total mess in all other aspects.

Church. Seriously?

Don't get me wrong. God's okay, even though I'm not sure about the role He had in my surgery. I have nothing against church, but this is going to be a small group of people who all know each other. I'll be the "new" person.

It's going to be awkward.

Never mind I haven't been to church in quite a while. I remember books of the Bible, but other than the names of some of them, I can't remember too much content.

"You'll be okay if I go get ready, right?" I ask Phoebe.

"Sure. I'll be fine. Get all prettied up for Mr. Stephen."

Prettied up? She has no idea how impossible that is.

AS I HEAD DOWN the hall to the entrance to the former garage-now church, I hear the buzz of conversation. My heels sound off my steps on the tiled floor as I timidly approach the door.

I've pulled my hair back in a ponytail, something I haven't done since the surgery. I have no idea where this confidence came from.

Taking a step inside the room, I square my shoulders and smile.

A smile which I forcefully keep plastered upward as all conversation ceases. Seriously, it's like a B movie come to life.

Why didn't I at least bring a purse? Something to latch onto, hold, anything that I could focus my attention on besides the faces staring back at me.

Faces that belong to bodies clad in jeans, T-shirt, shorts. Nobody, but nobody, is wearing a dress.

Even Phoebe has on her jeans and pink pullover she wore this morning.

Why didn't I ask about the dress code? Don't people dress up for church anymore?

"Jenny." Stephen walks to me. "You look amazing. Especially the shoes."

In a horribly failed attempt at humor, I had slipped on my cheetah-patterned platform pumps. In my defense, they do match my dress. The definitive word here being dress. I feel like I'm on the runway. And I feel more naked than if I were wearing only my underwear.

"Thank you. It appears I'm a little overdressed."

"Nonsense. God loves us however we dress. Come with me. I want to introduce you to my uncle and his wife."

He nods his head toward a small group of people. Then, in an unexpected move, he takes my hand in his.

He makes some introductions as we approach people. Then we are standing in front of a man almost as handsome as Stephen, but not quite. The woman standing next to him is stunning in her skinny jeans, silver and white striped top, and black flat boots.

"This is my Uncle Roger and his wife Celine. This is Jenny Harris. My house guest."

Roger smiles and gives me a hug. Celine follows. They seem extra happy or something. They can't quit smiling, and I'm wondering about this God thing. Does He really give people this much joy?

"It's nice to meet you, Jenny. We're glad you could join us today." Roger's voice is strong like Stephen's. And he's tilting his head a little, like he wants to say more, but doesn't.

"I'm glad I can be here." And right now, I am glad. I'm still exhausted and my brain still feels fogged, but the atmosphere of this room and these people has lifted some of my tiredness. Maybe some of their joy is contagious and by simply breathing it will come to me.

Roger points to the entrance. "Stephen. There's Brett Hamilton. He and his gal, Ann, are getting married next weekend. In the gazebo. I have the honor of marrying them."

Stephen nods. "I saw an invitation when I went through my mail. I haven't seen Brett in a while and I've never met Ann, so I'm going to go say hello. Jenny?" He tilts his head, indicating he wants me to accompany him.

"Nice meeting you two."

Roger starts shuffling some papers. "Likewise."

Stephen doesn't take my hand this time, but he does place his hand on my shoulder, as if I need guidance to maneuver across the room. We have to slip by a few people, as the space is tight, and the people are many.

"Brett." Stephen shakes Brett's hand. "Long time."

"Hey, there. It's been a while. Are you home for the holidays?"

Stephen laughs. "Sort of."

Brett places his hand on the shoulder of the woman standing next to him. "This is my fiancée, Ann. Ann, Stephen Day, Roger's nephew, and I'm afraid I don't know the lady."

"Nice to meet you, Ann. This is Jenny Harris." Stephen speaks my name like he's proud to introduce me.

We all kind of say hi at the same time. Ann is looking at me in a strange way. Not bad strange, more like puzzled strange. Handsome, well built Brett, only has eyes for Ann, his gaze rarely leaving her.

I can see why Brett keeps his focus on Ann. She's beautiful with her red hair and green eyes. Her smile is warm.

The fog begins to lift as I take Ann in from her feet to the top of her head. Her build, her look. It says SunKissed! My tired brain springs to life and energy buzzes through me.

"I hope you don't mind me asking, but don't you model for Simply Midnight?" Ann's voice is hesitant.

I might as well get used to this question. I'm sure it's not the last time I'll be asked. "I used to." Even though I keep my answer short, I feel compelled to divulge more. But I squelch that urge as I'm overtired and most assuredly becoming more dramatic by the minute. Especially since I found my model.

Seriously.

"Well, I'm a fan. It's very nice to meet you." Ann nestles in closer to Brett, and I mentally frame a photograph.

I find myself smiling. "Thank you."

"Cheetah, you'll always have fans."

Stephen's arm has slid off my shoulder and now nestles on my lower back. His hand cups my hip in a possessive way. I find myself comfortable with these people thinking I'm his.

But I can't keep from thinking about Ann and my clothing line.

Brett looks at Stephen. "Since you're in town, I hope you can make it to our wedding next weekend. Especially since it's practically in your front yard."

"Yeah. I'll be there. And I'll be bringing a guest."

"Jenny Harris is going to be at my wedding?" Ann asks, in a whispered tone.

That's the question I was ready to ask.

"Jenny Harris will be at your wedding." Stephen moves closer to me.

Thinking about how I can convince her to model my clothing, I agree. Then I remember Phoebe. "I will, as long as we can bring Phoebe. We can't leave her alone."

"Phoebe is more than welcome." Brett's gaze scans the room. "Where's Teresa?"

Stephen quickly explains the situation regarding the accident in Mexico.

"That's terrible news. We'll be praying for her family."

"Thanks." Stephen looks toward Roger. "It looks like we're about to get started. We better find a seat."

People have started toward the folding chairs that are leaning against a wall. Stephen grabs one for each of us. There appears to be no rhyme or reason to where anyone is sitting. Except that everyone is facing Stephen's uncle.

Stephen motions for me to sit, our chairs close together. The soft cushions make them more comfortable than I had imagined.

I look around for Phoebe. She's sitting with a group of girls who look to be teenagers.

And she told me she didn't have any friends.

Even though the girls are older than she is, they seem to have taken her under their wing.

Like Stephen has taken me under his.

Like I want to take Ann under mine.

Brett and Ann are sitting on the other side of Stephen. I have to stop myself from staring at them. Everything about them shouts "we're in love." Thinking back on my life and relationships, I'm not sure anyone would have ever looked at me and any of my boyfriends and thought those words.

Roger has strapped on a guitar, and Celine and another woman, whose name I can't remember, stand up by Roger. A teenaged boy sits behind a single drum. Words appear on the wall to the right of them, and Roger starts playing. The trio starts singing and everyone, including me, stands. A young guy manages the computer, keeping the words moving on the wall.

These people sing loud, and I find my toes starting to wiggle in my cheetah-print shoes. A couple of people put their hands in the air. The drumbeat of the music has a cool sound to it, and I can see why people are so moved.

Words like, "raised us from the dead," "brought us to life," "singing freedom's song"? Those words are new to me in music. And besides, it's Christmas. Aren't we supposed to be singing Christmas songs?

I have to admit the tunes are catchy, though. There is a lot of dancing going on. The teenage crowd jumps up and down to one of the songs. A song about God's great dance floor?

Really?

Only after we've been singing that song for a little while do I realize my foot is tapping and my hips are moving side to side.

I look to see if anyone is looking at me, and no one is.

Except Stephen.

He smiles when our gazes meet but then turns his attention back to the music. His singing voice is soft. I can't tell if it's in tune or not, but I don't think God cares.

After all, the only singing voice I have is the one God gave me, so He better like it. But, still, I'm not singing.

We all stay standing as a couple of kids who look like they're in middle school walk to a table up front that holds a wreath with five candles.

The girl with the dark brown hair speaks first. "The first Sunday of Advent we lit a candle to get our hearts ready for Jesus."

Celine lights one of the candles.

A girl with blonde hair speaks next. "The second Sunday of Advent we lit the candle of love."

Celine lights another one of the candles.

Both young girls turn and face us, speaking at the same time. "This third Sunday of Advent we light the candle of joy."

As Celine lights a third candle, Roger starts strumming, and everyone starts singing "Joy to the World."

At last, a song I know.

When the singing is done, we sit. Roger prays and passes around a basket for an offering. And once again, I wish I had brought my purse. Not that I have any extra money, but it feels awkward not putting anything in the basket as it goes by.

I notice a lot of people have Bibles on their lap. One more item I don't have in my possession.

As Roger starts his sermon, I find myself nestling closer to Stephen. All the energy I mustered up to say hello, then stand while singing, threatens to depart while we sit, but thoughts of Ann in my clothing flood my mind.

I try to focus on what Roger is saying, but I can't. Visions of my clothing line, Sunkissed!, float along with Ann's face and body. It's like I designed the clothing line just for her.

She's my perfect prototype.

But she's real. And she's here. She has to say yes.

Goose bumps play up my arms, and I think I'm starting to feel the joy we were singing about a few minutes ago. But how will I pull it off? Should I just ask her?

I would have to hire a photographer or photograph her myself.

My heart sinks. No money equals no photographer, and I don't think snapping a few photographs of a sunrise qualifies me to photograph a line of clothing.

My heart starts to race. I look at Stephen. No. He won't change his mind. Why should he? A world famous wildlife photographer has no reason to take pictures of my clothing worn by the literal girl-next-door.

"It's now time for yay Gods," Roger says. "I know God's been working this week, so now it's time to tell us how."

Is God working in my life? Did he just hand me a model?

An older man speaks up about how he received a promotion he'd been praying for. A lady talks about her aunt who'd been healed this past week of an illness that she'd been fighting for a while.

People smile and clap at the good news.

When no one speaks for a short while, I think we are wrapping things up. Which pleases me greatly because my brain is working overtime figuring out how and if I can talk to Ann. But Roger holds up his hand. "Everyone stay seated. We do have one more piece of good news."

Roger starts walking between the chairs. Each step brings him closer to Stephen and me. Then Roger walks behind us, and I breathe a sigh. But the relief only lasts momentarily because Roger stops and places one of his hands on Stephen's shoulder and the other hand on my shoulder.

"I heard some good news this week that I want to share with everyone."

I feel my face turning red. I mean, I can feel the heat. And this heat isn't from Stephen. My heart and brain knows what is coming.

And there's nothing I can do to stop it.

"It seems," Roger continues, "that my nephew is engaged."

Shouts and applause follow Roger's words. Brett is immediately in front of us, shaking Stephen's hand before leaning over to hug me as best as he can considering I'm sitting and he's standing.

"This is indeed a blessing." Roger's voice sounds like he's becoming choked up. "A blessing to see Stephen so happy. And we welcome Jenny to the family with open arms."

As Brett steps away, others come and congratulate us. Stephen keeps shaking hands. Eventually, we stand. The hugs keep coming.

Phoebe walks up holding the hand of one of the older girls.

"I'm confused." Her expression is puzzled. "You didn't tell me you and Mr. Stephen are getting married."

"I'll explain later," I tell her.

She smiles. "Okay."

"You have no idea how much explaining you are going to have to do."

Stephen's words are whispered into my ear. I'm sure anyone watching is thinking he's whispering sweet things to me.

I had no idea the damage those three words, "I'm Stephen's fiancée," would cause.

BRIGHT

"SO, WHEN IS the wedding date, Jenny. Honey. Baby."

Everyone has left, and Stephen and I are alone. The teenage girls asked if they could take Phoebe out to lunch with them. Phoebe looked so excited I didn't have the heart to say no. Stephen agreed, and after a promise of returning Phoebe by three o'clock, they left.

"Stephen, *honey*, *baby*, I don't know." My fun thoughts of Ann and my SunKissed! line have vanished in the wake of the fake engagement rearing up again.

"How did this thing spiral so far out of control? First Gary, then my coworkers, now my family and the church family? Jenny, this is huge."

I take a couple of deep breaths. "How did he find out?"

"I don't know."

"Somebody must have called him. Would Gary do that?"

"I doubt it. But I don't know who Gary has called. He told everybody at the mag. But you are the one who told Gary you were my fiancée. You."

"I know. But I tried to tell him I lied. He didn't believe me."

"Lying is never good. Now, we are going to have to tell another lie when we break up. This thing has the potential to turn even uglier."

My brain is back to being tired, sleep deprived and foggy. I sit in one of the folding chairs and kick off my cheetah pumps. "We're going to break up in a day or two, remember? Then this will all be over. And you can be rid of your fiancée. I'll just be a friend."

"Friend?"

His expression reveals everything he is thinking. Am I that painful of a friend? He really doesn't know me. "I'm sorry the thought pains you."

"Were you listening to Roger this morning?"

"Stephen, I don't need any false hope of words in a book. I need a future."

"Lord, this is so difficult."

"You're telling me."

"I wasn't speaking with you, I was speaking with the Lord."

Stephen shakes his head and looks upward before walking out of the room, leaving me all by myself, sitting in the folding chair. My dress is rumpled, my shoes lay on the floor and if it was possible, my heart would be right next to them.

"MR. STEPHEN WANTS to know if you want some dinner."

I open my eyes, Phoebe's voice coming through a muffled filter that is my brain. "Dinner?"

"Yes. Dinner's ready. What happened to your room? It feels like I'm stepping on clothes."

Yes, she is stepping on clothes. "I was working and didn't clean up. I'll be out in a minute for dinner."

"Okay. What kind of work do you do with clothes?"

"That's what I'm trying to figure out, Pheebes."

I throw back the covers. Phoebe leaves the room, and I go into the bathroom. As I brush my teeth and wash my face, I try to convince myself that dinner with Stephen and Phoebe is what I need to be doing. Brushing my hair, I decide I am hungry, so I make my way to the kitchen.

My stomach verifies the hunger issue as it growls at the scents of something yummy filling the air. Yummy and greasy and oh-so-not-good for me, I'm sure.

I spy chicken wings coated in hot sauce on the counter, along with a salad and a dish of macaroni and cheese.

An odd combination until I remember that Phoebe is eating.

"You decided to join us, I see." Stephen body is tense, but his eyes are warm.

"Yes. The Lord didn't tell you I was going to?"

"Excuse me?"

"Well, if you talk to Him I thought he might talk back. You know, tell you things."

He raises an eyebrow. "Are you making fun of Jesus?"

My heart jolts. Am I? That can't be good. Along with lying, no telling what Stephen thinks of me. "I didn't mean for it to sound like that."

"You do love Jesus, don't you, Miss Jenny?"

There's that sweet Phoebe voice again. Do I love Jesus? I like Jesus. I'd never really thought about loving Him. It's at this moment that I realize I really don't know all that much about Jesus. How can I love someone I don't know?

The word love shifts my focus to Stephen. My focus and my gaze. The clash of all his strength handling delicate, breakable plates.

"Miss Jenny?"

Phoebe. She asked me a question. About loving Jesus. My heart painfully steers toward honesty. "I do like Jesus."

"That's a start."

My heart whooshes at *her* honesty. "Did you have fun at lunch?" I'm more than ready to move this conversation away from me and Jesus.

"I did. The girls are nice."

"Did you tell Jenny you got to speak with your mother?" Stephen asks.

"My mommy called." Phoebe sounds happy. "Grandpa and Grandma are still in the hospital. Mommy is still worried about them. She didn't say so, but I can tell."

I'm sure she can tell. "I'm sorry they are still in the hospital, but I'm glad you were able to talk with her."

"She told Mr. Stephen the directions so he can take me to my school tomorrow."

Stephen has set the plates and silverware on the table. Wanting to be of some help, I carry the food to the table. "Are you excited about going to school?"

"No. I'd rather stay here with you and Mr. Stephen."

"You'll learn a lot more in school," I say.

"There's a lot to learn here." She wiggles her way onto the chair.

Stephen laughs.

Did she just really say that? "There's more to learn at school."

"Like you're still learning about Jesus?" She feels the table, finding her utensils.

I set the bowl of macaroni and cheese down close to her. "Sure."

"Ladies, I think it's time to eat." Stephen sits to Phoebe's right.

Trying to avoid being close to Stephen, I sit to Phoebe's left.

Stephen takes Phoebe's hand in his. "Phoebe, do you want to say the blessing?"

"Yes."

She reaches over and grabs my right hand. I look across the table, and Stephen has his hand out, so I place my left hand in his. The warmth from their hands feels natural, like this is something we do all the time.

"Jesus. Thank you for this food. Thank you for Mr. Stephen and Miss Jenny and I'm glad they are getting married. We want this food to make us strong so we can tell people about you. And thank you for telling Santa where I am. Amen."

Their hands let go of mine. As they do so, the warmth flees, like it's draining out of my heart, like the lie I told has left me cold, alone, in the middle of all that is warmth and love. She told God she was glad we are getting married.

God knows the truth.

I know the truth.

My scar aches, mirroring my heart, and I realize I have no idea what I've been dropped in the middle of.

EVEN THOUGH I had a nap this afternoon, my body wants to snuggle down in the covers with Phoebe. My eyes want to close and I want to sleep peacefully. But Phoebe isn't as ready for me to sleep. She wants me to continue the story of Princess Bea and Prince Jonah.

Her hands grasp her blanket that we found in her suitcase a couple of nights ago. "So, does Prince Jonah change his father's mind?" she asks.

"Whoa. You are moving ahead in the story. Remember Princess Bea asks Prince Jonah why he is at the castle. He's holding the decree, and he doesn't want to lie to the princess."

"Because lying isn't good."

I'm glad she can't see my face turning red. "No. Lying isn't good. So he tells her he came to see her father, but when he heard her beautiful music he had to see who was playing it."

"And that's what happened."

"It is. Princess Bea thanks him for the compliment regarding the music. He asks her how long she's been playing the harp, and she tells him since she was three."

"Three? Wow. That's a long time. She was little when she learned."

An idea starts to form in my mind. "Yes, she was. Her mother taught her and told her she would continue to play the harp beautifully until she married. After she married she wouldn't be able to play anymore."

"That's sad. Why?"

"Because there was a curse. It had happened to Princess Bea's mother, grandmother, great-grandmother and all the other grandmother's before that."

"A curse? What kind of curse?"

"The Music Curse. The women would play their beautiful music, and that music would call to the man that would be their husband. When they married, they had no reason to play. Of course, Prince Jonah had no idea of what was happening, but when Princess Bea saw him walk in, she knew she was going to marry him."

"Did she tell him?" Phoebe asks.

"No. She couldn't. It's not allowed. She had to make him think he wanted to marry her."

"Wow." Her voice is soft, like we're telling a secret.

"But there was one problem."

"What?"

"Princess Bea didn't want to quit playing her beautiful music. She wanted to marry the prince *and* be able to play her harp."

"So what does she do?"

"Tomorrow night."

"Oh, Miss Jenny? Why do we have to wait until tomorrow?"

So I can think of what happens next in the story.

"Because it's time for you to go to bed. You have school tomorrow."

"Okay."

She may act like she's disappointed, but I can tell she's tired. Going out with the girls this afternoon was something she's not used to doing. It was exciting as well.

After we say our goodnights, I leave the study and go in search of Stephen. When I don't see him in the kitchen or living room or on the terrace, I start to worry. I walk down the hall toward my room and spot him in what I'm assuming is the master suite. First door on the left.

Stopping outside the room, I look through the open door. He has a clipboard and is jotting something on a paper attached to it. It almost looks like he's drawing.

Even though I don't say anything, he turns and stares straight at me. "Hello, Jenny Harris."

"Hi. Are you taking Phoebe to school tomorrow?"

"Yes. I've already put her booster seat in my car."

I should have known. "Nice. Thinking ahead."

He shrugs his shoulders like it was no big deal. "The morning might be a little crazy."

"It might. What are you doing?"

"Making sure I know how I want the furniture arranged when it's delivered."

Stephen fills a room. No matter what size, his presence captivates every inch of space that surrounds him.

Or that he invades.

I have a hard time envisioning anything that can contain Stephen. "Tell me about the lion. The one in the picture with you."

His eyes light up. "His name is Sebastian. I've been around him since he was a cub."

"Is he that friendly to everyone?"

He shakes his head. "No. Just a couple of us."

"It's a great picture."

"I like it."

I take a step into the room, void of everything but Stephen. The tile floor is cold on my feet. The walls are painted white, the same color as the blinds that hang in front of the window.

He tucks his clipboard under his arm. "Teresa told me she hoped to be home Christmas Eve day. She didn't want to say anything to Phoebe in case she isn't, but her parents are going to be all right. They'll be in the hospital for a few more days, then she'll settle them at home and make sure they have good care before she leaves."

"That's good news. Phoebe will be so surprised."

"I told Teresa to let me know when she's made her plane reservations. Then we'll tell Phoebe."

"That will be a great Christmas present for her. Speaking of presents, did Teresa buy her any, or is that something we need to handle?"

"It's is all taken care of. She says she can wrap it all Christmas Eve after Phoebe goes to bed."

An unexpected feeling of disappointment courses through me. Like I am now missing out on something.

Maybe the thought of buying Christmas presents had me more excited than I thought. Thoughts of seeing a little girl's smile on Christmas morning and knowing I had something to do with it.

Oh, well. Christmas isn't about me.

It's not even going to affect me this year. I came here to forget it's the holiday season, yet at every turn I'm reminded of it.

At least now I can return to my original mindset of sleeping in late on Christmas morning. Maybe even forget it's actually Christmas Day.

In a couple of days, Stephen will have "broken up" with me, the New Year's Eve engagement party will be cancelled, and I'll be back to my old self again.

Except now, things have the possibility to have a new look about them. I just have to approach it in the right way. "So, about this wedding we are going to. How well to you know Brett and Ann?"

"I've known Brett for a couple of years of seeing him off and on at the church, when I've been in town. He was an accountant but now is a missionary in Peru. I guess he came back here to get married. I only met Ann today. They just met last spring."

"And they are already getting married?"

"Yep. It happens like that sometimes."

"Not with me, it wouldn't. I'd have to know somebody a long time before I committed spending the rest of my life with them. Talk about a life sentence."

He rolls his eyes and shakes his head. "Is that how you see marriage? As a life sentence?"

"Well, it is for life. I believe that. So it's better to know all you can about them. No surprises, you know?"

"Surprises don't always have to be a bad thing."

The conversation is moving far beyond the scope of where I was trying to take it. "So, you don't know how long they are in town?"

"No. Why?"

I take a deep breath. Should I tell him my idea? Will he think I'm crazy? Will he help me out at all?

BUTTERFLY

I TAKE A DEEP breath, readying myself for a rejection. "I have an idea, but I need your help."

That sentence pulls his attention away from the musings of the bare room and focuses it directly on me. "My help?"

Really, his tone doesn't reveal much. He could go either way. "Yes. Ann would be the perfect model for my SunKissed! line. Perfect. I could put together an awesome portfolio with her wearing my clothes. It's like they were created for her."

"And, this has to do with me, how?" His expression is curious, like he doesn't have a clue as to why I would need his help.

"You know Brett. Maybe you can find out how long they are going to be in town. Maybe ask if she'd be interested in having a few pictures taken of her? Wearing my clothes?"

He sweeps his hand across his brow, his brown hair falling back into place when he's through. It's insane how I notice everything this man does.

I now notice he turns away from me, focusing his attention back to the bare, plain room. "They're right next door. You can take a walk over there just as easy as I can. Ann seemed enamored and in awe of you, anyway. It might be better coming from you."

"I'm sure she has a lot to do with her wedding less than a week away. I'd feel like I was imposing."

"But it's okay if I impose?"

"My thoughts were more geared toward you mentioning it to Brett and he could ask her when the time was good."

He turns back toward me. "You're thinking a guy would have the sensitivity to know when it's a good time? Aren't we accused of just the opposite?"

Can I ever win with this guy? But he does have a point. "Would you go with me, tomorrow?"

"I thought you didn't have a photographer."

Wow. Maybe going to church this morning was a good idea. I couldn't have asked for a more perfect segue into asking Stephen if he would photograph Ann.

If she said yes.

"Well, you're a photographer. I was thinking maybe…"

"No. Sorry. I don't photograph people. We've had this conversation."

When Stephen takes a stance on something, one needs to know it's going to be impossible to change his mind. Even if I could explain how my heart dropped when he said the word no, I don't think it would change his mind at all.

I guess going to church didn't help me as much as I thought.

Another idea walks into my mind. This one is a little crazier.

More risky in the scope of all considered.

But it seems I have no choice.

Being with bold, unwavering Stephen makes me even bolder. "You said I had a natural eye. Can I borrow Millie?"

EVEN THE STRONGEST coffee and another beautiful sunrise can't erase the "are you crazy" expression Stephen gave me last night when I asked about borrowing Millie.

He didn't answer and the brief bout of boldness I felt left me immediately, so I didn't restate my request. I did retreat to my room, where I looked up cameras on my computer. All I discovered was an amazing influx of confusing information.

Maybe Stephen can lead me in the right direction for a camera, if he won't let me borrow his.

Although, I don't need to be spending a lot of money. Some of the cameras were ridiculously expensive. And the accessories were equally pricy.

Right now, budgeting is most important.

I pull the throw I grabbed off the back of the couch around me a little tighter. The morning is cool, my coffee is hot, and my nerves are on edge anticipating Stephen's return from taking Phoebe to school.

My gaze takes in this backyard area. All the seating, the pool, the natural beauty. Setting my coffee on the table, I stand and start walking around. Visions of my clothes come into mind. What a perfect place for the photos to be taken. SunKissed! can really come to life here, in this place.

So many possibilities.

A skinny palm juts out from a plain brown planter. The grayish trunk of the tree along with the brown color of the planter beg for color. My heart rate accelerates at the image in my mind. Ann, wearing the knee-length skirt and lacy top, sitting on the edge of the planter, parades before my imagination.

I run across the patio, the throw slipping from my shoulders. I stop and pick it up and toss it on the settee as I pass by. Using what girlie strength I have, I pull a planter from where it leans against a wall. I scoot it backwards until it's sitting at the edge of the pool. A metal sunflower sticks out of the pot. The metal is painted yellow. I'm disappointed to find the metal is chipped in places.

Maybe it won't be visible from further away. I start stepping backwards until the blue of the pool, and the yellow of the sunflower are in a good visual spot. Deciding I need more perspective, I take one more step back.

My breath hitches as my back slams into something hard.

Lean.

Stephen.

Usually able to detect him even when I don't see him, I'm surprised I didn't know he was here.

My excitement must have overtaken my Stephen radar.

Not a good thing.

Strong hands steady my shoulders, keeping me close.

"Can I ask what you are doing?" His voice is like the soft warm breeze of December in Florida, tickling my ear.

I make no attempt to leave his embrace. "I'm visualizing photos here in this backyard. It would be a great place to photograph Ann in SunKissed!

designs. I spotted the sunflower from across the pool, but I didn't realize how beat up it really is."

He slides his hands down my arms. "You call it beat up. I call it character."

"Call it what you want, I need perfection for these photos." I hope he hears the seriousness of my tone. I do need perfection.

"Dig deeper." His tone is challenging.

I'm not grasping his challenge.

"What?"

Stephen steps around me and heads for the sunflower. "Come here."

It's only a few steps, I reason. But somehow everything with Stephen is exaggerated. When I reach the plant, I stop and look at him.

He points to a brownish-coppery place on the sunflower. "What has happened here?"

"The paint has chipped off."

"You think so? Why do you think it was sitting under cover of the patio?"

Are we really engaging in a conversation about the placement of a metal sunflower? I guess we are. "Because that's where someone moved it."

Rolling his eyes, he hitches his thumb in his jean pocket. "Cheetah, work with me here."

Feeling too excited for his broodiness, I try to mold my mindset into his. "Maybe someone moved it there so it would be out of the weather?"

"Maybe. Sometimes we need pruning to be of good character. But there is a balance. Just the right amount can make us into who God wants us to be."

God? Pruning? "We're talking about a metal sunflower."

"Are we?"

"I am. What are you talking about?"

He reaches toward me, his index finger tracing my cheek just below my scar. "Appearances can be deceiving."

It's all I can do to keep my composure as his touch drifts from my cheek to my ear. He traces the top of my ear, down to my lobe, before finding his way to my neck. At this point I'm hoping his statement has truth. I want to appear unmoved by his ministrations, but my knees threaten to buckle at the sweet sensation that now tingles far past the point of his physical touch.

"What about you?" I ask. "You appear to be cool, controlled. You hang out in the jungles of the worlds, with ferocious prey all around, yet the thought of committing to one female seems to shatter your world. Are you who you appear to be?"

His gaze doesn't leave mine as he draws me toward him. He wraps his arms around me, pulling me close in an embrace as gentle as one would hold a baby, yet strong enough to know he means it.

My head rests on his shoulder, and I'm not sure who's consoling who.

"Sometimes," he starts, "I have no idea what's in store for me. I do know what I'm called to and what my passions are. But there are times when I'm surprised where God leads me."

He speaks the last sentence low and throaty, like the words can barely come out. Like speaking them is an admission of something dreadful.

I wonder if he is thinking about Leah.

"You are so in tune to who God is." I've never known anyone to speak so boldly of God.

The comforting feeling of his hands lightly stroking my back could become addicting. Stephen brings a measure of security I've never felt with anyone.

Yet, being around Stephen brings out my insecurities in a way I've never experienced.

AS STEPHEN AND I walk out the front door, an anticipation I haven't felt in a long time consumes me. Stephen is escorting me next door to Ann's house, which she apparently inherited earlier this year.

Talk about an inheritance.

The mid-morning sun shines, and I'm glad I remembered to use my sunscreen lotion on my face and arms. While it's only a short walk, the sun doesn't need much time to do damage.

"Thank you for going with me." I hope he knows I really mean it.

"I'm going to 'break the ice' then I'm leaving. Hanging out with two women talking about clothes isn't my idea of fun."

"Besides roaming around the jungles, what is your idea of fun?"

"Right now it's calling Gary and telling him you broke my heart. I need to do that soon. Today, preferably."

Thankfully my steps don't falter with my heartbeats. It's ridiculous of me to think anything less would happen, but Stephen's gentle side has drawn me in to a place unfamiliar, yet intriguing. His boldness, though, reminds me reality reigns. "I'm glad I didn't break your heart before you helped me out here. That would have been devastating for me."

"And there's no good reason for both of us to be devastated, right?"

The way his words make me laugh warms my heart.

As we near the end of the driveway, Stephen stops. "Hey. There's Ann in the gazebo."

My gaze turns to the middle of the cul-de-sac, where the big, white gazebo sits. Ann is walking around the grassy area, notebook and pen in hand. Her hair is piled on her head in a loose knot, her jeans and T-shirt giving her the perfect girl next door look.

Exactly what I'm looking for.

Stephen and I start walking across the street when she spots us. Immediately her hand goes to her hair, like she's trying to smooth it. Her smile is hesitant, but it's there.

"Hello," Stephen calls out.

She returns the greeting and waves.

"All ready for the big day?" Stephen asks as we step onto the grassy area of the cul-de-sac.

"Pretty much. I'm just making some last minute notes. Four days left."

"Has it been stressful?" I recall most of my friend's weddings. Crazed-out brides and nervous mothers seemed to rule the wedding mantra.

"Not really. It's a small wedding. Simple. We both have small families, and we only invited a few friends."

Ann's gaze doesn't meet mine. She has no problem looking at Stephen. And I don't mean in a flirtatious way. It's like she feels comfortable with him, even though they've only met.

She doesn't appear comfortable around me at all.

Which won't bode well if I'm photographing her.

"What made you decide to tie the knot here?" My goal? To generate some casual conversation before I ask the big question.

Or favor.

Whatever category my request falls under.

"My mom married my dad here, years ago."

Still her gaze remains anywhere but me. If I was the type of person that cursed, I would probably be cursing my scar here and now. "That's nice. I guess they had a great marriage."

Ann laughs. "No, actually, it didn't even last three months. It's a complicated story. But I know they loved each other. So that's what I believe in. The love."

A dreamer? She seems so grounded. "I think it's sweet that you chose their spot."

The conversation is awkward, with nothing more to say. It would be a great time for Stephen to step in. I gently tap his arm, hoping he'll catch my signal.

He better unless he wants to stand here all day.

Which is something I don't want to do. I'm already wishing I had covered my arms. Brilliant rays of warmth are such a contrast to what I'm used to this time of year.

"Well, Ann, I believe Jenny would like to talk to you. So, I'm going to head back to the house. I'll see you Friday night. Tell Brett hello for me."

Stephen steps in front of me, brushing a quick kiss across my lips before leaving. I can't comprehend his behavior until I remember Ann thinks we are engaged.

Stephen certainly knows how to play the role of a committed guy.

Too bad it's only a role.

I honestly think I can become used to his touches and kisses.

Maybe I already have.

With that unsettling thought, I turn my attention toward Ann.

"It's pretty obvious he's crazy about you." Ann continues to jot notes as she speaks.

That word obvious. The same word Alice or Gary used when stating we were in love.

Like Stephen said earlier this morning, appearances can be deceiving.

"Oh, look." Ann points to the railing of the gazebo where a blue butterfly has landed.

Its fluttering wings mirror how my insides feel when Stephen kisses me, while the blue on the wings remind me of his eyes. I doubt I'll ever be able to see a blue butterfly and not think of Stephen Day.

Good thing I'm not an outdoor gal.

BEWILDERED

MY FEAR OF becoming sunburned has officially taken over. "Do you mind if we sit in the gazebo?"

"No. Not at all."

I follow her a few steps to the beautiful white structure. She settles on one bench, I settle on another, grateful for the shade. I'm hoping the pinkish tint to my skin is my overactive imagination.

"What colors are you using in your wedding?" I ask, deciding we need that little icebreaker Stephen talked about, before I pour out my broken heart to her.

"We're using reds and whites. Keeping the Christmas theme is really important to us."

"I'm sure it will be beautiful. Are you going on a honeymoon?" Might as well establish a timeline while the conversation warrants it.

"No. Actually we leave for Peru the day after Christmas. My mom and her husband will be in town for the wedding and Christmas. My aunt Venus as well. We planned this all so we can have some family time before heading to Peru."

Okay, so I heard what she said after she stated they were leaving the day after Christmas, but honestly it didn't register or stick. I now realize I have about a week to accomplish the one thing that has the possibility of landing me a new career.

And I'm unfamiliar with this strange nudging which is leading me to place my hope in a woman I met briefly yesterday and now seems incredibly uncomfortable in the presence of me.

"I have a confession to make." Ann's statement is loud and hurried, her gaze darting from the ceiling, back down to eye level, left, then right. Everywhere but toward me.

I notice her legs are crossed and her dangling foot is moving at a speed that can only be considered breakneck nervous.

Or uncomfortable.

Or how about, I-want-to-be-anywhere-but-here.

My heart sinks as I realize a photo session with Ann probably isn't going to go well. SunKissed! represents fun, lazy, summer days. Maybe a beach wedding. Relaxation.

The exact opposite of Ann's body language.

And isn't photography about the body language?

Better to hear her out now than have her decline my request. "Okay. Confess." I smile when I say the words.

Inside I'm not smiling.

Her gaze rolls once more to the ceiling of the gazebo, then, amazingly, settles on me. My face. Our gazes connect, and I see unexpected warmth in her green eyes.

Eyes I want to capture in a photo.

Tingles reign over my body. Stephen's words are coming to life. I'm seeing beyond what is actually on the surface.

Ann has to say yes.

She smiles briefly.

"Here goes. I'm pretty star struck around you. You're beautiful and poised and sure of yourself. I'm just a girl whose crazy circumstances led me to the mansion here. I feel like an imposter, I guess."

So while I'm sitting here in awe of her, she's sitting here in awe of me.

Really?

"Well then, we have something in common. I'm feeling like an imposter as well."

She shakes her head and strands of escaping glorious red hair move elegantly. Perfect for SunKissed! "You? An imposter? No way."

If she only knew. "I really do."

"In what way?"

The thought that God might have actually orchestrated this meeting with this segue into my request flits through my mind. I don't let it stick long enough to have any merit. Along with the crazy thought, Stephen's face comes into view, but his image vanishes when I release the notion. "Funny you should ask. I have a favor of sorts to ask of you."

"Me?"

"Yes. And I know you are going to wonder at my sanity with your wedding coming up and your timeline of returning to Peru."

"My curiosity is definitely piqued now."

I take a couple of deep breaths hoping Ann doesn't notice I'm taking a couple of deep breaths. "Okay. I've designed a line of clothing. Stephen's sister Katherine was supposed to model them here for me, but her boyfriend surprised her with a Christmas Mediterranean cruise, so she sent her apologies."

"Okay."

She has a confused expression and I don't blame her. She has no idea where I'm going with this. "So, when I saw you yesterday, it hit me. Totally. Like a lightning bolt."

"What hit you?"

"You would be the perfect model for my line."

Her hand covers her heart and she leans back, while her other hand barely keeps her notebook on her lap. "I'm an accountant. Or I used to be. Now I'm a missionary. Not a model."

"Hear me out, please? I'm calling my line SunKissed! It's fun, breezy, beachy, sunny. The clothes look like they were made for you."

She sets her notebook on the bench and stands. "You are one of the most beautiful models in the world. I can't imagine trying to model anything at anytime, let alone in front of you."

Ann is genuine. I don't think she's trying to play this off like some might. Trying to be coy but secretly, in their minds, they are already in the clothes thinking they look way better in them than I do.

No, Ann has an honest hesitancy.

Which is going to be hard to break through. "I know my timing is bad with your wedding. I'm sorry."

"I have a sister. Half sister, actually, Anastasia. She's much more beautiful than I am, and she's poised and well, perfect for taking photos."

Ann doesn't get it. "I can appreciate your uncertainty about this. I really can. But, it's hard to explain. Sometimes there's a certain look that captures someone's attention. And your look has captured my attention."

She starts to speak, but I hold up my hand, stopping her. "It's like this. You know how sometimes you don't know what you are looking for, then it hits you like a ton of bricks, and you realize it's all coming together. That's how it happens."

So I know I'm bold in life. But bold and pouring out your feelings are two different things, and I really haven't ever poured out my heart like this to someone who is virtually a total stranger.

Ann's expression is probably why people don't pour their hearts out to strangers. She looks like I've totally bewildered her.

I guess her face mirrors my heart. Because I'm bewildered as well at the turn I seem to be taking.

This change has to do with Stephen. I know this, yet I don't want to dwell on it. I don't want to dwell on how he makes me see things differently than I've ever seen them before.

Now if I can only make Ann see things differently than she's seeing them. "How about this," I say. "If you have a few minutes today, why don't you come over and look at the clothes. That's all I'm asking right now. That you simply consider what I've asked."

My words are spoken slowly and carefully, a total contradiction to my internal desperation of wanting to cry out, "You have to yes, you have to."

She taps her foot, her gaze once again focused everywhere but toward me. Her arms are crossed, her lips drawn into a thin line. Noncommittal personified.

"I guess it wouldn't hurt to look at the clothes. But that really isn't me considering doing what you've asked. That's me being curious as to what you've designed. From a fan aspect."

She can call it whatever she wants. I call it victory.

A small victory, but victory nonetheless.

"I'M GOING TO have to be ready to snap photos at any time," I tell Stephen as we walk around the patio. I have a notepad in hand, jotting down places for certain shots. "If Ann says yes, I'm going to have to jump on that yes, right then. You know?"

"I'm not sure how this is going to work. From what you've told me about your conversation, she doesn't seem to be very willing."

Ignoring his remark because I don't want to think about it, I turn toward him. "What do you think about this spot? We can move that sunflower over under the pergola, put that potted palm here. With the worn wood planter, this is a remarkable mixture of textures and color."

He nods. "You're going to need to shoot the photos in the morning. Your light will be perfect then."

"My light. Like I own it. I have a feeling I'm going to have to work with what light I get." And his camera if I don't find a photographer, but I don't tell him that right now.

"You're going to have to own something if you want this to work. An unwilling model and wrong light would be a disastrous combination."

"Just like a scar and a modeling career, right? Pretty disastrous."

"Cheetah, what man plans for harm, God uses for good."

"Is that from the Bible? Or you."

I see the flash of disappointment in Stephen's eyes. I didn't mean my comment to come across as snarky, but it did. Maybe it was my tone. I tried to keep it light. I really like his God moments with me, but sometimes they don't set very well.

And this is one of those times. Once again, it appears that he's making light of my situation.

He can't begin to comprehend.

And I'm tired of trying to explain it to him.

"Don't you need to get Phoebe from school?" I ask, hoping he'll leave.

"That was from the Bible and I don't need to leave for another hour. You're not getting rid of me that easy."

So I'm transparent as well as snarky. "Can't say I didn't try."

"Why don't you take some pictures at the beach? It's not far from here. About a ten-minute drive." He crosses his arms in a relaxed way.

I like the way parts of his brown hair glimmer golden in the sun. Natural highlights for a natural guy.

"That was part of the plan. Until I saw your backyard. It's different and has a lot of interesting aspects. A lot of summer line photos are taken at the beach. I'm thinking I want to do something different."

"Nothing wrong with wanting to be different. Make sure you're relevant."

"How could I not be relevant?"

"You can lose focus. It does happen."

My confusion must show because he continues. "All I'm saying is in trying to be different, don't lose sight of what you're trying to accomplish."

His determination makes me wonder if the king's daughter, Arabella, caused Stephen to lose focus while he was in Zaunesia.

His accomplishment?

Getting kicked out.

The sound of the doorbell ringing echoes outside.

"I'll get it," Stephen says.

"I'm right behind you. It might be Ann."

My hope escalates as I see Ann's red hair as Stephen opens the door.

"Hi, Ann." He steps back so she can come in.

"Hello." Her voice sounds timid. "I hope I'm not intruding."

"Not at all." I try not to sound eager.

Stephen starts for the keeping room off the kitchen, and Ann and I follow. The couch looks bare without Phoebe sitting there.

"I like your Christmas tree," Ann says. "We put our tree up last night but won't decorate it until tonight. Brett was going to put up some lights outside, but we waited too long and now, with us leaving, it really doesn't make sense."

Stephen nods. "Nobody ever comes down this far anyway."

"I've only been here since April, but you're right. Being on the cul-de-sac is nice and quiet. I haven't even met the people on the other side of you," Ann says.

"I haven't either. But Roger, being the pastor that he is, went over when they moved in a couple of years ago. Kind of a tragic story. Nice family. Apparently the guy used to be big in racing and he now owns several car dealerships here in the area. He and his wife had twin girls, but his wife was sick, and I guess she died not too long after they moved in."

"Oh, that is sad," I say. "How old are the girls?"

"I'm not sure. Roger will know. He's been over a couple of times, asking them to come to church, but they haven't come."

Stephen's story sweeps my focus away from the reason for Ann's visit. As I settle back into that mind frame, my mind starts to race at what her answer could be.

But she did promise to look at the clothes.

"I'll tell Brett and we'll be praying," Ann says. "You never know what it is that will trigger someone's desire to go to church. Or maybe they already have a church home."

"As of Roger's last visit, and I'm not sure how long ago that was, they were still looking," Stephen says.

Ann smiles. "Well, as one who didn't have one for a long time, and now has two, one here and one in Peru, I'm here to say it's changed my life."

And now I have God insights from Ann. Great. But I will not comment like I do with Stephen. I would like to change the subject, but it seems rather rude.

"Amen, sister." He gives her a high five, and I shake my head. Certainly an hour has gone by and Phoebe needs to be picked up from school.

I glance down at my phone. Nope. Only thirty minutes.

Patience isn't something I like. But I'm going to practice it now and smile through it.

"Well." Ann looks at me. "I came over to look at the clothes."

"Great." I'm disappointed she didn't say she was going to do the shoot, but then again, she didn't say she wasn't. "I'll bring them out here."

"Okay."

It's all I can do not to skip down the hall. If she had said she was on board, I would be skipping.

But that seems premature right now.

I start to cross my fingers but find myself saying a quick prayer instead.

All that talk of church has my brain thinking differently.

But I guess it can't hurt, although I'm not sure how much interest God has in my selfish prayer.

BREAK

IT'S MUCH EASIER to pull the suitcase out to the keeping room than carry all the clothes, so the sound of the wheels covering the tiles announces my entrance.

Stephen and Ann watch as I lay out my collection on the couch. Not a very good way to present it, but I'm not sure what else to do.

"Oh, is that a wedding dress?" Ann picks up the dress.

"It is. A beachy-type wedding dress."

"This is beautiful. So fun." She holds the dress in front of her.

"Thanks." I wonder if the fun look of the wedding dress will persuade her, seeing as how I'm not doing a very good job of it.

"Ladies, I need to go and retrieve Phoebe from school."

Once again the feel of his hand on my back surprises me until I remember that Ann thinks Stephen and I are engaged. Somehow, I keep forgetting that part, but Stephen doesn't seem to forget.

As I turn to face him to say goodbye, my words are cut short by his lips as they press against mine. A chaste kiss as judged by anyone looking on, but anything but chaste as my body sizzles while his lips sweetly devour mine.

And yes, his simple kiss devours everything inside me.

All I thought I knew about kissing has now been replaced by a new standard that I doubt I'll ever experience again.

A sad thought.

And then there's Ann.

And the thought that she may save my hide.

"Be back soon, Cheetah." Stephen's voice is a whisper as his hand

114

lingers on my back for several moments.

His touch leaves me, and I watch him walk to the front door. As the door clicks shut at his exit, I sigh.

"You two are perfect for each other." Ann is still holding the dress, but her focus has shifted to Stephen and me.

I'm mortified at being caught in my Stephen daydream. For the first time I feel bad deceiving her. Deceiving everyone, really. An unfamiliar urge to blurt the truth comes over me, but I stop myself. It really doesn't affect her. Not like Gary or Roger.

And isn't Stephen supposed to be breaking up with me soon?

I'll let this lie run its course. And remember never to put myself in this position again. "Thanks. What do you think about the line? Want to try anything on?"

Ann lays the wedding dress across the back of the couch before slinging the beach bag over her shoulder. "This is so cute."

"It's designed to be able to hold the clothes. You know, kind of hang at the beach, then go out at night. SunKissed! is a line that encompasses all aspects of a day in the sun as well as a night of fun. Even a wedding."

"I see you mix and match everything." She's now looking at the other items, picking them up one by one.

"Yes. That's the idea." I ignore the hum of excitement that is racing through me.

"I really like the wedding dress. It's amazing." Her hand runs over the dress softly.

I smile. "It's one of my favorites."

"You have a talent for this. All the clothes are beautiful. I have no idea why you would want me to model them."

"They look like they were made for you, that's why. You're beautiful and you embody the line. Women like you were my inspiration in designing the clothing."

Ann shakes her head. "I'm not beautiful. There is nothing extraordinary about my look. I need to introduce you to Anastasia, my half sister. She's your model."

I can't believe she doesn't see how beautiful she is. "I'm sure your sister is as gorgeous as you say, but I had a particular look in my mind, and you are the look. Please say yes."

"Are you into bartering?" Her coy expression peaks my interest.

"Bartering?"

"Yes. I might be willing to model the clothes in exchange for something."

Ann is feistier than I thought. "Okay. What could I possibly have that you want?"

"Can I wear the wedding dress in my wedding?"

"SHE WANTS TO wear your dress in her wedding?" Stephen leans against the kitchen counter and looks as mystified as I did when she bartered with me.

"Can you believe it? I'm so psyched."

"Her wedding is in four days. I know I'm a guy, but didn't she already have a wedding dress?"

"She did. But she didn't really like it." I sing-song my answer because I'm feeling rather happy right now. "She said she'd been looking for months, and nothing struck her. But, she loved my dress right away and she said my design was ethereal."

"Nice," Stephen says.

"Now, all I need is the photographer. I have a call into a guy who one of my friend's brothers knows."

A quickening sensation runs through my body at Stephen's put-out-looking expression.

"And what do you know about this guy?" His voice reveals how put out he is.

Knowing he's put out delights me. "Nothing. Scary, huh? But apparently he lives within thirty minutes of here and has had some pics bought by magazines. It's amazing what social media can produce in an afternoon, isn't it?"

"What's his name?" Stephen frowns.

"Oh, Mike something. I'll have to look it up and tell you. Maybe you've heard of him."

Stephen's frown doesn't disappear. "I doubt it."

Phoebe is sitting at the island eating a snack. She takes a drink of her milk, and I laugh at her cute milk mustache. I walk over and wipe it away with a napkin. "You're looking like Santa with that white mustache."

She giggles. "I don't think Santa looks like a little girl."

"Me either," I reply.

"Can we go sing Christmas carols Saturday night?"

I look at Stephen who shrugs his shoulders and gives me his I-have-no-idea-what-she's-talking-about looks.

"Where would we go to sing Christmas carols?" I ask, barely able to keep my mind off how Ann is going to look in SunKissed! and Stephen's reaction at me contacting another photographer.

"A girl in my class invited me to her house for a caroling party. I really want to go."

Memories of the first day I met Phoebe and her sad expression as she told me she didn't have any friends run through my mind. Maybe she has one.

"Who is the girl?" I ask.

"Raney Lee. Everybody likes her. She only invited a couple of girls."

I catch on that this is a big deal for her. Somehow I don't think she's had a lot of invitations in the past. "I'm sure Stephen can take you."

His look is one of shock. "I'm sure Jenny and I will be happy to escort you caroling."

Raising his eyebrows, he nods.

"Yay! I'll tell her tomorrow."

"Okay. Find out where she lives, too."

"There's an invitation in my backpack. I'll get it."

She finishes the last of her Goldfish and scoots off the chair. Moments later a holiday invitation is sitting on the counter. A palm-tree snowman with musical notes floating across the top indicate it is a specially made invitation.

"That's a cute invite." I tap her on the top of the head with the invitation in a playful gesture. "And you said you didn't have any friends."

"Raney isn't really my friend. I'm not sure why she invited me." Her voice dips a little before picking back up. "But she said we're going to be caroling and roasting marshmallows."

"That's nice. A combo event." I take her glass to the sink.

"What's a combo event?" Phoebe asks.

"It's when more than one thing is happening at once." Stephen scrunches her napkin before tossing it in the trash.

I refuse to reflect how we work well together.

"Oh, okay. Like you and Jenny saying you're getting married when you're really not getting married? That's two different things happening."

If Stephen's eyebrow could rise off his forehead I think it would. "Yeah. Like that." He gives me *the look*.

I don't give him *the look* back. It won't do any good. He thinks the whole fiasco is my fault and nothing will change his mind.

He needs to hurry up and break up with me. That will solve all the problems and we can quit pretending.

ARE ALL KIDS THIS good about going to bed? According to what I've heard, putting a child to bed ranks right up there with trying to model swimsuits in the cold New York air.

Not fun.

But Phoebe doesn't mind at all. Maybe that's because she obeys her mom. Stephen says Phoebe is always well mannered and polite, and I see that. I have no reason to think she is a difficult child.

She's snuggled in her bed with her blanket and smile. I automatically brush her bangs away from her eyes. She crinkles her nose.

"Your fingers are so soft," she says. "Like your voice. Most of the time. Sometimes with Mr. Stephen it gets a little loud."

I can't help but laugh. "It does."

"But sometimes it's really whispery soft. Like you guys have a secret or something."

I clear my throat. "We don't have any secrets," I assure her. "Let's continue on with our story. So, we know Princess Bea can't marry Prince Jonah and continue to play her beautiful music. And she knows that."

"But Prince Jonah doesn't," Phoebe adds.

"No, he doesn't. Princess Bea and her family have a big feast for dinner every night, so she asks Prince Jonah to stay for supper. She needs to make him fall in love with her, and she needs time to figure out how she can marry him and keep playing her music."

"What if there's a secret ingredient in the food? Like a love potion that will make Prince Jonah fall in love."

Love potion? Seven years old? Kids are growing up so fast. "Okay. I like it. But what if Princess Bea doesn't want to give him the potion at dinner? What if she wants to find out what goes into the potion, so maybe she can tweak it so that when he falls in love with her, her ability to play music won't automatically stop?"

"Tweak?"

I keep forgetting she's seven. "Adjust. Make changes. Maybe there is an ingredient in the potion that stops the women from playing the music?"

"I know how to fix it! It's when the prince kisses her. After he kisses her, she can't play the music anymore." Her excitement causes her to talk fast.

"And they never kiss until they are married," I add.

"Right. Maybe something in the potion goes from his lips to her lips and it gets into her body and she can't move her fingers over the harp anymore."

I like how her imagination works. "I think you're onto something, Phoebe. It sounds like Princess Bea isn't going to be satisfied until she figures out the potion."

She clasps her hands. "But she can't wait too long, or the prince might not fall in love with her."

"You don't think he'll fall in love with who she is? You think he has to have the potion?"

"I guess if we want to make sure he loves her he has to drink the potion. If he doesn't, he might fall in love with someone else." Spoken like a true teenager, and she's only seven.

"Okay, so Princess Bea keeps the potion in her room and doesn't bring it down to supper that night."

"But the prince sits by her."

"Of course he does. And he stares at her." I think about how I stare at Stephen.

"Because she's smart." Phoebe's tone is matter of fact.

"Smart? Okay. And she's beautiful."

"I think they are eating a chicken for dinner. Do they have macaroni and cheese where the princess lives?"

Can you say random? "I think they do. All princesses must eat mac and cheese."

"I agree. The story is exciting. What happens after dinner? Does Princess Bea play her music for the prince again?"

"Maybe. We'll see tomorrow night."

"Not again." Phoebe puts her palm to her head. "Just when it's getting good."

"That's what a good storyteller does. Leaves you hanging, waiting for more."

Her face scrunches and she frowns. "Okay. Goodnight."

"Goodnight, Phoebe."

Bending over I brush a kiss across her forehead. She smiles.

I exit the room before she can guess at the tears in my eyes. That child can detect things I wouldn't imagine. Standing outside her room, I gather my composure before possibly running into Stephen.

What is it about the simplicity of Phoebe that tugs at my heart so? Is it her ability to flourish? Her blindness doesn't seem to hinder her in any way, nor does she seem bitter about it.

Unable to help myself, I trace the line of the scar on my face. I've thought about it less and less as I've been here, but it's a bitter reminder that everything I ever knew in life is no longer.

Even though I now have the opportunity to design, a desire I've had for a long time, it has come at a high price.

And getting the line photographed has been met with strife at every turn.

Why can't I catch a break?

You did catch a break. Ann agreed to model the clothing.

The thought runs through my mind, and I know I have blessings to be thankful for. That Dominick Redding is willing to look at my line for his Inter-Season show is more than I could have hoped for.

My thumbs become moist as they press against the corners of my eyes. Quickly going through all five fingers, I finally stop my tears. Walking toward the kitchen, I hope no signs of my self-pity are evident, as I'm sure Stephen is somewhere close.

BRAZEN

"IF YOU WANT TO go out at night or something, feel free."

Stephen's voice greets me as I walk into the kitchen.

"What?" Am I too focused on my self-pity to focus on his comment?

"I'm sure you're used to going out at night. I can handle Phoebe as long as she's sleeping."

Is he dismissing me? I'm not sure my state of mind can take any more rejection right now. The tears I had tamed moments earlier are now waiting to spill out all over again. I lower my head, avoiding eye contact. "I'm not a party girl if that's what you're insinuating."

Once again his presence overpowers everything else in the vicinity. I don't have to be looking his way to know he's walking toward me. The air simply shifts, making me aware.

It's rather unnerving.

"You've been cooped up in this house since you arrived. I thought you might want a change of scenery."

Close. He's so close he can probably smell my hidden tears. This man has a way of extracting everything within me. Everything about me is revealed when Stephen is around.

I have to counter attack. "I have no idea what's around here. No, thanks."

"Use your navigation on your phone. You can take my SUV." His voice is a whisper on the wind as he basically orders me out of his house.

I'm not budging. "I'm perfectly content to languish in this house for another evening."

"All right. Just thought I'd offer."

Self-pity gives way to a more brazen feeling. Actually the tears are no longer threatening, which gives me the courage to look at him. I give him my hard look. The one the photographers love.

The one that made me money.

That look. "You can offer to kick me out for an evening, but you can't break up with me? Interesting."

The lazy warmth in his eyes ices. "I wasn't aware you needed the actual breakup acted out."

Coldness seeps into me as if his gaze has the power to dip my body in ice water.

Stephen has me so confused. I'm a grown, confident woman. And I've never known another human who had the ability to turn my senses into a hay-wired mess.

No wonder he photographs wildlife. No human model could sustain his scrutiny.

I'd either be an ice statue or a melting mess.

"I do need to talk to you," he says.

So, has the handsome photographer laid a trap for me? Now that he's assured I'm in for the evening, he wants to spring something on me? How easily I fall under his spell. "Talk."

"You don't have to be so blunt. I'm actually going to make nice."

"Nice?" I ask.

"I know you are in a bind, so I'm offering Millie to you."

He's offering Millie? Can my heart assume that the mention of a guy named Mike coming around to take pictures has actually affected him? "Thank you."

"Since you aren't going out or anything, I can give you lessons tonight. Why don't you call Ann and tell her to come tomorrow morning?"

No harm in pushing my dream come true scenario. "Are you sure you don't want to shoot the pictures?"

"I told you, I don't shoot humans."

Hearing those words sounding so serious makes me chuckle. His eyes narrow and he turns, placing his hands on the counter. Something about this topic makes him nervous. Is there a chink in Stephen's Day armor?

If so, I'm not pressing it now. It doesn't seem like a good time. "Okay. I appreciate it."

He picks up his camera. "It would be optimal for me to go over this with you in the morning, considering you are going to be taking the pictures in the morning. But there are a few basic things you can learn about photography anytime."

"Okay. I'm listening."

He drapes the strap over my head, and I grasp the camera in my hands. Standing behind me, he wraps his arms around me, his hands covering mine briefly, like he's making sure I have a good grip on his baby.

"This is your menu." His thumb pushes a button. "I don't think you'll need to be changing anything here, but it's good to know where it is. To exit, simply push it again."

We spend the next twenty minutes going over the buttons on the camera. He's still standing behind me, his body pressing into mine. I'm listening to him speak, but occasionally I find my mind wandering. I think about how tan his skin is next to my pale white complexion, how I could stand in his arms forever.

"So." He steps from behind me. "Now you know basically how the camera works. Any questions?"

I look at him full in the face. He's so beautiful it takes my breath. Maybe one day his looks will be second nature to me. "I guess my biggest question is how do I take a great picture?"

"Instinct." He doesn't hesitate and his tone is adamant.

Can I make my tone as adamant? "Panic and desperation I have. Instinct? I'm not so sure."

He shakes his head. "Cheetah. You've been a model for years. You have instinct. You couldn't have survived without it."

Eyeing Millie, I turn slightly putting the big black camera to my face, pretending I'm focusing on the kitchen sink. Not doubting I only have one shot at this, I back up a couple of steps, pivot, and click the button quickly, capturing the beautiful Stephen Day in the view finder.

His laid-back expression flat lines. His gaze moves sharply over my face as he jams one hand in his pocket. "The flash wasn't on, and don't ever do that again."

Everything inside me knows he's never been more serious, the words he spoke not up for any sort of discussion. Not warranting even an acknowledgment.

Maybe one day I'll have his impact on people. Until then, I'm going to learn from him. Although honestly, I don't want to give him too many opportunities to be so serious with me.

It only seems natural to return Millie to him at this moment, like it only seems natural that he would push a few buttons erasing the image I took of him. The image that probably didn't turn out.

I totally forgot about the flash.

Instead of placing the camera around his neck, he sets it on the counter. His index finger pretends to scrape something off the counter top, but there's nothing there.

Maybe a nervous habit? Although what Stephen would ever have to be nervous about is beyond me.

"Do you ever think that your surgery turned out the way it did for a specific purpose?" he asks.

Is he serious? A downward spiral kind of feeling runs through me. "What purpose?"

"Can I ask what happened? Why you had to have surgery?"

This is it. The moment I sound like somebody I don't want to. But facts are facts. I can't change the truth. "I had a small pimple on my cheek. It had been there awhile, so I went to the dermatologist to see about having it removed. He assured me it was a simple procedure done all the time."

His hand clasps mine. "Not so simple, huh?"

"No. The root was much deeper than he anticipated. It happens sometimes. It's rare, but it's real. I'm living proof."

"I have this feeling that you think it's your fault. It's not." His voice is husky, emotion-filled.

The truth needs to be told. "I was scared. Scared of losing jobs to younger girls. Scared of not having the things I was used to. All those things that I'm living right now. And I now see that I was simply being vain. Nobody cared about that little pimple. Nobody but me."

"I want to show you something," he says. "Come outside for a minute."

We walk, hand in hand, out to the patio, the pool light shimmering through the rippling water.

His gaze travels upward. "There's too many city lights here to really see the stars, but do you know how many stars there are?"

"No idea. Millions, I'm sure."

"Hundreds of thousands of millions. And that's just in one galaxy. There are millions of galaxies."

While night has fallen, Stephen's right about not being able to see many stars. Dark grey, almost black skies hover overhead, with the occasional airplane white or red blinking by.

I imagine he sees a lot of stars when he's out in the wild. "I don't know too much about astronomy."

"I don't either, but I know that each star was put there by God for a purpose." He squeezes my hand. "If you didn't have this scar, what would you be doing right now?"

Scooting closer to him as the breeze picks up, I shake my head. "I'm not sure. Probably vacationing somewhere for the holidays with my friends."

"You're cold." He folds me into his arms.

"Not anymore." His touch renders me mindless. I'm glad he quit talking astronomy. No way could I keep up.

"If you didn't have the scar you wouldn't be standing here. In my arms."

Is he at war within himself? Is he glad I'm here? His touch says yes, but I'm not convinced. "You're right. I wouldn't be here."

He tilts my chin up. "What if you are supposed to be here? With me?"

What part of we're supposed to be breaking up doesn't he understand? And he can't seriously think that he and I are supposed to be together. Can he?

"What purpose would I being here with you serve?" I focus my gaze on his chin. Anything to keep from looking into his eyes or at his mouth.

"One we may not even be aware of at this time."

"Are you talking fate?" Fate is proving cruel teasing me with Stephen.

"I don't believe in fate. I believe in Jesus."

To me it's weird for us to be in an embrace and talking about Jesus. Like it's sacrilegious or something. And I would much rather be embracing Stephen than talking about Jesus. "I'm not sure of your point."

"My point is this. What if it was meant for us to meet?" He drags the words out like they aren't easy for him to say.

They're even harder for me to hear. "Like Jesus wanted us to meet?"

The idea spoken out loud sounds even weirder than when it was in my head.

Stephen shakes his head, his gaze drifting upward. "I know it sounds crazy, surreal. But that's how it feels to me. Crazy. Surreal. You're here. I'm here. And given normal circumstances neither of us would be here."

His words fall on me, settling onto my unsettled heart. "You're supposed to be in Zaunesia capturing the wilds through your viewfinder."

"And you'd rather be languishing on some covered veranda, feeling warm temperatures caress your skin. Not cool breezes."

When we're this close, it's like we're in a cocoon, closed up and melded together. "There's something to be said about cool breezes."

I barely finish speaking as his lips touch mine. Not really in a kiss at first. Even though this isn't our first kiss, it's like he's treading carefully, and it's up to me to embrace his offer.

Like this morning, my lips capture his, the sweet taste of him making me weak with desire.

Weak for more of who he is.

Only as I deepen the kiss, I realize I'm craving for more of what I don't know. Because honestly, there's not too much about Stephen that I do know.

Except that his kisses are amazing.

And I guess, if you only know one or two things about a man, that's a good thing to know.

TUESDAY MORNING I open my eyes and am filled with excitement. Today I'm shooting my SunKissed! line.

As I lie in bed, visions of poses running through my head, I hear a soft, pelting sound. My heart sinks as I realize the continual soft, pelting sound is rain.

I push the covers away and slip on my lounging pants, then shuffle over to the window.

The loud sound of the blinds lifting echoes the scream inside me. It can't be raining. But the scream is rounded out at the edges with bits of relief.

A relief I don't want to think about.

Steady, dripping rain soaks the earth and any chance I have of taking outdoor pictures today.

And SunKissed! has to be shot outside.

Walking over to my phone, I see that it's after eight. Stephen must be taking Phoebe to school.

Why didn't he wake me?

My tongue moves along my lower lip as I think of his kisses. I cross my arms, my hands warming my arms like his did mine last night.

This man has invaded every moment of my thinking. I want to be mad at the rain for ruining my day, but thinking of Stephen doesn't let me.

Thinking of Stephen makes everything okay. But just in my thoughts. He's not in my real life. He's in my pretend life.

The one I'm living here.

Pretending to be a designer and photographer instead of a model. Pretending to be engaged. Pretending to be a woman who goes to church.

Honestly, can I think of anything truthful that is going on at the moment?

My desperation.

Oh, there is that.

Sitting on the edge of the bed I can't help but think about the bit of relief that I felt at the sound of the rain.

While I think Ann is the perfect model, what if the clothes don't show well? What if the colors don't mesh? The designs aren't practical?

What if I take horrible pictures?

I rest my head in my hands, mentally pushing images of failure from my mind. *You can't fail if you don't try.*

Raising my head, I slide off the bed, refusing to wallow in this all day. When Stephen returns from dropping off Phoebe, I'm going to ask to borrow his SUV. I need to buy Ann a gift for modeling the clothes and pick up a wedding gift for her and Brett.

Deciding coffee can wait for a little while, I shower and dress. The warm water relaxes me, but I already have the beginning of a headache when I do make my way into the kitchen.

The kitchen's void of Stephen, but not coffee. The half-full pot is still warming. Opening the cabinet, I grab a cup and pour.

"Sleeping beauty awakes."

Stephen's voice startles me and I turn in a too-swift movement. "Ouch." Coffee sloshes over my hand, onto the counter and subsequently the tiled floor.

I set the mug down and take the paper towel Stephen has torn off the roll. "I'll get it."

He's trying not to smile. "I'm sorry. I didn't mean to startle you."

He doesn't understand that his whole being startles me all the time. "It's okay."

It doesn't take but a minute to wipe up the spilled coffee. It takes much longer to absorb Stephen. His presence.

Might as well get the favor asking out of the way. "Do you mind if I borrow your SUV this morning?"

"Not at all." He sets his keys on the island. "Where are you off to?"

"Shopping."

"Ah. Since the shoot is off you are going to drown your sorrows shopping."

"I'm actually buying a wedding present for Ann and Brett. Can't show up at the wedding empty handed."

Stephen taps his finger on the island. "Good point. I was going to give them the standard guy gift. Cash. But I guess I still need a card, huh?"

"Yes. Unless you just slip Brett the cash in a handshake. I've seen that, too."

"Yeah. Not going there. Why don't we go together?"

Great. My morning trying to escape Stephen is not going to be successful. "Sure. I'm going to call Ann and see when we can reschedule. Do you know what the weather is supposed to be like tomorrow?"

"Rain should let up by this evening. Everything should be dry by tomorrow."

"Okay. I'll be right back."

I take my coffee with me. After a quick conversation with Ann, and a touch-up of my makeup, I grab my purse and head back to the kitchen.

"Okay. She's on for tomorrow morning," I say to Stephen. "If we can't do it then, I don't know what's going to happen."

"Whatever is supposed to happen, will happen. Come on."

Stephen doesn't see me roll my eyes at his words because he's already headed to the garage.

With a hand from Stephen, I climb into his SUV. It's black, big and rain-streaked from his morning trip to Phoebe's school.

The scraping sound of his windshield wipers serenades us into town. Stephen pulls into a parking lot of an outdoor mall.

"Which store?" he asks.

"How about something knick-knacky?"

"Knick-knacky?"

"Yeah. Vases, home décor, stuff like that." I have no idea what to buy as a wedding gift.

"You tell me where to stop when you see one of those stores. I think I'm still on the card agenda."

"I wanted to pick her up a little something for doing the shoot, too."

"You aren't going to pay her?"

"A little. I don't have much. But still, these circumstances are skewed. A gift would be cool. Oh, here's a good store."

Stephen whips into a parking spot. I unbuckle my seat belt and climb out of the car. He meets me and shuts my door as I pull my shirt down. "I guess you help Phoebe in and out of that thing," I say.

"That thing is an expensive thing," Stephen says. "And yes, I do help Phoebe. I'd help you too, but you're too fast, Cheetah."

"I don't have time to be wasting." Besides, his touch drives me crazy, so the less time I'm in those situations, the better off I am.

"The weather has you a little feisty today."

Since I didn't bring an umbrella, I pull my hood over my hair in an attempt to keep from becoming drenched. "I'm no different today than I am any other day."

"Watch out."

He grabs my arm as a horn honks. The driver I was about to walk in front of motions us across the street. I whisper a "thank you," to Stephen as we hurry our steps out of the way of the traffic and make it to the sidewalk.

"Maybe if you'd push that hair out of your eyes, you'd be able to see cars clipping along at a decent speed."

I try to talk over the loud Christmas music playing above. "It's a parking lot. He shouldn't have been going very fast."

"Just because he shouldn't have doesn't mean he wasn't. And he was."

He reaches around me making a move toward my hair. "You can tuck it into that hood."

"I'm fine." I'm used to walking with my head down, hair hanging in front.

"You know, all that hair draped across your face begs more attention than your scar does."

"I'm not sure about that." I refuse to alter my look because of his opinions.

"You have a grunge look about you. With your torn jeans, your hoodie and your loose hair."

I sigh. "That assessment clearly states you have no idea what grunge is."

"Hey, I live in the wilds. What can I say?" His tone is playful.

"Nothing. And maybe you shouldn't."

"Funny, Jenny."

I wonder what motivates him to call me Cheetah or Jenny. He switches it up and I have no idea why. "I'm not trying to be funny. Here's the store. Are you going in or waiting outside?"

He looks at the sky. "Might as well go in."

"All right, bull in the china shop. Let's do it."

He doesn't even look put out as we walk in. Not too many things ruffle Stephen. The mention of a male photographer helping me out stirred something in him. Oh, and me announcing that I'm his fiancée. That did some ruffling.

Ruffling he still hasn't undone.

"You probably have no idea what you are looking for, do you?" he asks.

"It's one of those I'll-know-it-when-I-see-it type of gifts. I just know it has to look good."

"Of course it does." He slips past a rack of crystal glass items.

Not really wanting to buy anything Christmassy, I have to look past all the holiday decorations. Even items that aren't holiday oriented are draped with red scarves or greenery of sorts. A few sprigs of fir sit here and there.

In the midst of all the festive décor, I spy a vase that in no way, shape or form reminds me of Christmas, and hurry over to where it sits. "Now this is beautiful. The colors are amazing. What country are they missionaries in?"

"Peru."

"These colors look Peruvian, don't they?"

Stephen smiles slightly and laughs softly. "I have no idea what Peruvian colors are. If they are bright, then you're on the right track."

"It's festive. And fun. And gorgeous. What else do you need?"

"What else, indeed," he replies.

I lift it up to see how much it is selling for. I swallow hard at the high price, but decide it's worth it. And since Stephen is lending me Millie, that's one expense I don't have to worry about.

"All that money for a couple you barely know? Can I tell you when my birthday is?" Stephen asks.

"Now you're the funny one. Beauty is worth paying for. This is probably an original. I bet I can negotiate at the register for a lower price."

The negotiations at the register don't go well and I end up paying full price.

"At least I tried," I say to Stephen as we leave the store.

"Is that the wedding gift or the thanks-for-helping-me-out-in-a-pinch-when-I-needed-a-model gift?" he asks.

"This is the wedding gift. I'll buy some lotion or good smelling stuff for the other gift. Card shop coming up."

We're barely in the door when Stephen stops. "Well, well. Look at what we have here."

He points down an aisle at the end cap. There sits the vase I bought. The same exact colorful vase.

"Really?" I say.

"Wanna know if you got a deal?" His has a mischievous look on his face

"No, not really."

"I want to know." He starts walking toward the vase.

Like the proverbial train wreck I follow him. "If you don't say anything, then I'll know I didn't get such a good deal. If you smile, then I'll know I did."

"Smart girl. Except I don't give stuff away. You'll never know."

"Try me."

He picks up the vase. True to his word his expression is void as he sets it back down. "Come on. Let's look at the cards."

Draping his arm over my shoulder, he turns me and we walk to the other side of the store where racks and racks of cards are for sale.

I can't concentrate on buying the right card. And it's not that I want to run back to the aisle to see if I got a good deal. It's more that Stephen *isn't* giving anything away.

The fact that he can show no emotion one way or the other is somewhat bothersome. Does he hide all his feelings? He's not shy about kissing me, but what do those kisses mean? Nothing?

Is his heart as flat-lined as his expression was when he set that vase down?

"This is a good card." He grabs an envelope. "Did you find one yet?"

"Uh, no. I haven't. Give me a little more time." I force my lips into a smile.

It's probably because my heart isn't in a good place right now, but I'm having a hard time finding a card. I barely know the couple, so that nixes about half the cards as they walk down memory lane.

Generic cards have a cold edge to them.

"You know, we could share a card." He offers the suggestion casually, like it's normal.

Once again he catches me off guard. "Share a card?"

"Yes. Both sign it." He holds his card in the air. "This card can be from both of us. Yes? No?"

"The wedding isn't until Friday."

"And?" His expression clearly states he and I aren't on the same page.

"Aren't we supposed to be broken up long before Friday?" I hadn't even connected the two events until now. Would a couple, who has just broken off an engagement show up at a wedding together? Not in my world.

"So we'll break up Saturday. No big deal."

That's the problem. It's no big deal to him. Apparently pretending to be engaged to me doesn't affect him like it does me. Somebody needs to interject some reason here. "Okay. So what's going to happen at a beautiful Christmas wedding on Friday night that would have us breaking up the next day?"

He shrugs. "We'll think of something."

Memories of attending other weddings come to mind. All the festivities, the beautiful brides. Flowers. It all seems so happy. What could break into that mindset?

Commitment. That's what. "I have it," I say.

"You do?"

"Sure. It's the whole commitment thing. It comes to life before our eyes. The reality of what takes place. Forsaking all others, until death do us part. Yeah. All that is too much for me and I call it off."

"Strong Jenny. Doesn't need a man in her life."

The sound of "Jingle Bells" bursts through the speakers above us. I wish a springy Christmas song could put me in the mood for Christmas. But it's not. No "Joy to the World" in my soul right now.

Stephen shifts his weight, his gaze not leaving mine. "I may not have known you long, but I know what you're thinking. But you're wrong. Men don't want to spend the rest of their life with a face. They marry to share heart. Soul. Personality."

The florescent light above us blinks. So do I. Now he's talking personality? "You're trying to make me feel better. Thanks."

It's not working, but I can appreciate his attempt.

He shakes his head. "I'm not trying to make you feel better. I'm trying to make you see there's more to you than your face."

"Yeah. I've heard that before. That's what most guys want." Does he think I don't know about men?

"I'm not talking physical attributes here. Although you do have great physical attributes. I'm talking about what's on the inside."

"People don't see that." I sound matter of fact because it is a matter of fact. I had a big heart to go along with my overweight body years ago and nobody was interested. But, I'm not telling Stephen that. TMI.

Or EFM. Embarrassing For Me.

Not sure which acronym suits this situation best. Maybe both of them.

"You know I'm right." My look dares him to challenge me.

His gaze shifts. "I don't know any such thing. I know what's important comes from the heart. And I'm sorry if you've never met a guy who has portrayed that in your life. After you." He nods his head toward the register, carrying the together card.

It's only then I remember the vase, and how I don't even know if I got a good deal on my purchase. It certainly wasn't even close to being an original anything.

A feeling I'm beginning to know all too well.

BOTHER

THE RAIN HASN'T relented. In fact it has picked up as I sit in the car while Stephen goes into the school to get Phoebe from her class.

We spent too much time in the card store debating, and by the time we were finished at the outdoor mall it didn't make any sense to go home only to have to turn around and go back out to Phoebe's school.

The feeling that settles through me as I see Stephen hurrying out of the doors of the school, Phoebe's hand in his, her pink book bag bouncing on her back, is a feeling I don't want to become used to. He's all male, strength, beauty and single.

Why is this man single?

He says he enjoys spending time in the wilds away from civilization. I wonder if there is more to his story? Sometimes running can say a lot about a person.

He quickly opens the door, takes off Phoebe's backpack and sets her on the seat before jumping in the driver's side. Phoebe's backpack drips water as Stephen hands it to me. I turn and set it on the floorboard of the back seat as I say hello to Phoebe.

"I knew you were here." She's smiling and her voice sounds happy.

"Mr. Stephen told you, didn't he?"

"No. I smelled your hair. It smells good. I like your shampoo."

"Thank you." I brush my hair down in an auto-response to her comment. "It's pretty crazy looking right now. It's been shoved in my hoodie almost all day."

"I bet it's fine." She clicks her seat belt into place.

"How about some ice cream." Stephen looks into the rearview mirror for Phoebe's response.

"Yay! Ice cream."

I love seeing her smile. Her cheeks are extremely pinchable.

"Good," Stephen says.

"I like it when you pick me up from school. I'll have to tell mommy we need to stop for ice cream some days on the way home. She'll probably say no, though. She's always in a hurry to go back to work."

Stephen's expression remains solid as he listens to Phoebe. Wet tendrils of hair cling to his forehead even as his fingers reach up and try to tame his brown locks. "I'll have to give your mom an afternoon off here and there. Then she'll be able to take you without having to worry about rushing back."

"She'll still wanna go back to work, probably. Mommy isn't very fun."

I turn and look at her. "You said she tells you stories every night. That sounds like fun."

"Well," Phoebe says, "She's fun sometimes. But not very often."

"Plus," Stephen adds, "Moms have responsibilities. It's always more fun to hang with somebody else, but bottom line is moms are the best. Remember that."

"I'll try." Phoebe shrugs off her comment.

We pull into a parking lot and secure a spot close to the door. A sign that says "seat yourself" indicates we need to find our own table, so we settle at one in the middle of the café.

There are only a couple other tables occupied.

The plastic menus are tucked between a napkin holder and the salt and pepper shakers. We peruse their extravagant selection of ice cream.

I peer over my menu. "Phoebe. I'm going to read this list of flavors. Stop me when you know what you want."

"Okay," she replies.

"Vanilla—"

"Strawberry," she counters.

I set my menu on the table. "Phoebe, there are a ton of flavors here."

"I love strawberry."

"Maybe you should try something else? Have you ever tried the cookie dough? How about the birthday cake flavor?" I stop looking at the menu and look at Phoebe.

She shakes her head. "I want strawberry."

I continue looking at the flavors. "Oh, look—"

Stephen taps me on the shoulder. Looking up from the menu I see him shaking his head back and forth. He mouths the words, *strawberry is good.*

To which I smile and nod. *Okay. Got it.*

"Phoebe is having strawberry," I say, out loud this time. "What are you having, Stephen?"

"Not sure. You?"

I continue running my index finger down the menu. Each new flavor I read becomes the one I want. Until I reach the end and realize any one of the flavors would taste amazing. "I think I'm having peach."

Stephen makes a funny face. "Peach? You ever had that before?"

"No. But I'm all for trying something new. Are you?"

He closes his menu. "Sometimes. But I'm sticking with chocolate chip mint."

The waitress comes to our table, drops off glasses of water, then takes our order.

White and red décor brings brightness to the space. But even the Christmas garland edging the wall of windows can't hide the dreary skies. The rain has stopped while gray clouds still hover, moving slowly across the sky. A traffic light swings from side to side, indicating the wind hasn't died down.

Glad to be inside, I glance at Phoebe. She and Stephen are having a contest to see who can tell the best knock-knock joke. Phoebe is in the process of telling the one about the banana and the orange. Stephen declares her the winner.

They laugh, and I still can't think of a better sound than Phoebe's laugh.

The waitress delivers our three bowls of ice cream. She sets them down in front of us and hands us our spoons.

"Can I get you anything else?" She tucks her tray under her arm.

"I think we're okay." Stephen looks at me.

I nod.

"Great. I have to tell you, that you guys are such a cute family. Watching you makes me excited to have my own family one day." Her eyes sparkle and her mouth widens in a smile.

My insides jar at her words. Stephen's eyes widen and Phoebe laughs.

"We're not a family." Phoebe licks her lips. "Mr. Stephen and Miss Jenny are watching me since my mommy is gone."

The waitress blushes. "I'm sorry. The way you all were interacting was just so natural, I just assumed…"

"It's okay." Stephen's tone is calm.

I'm glad he thinks it's okay. The combination of the festive music playing, the over decorated Christmas tree in the corner, and the three of us sitting here has propelled me into a world so unlike my normal world.

A world where I don't know how to act or what to say.

Ever since I woke from the surgery to anxious doctor faces, and promises of what could be, I've been in a strange world.

I didn't expect the strangeness to not only linger but move forward as well.

But it does.

Last year at Christmas I was on the sunny beaches of the island of St. John with Jeff, enjoying the down time between jobs, not really paying much attention to Christmas, much to my parents' dismay, which is why I wanted to go far away for the holiday. My bank account had cash in it, and I didn't have a care in the world.

If you had told me in one year my face would be scarred, I would be out of a job, my bank account would be begging for more zeros, and I would be sitting in a small-town ice cream shop with a blind seven-year-old and a hot photographer, well, the only part I would have wrapped my mind around is the hot photographer part.

And he wouldn't be sitting with me eating ice cream, he would have been taking pictures of me.

"Listen," Phoebe says. "'Jingle Bells' is on the speaker. We can practice our caroling."

She starts singing the song, pulling me out of my reminiscing. Her voice is clear, a little off tune, but spunky.

Stephen elbows me. "You aren't going to sing?"

"No. You?"

"I'll wait until the real deal."

"Me, too. Hopefully there'll be a bunch of carolers and my voice won't be heard."

"You shouldn't worry about what other people think about your voice. That's what my mommy tells me," Phoebe says.

I smile. "Your mommy is right."

Phoebe goes back to singing, her shoulders rocking with the beat of the upbeat Christmas tune. She only stops to shove a spoon of ice cream into her mouth.

A lady holds the door to the shop open as three young girls walk in. Young as in Phoebe's age or a little older. The girls are talking and laughing. One of them pulls the hood of a blonde girl's sweatshirt down then brushes her hair with her hand.

The blonde girl pushes some hair out of her eyes before saying thanks to the other girl. She then pulls a Santa hat out of her pocket and shoves it on her head.

After the three girls tell the lady what kind of ice cream they want, they rush to a table. Sounds of chairs pushing across the floor threaten to drown out the festive Christmas music playing. The girls lean into each other as they talk before their laughter leads them back into their own space.

I glance at Phoebe, oblivious to the girl's antics. Phoebe's changed her rocking to the rhythm shoulder beat to a slower kind of move as a song talks about coming home for Christmas.

A burst of laughter from the girl's table echoes through the shop. Now Phoebe does pay attention, her spoon half-way to her mouth. She slowly lowers her spoon, then grabs her napkin and wipes it across her mouth.

I can't help but be taken back to my childhood of loneliness as I watch it play out right in front of me.

A LOUD KNOCK sounds on my bedroom door. I open my eyes.

Darkness reigns outside the windows indicating it's still night.

Indicating I should still be sleeping, and unless there is an emergency, no one should be waking me up.

The knock sounds again, sounding a little more frantic.

Swinging my legs over the side of the bed, I grab my robe from the end of the bed and make my way to the door, opening it hesitantly.

"Miss Jenny?"

I look down. Phoebe stands there with her blanket. All I can think is that she had a bad dream. So I ask her. "Honey, did you have a bad dream?"

"No." She's shaking her head back and forth.

My brain still foggy from being woken up from a deep sleep, searches for a reason she could be at my door. "Are you okay?"

"Yes. My alarm just went off and I wanted to hear more about Princess Bea before I went to school since I fell asleep last night and you didn't get to tell me more of her story."

"Your alarm went off? What time is it?"

"Six o'clock. I don't have to be at school until eight-thirty. We have time. I promise."

"Oh, okay." I can't even comprehend the time and she wants me to add to a story I can barely remember.

"Can I get in bed with you? I'm cold."

I tug my robe tighter around me. "Sure. Come on."

Taking her hand in mine, I slip into the bed and she hops up with me. We push the pillows behind us and sit up in the bed.

"Better?" I tuck the covers around us.

"Yes. I'm warmer, now."

"Good."

"I didn't mean to fall asleep last night." Her voice is soft, like she might still be a little sleepy too.

"It's okay. You were tired."

"But I wanted to hear more about Princess Bea."

Oh, yeah. I'm supposed to be thinking of a storyline right now. I can't really remember where we left off. "Didn't we leave the princess at a dinner?"

"Yes. Remember she decides not to give the prince the potion? Because she wants to figure it out?"

Images of princes and princesses push through the fog that is still my brain. The story is slowly coming back to me. Phoebe turns in the bed, curling her body close to mine before she leans her head against my arm.

Wondering if she's falling back asleep I look down to find her eyes wide open and expectant.

Kind of like how I would describe my heart right now. Everything I know has been thrown out of the window so to speak, and this crazy, new world encompassing a rogue photographer and a small girl-child, both who've tugged at my heart more these last few days than a slew of people have over the last few years.

I can hardly wrap my mind around it. Just like I can't bring myself to wrap my arms around this little girl next to me.

Maybe one day, but not today. Focusing back on our princess, I search my mind for the next part of the story. "Okay, so they've finished dinner. And the king asks Princess Bea to play for the family and guests. So they all make their way to the music room. Princess Bea walks to her harp. She sits down and before playing she smiles at the prince."

"He likes her smile, doesn't he?" Phoebe asks.

"Yes. He does. But her father notices it as well. And it doesn't make her father happy at all."

Phoebe squirms momentarily before sitting all the way up. "Why not?"

Why not? Good question. I look at the window still dark with the sun yet to rise. "Because he doesn't want Princess Bea to like the prince. He already has somebody he wants her to marry."

"Does Princess Bea know?"

"No. Princess Bea has no idea that her father wants her to marry...to marry Camden."

"Who's Camden?" She asks.

"Camden is a childhood friend. She's grown up with him, and he was always mean to her and pulled her hair and made fun of her. But her father is going to put Camden in charge of the army and if Princess Bea marries Camden, her father knows Camden's loyalty will stay in the kingdom."

"Was Camden at the dinner and is he in the music room now?"

"Yes. He is. And Princess Bea hasn't smiled at him once or even acknowledged that he is there. Her father isn't happy at all."

Phoebe sits straight up. "Omigosh. What if her father gives Camden the potion before Bea can give it to Prince Jonah?"

I'm amazed at Phoebe's ability to create drama. She's got some girl power for sure. "That would be tragic, wouldn't it?"

"Yes. Because Prince Jonah won't fall in love with her and a princess should always marry a prince. And Camden isn't a prince."

Talking like this makes me think of Stephen and Arabella. Certainly the king wouldn't want his daughter hanging out with the likes of a common American photographer. No wonder he chased Stephen out of his country.

"Yes, a princess should always marry a prince. So, the king isn't happy when he sees Princess Bea smile at Prince Jonah. And remember, he doesn't know the prince has a letter for him. So he doesn't know the other king wants to take the lands. Plus Princess Bea's father really doesn't want to share the lands, he wants them all to himself."

"That's called being selfish." She folds her hands in her lap.

"It is."

"Does the prince smile back when Princess Bea starts playing the harp?"

"He does. Her music once again warms his heart and makes him glad he chose to deliver the letter himself. But he has to figure out how to get an invitation to stay the night in the castle, because if he goes home without delivering the letter his father will be mad."

"Oh. Maybe Princess Bea asks him to spend the night."

"Ah. I don't think it's appropriate for young ladies to ask young men that." As I speak those words, I'm wondering why I'm preaching what I didn't practice in my young lady days.

"Why not?"

I look down at her innocent face. Of course she doesn't know what I'm talking about. "Let's just say, when you are a teenager and you like boys, you wouldn't be allowed to spend the night with one. Not until you are married."

"I'm going to get married when I'm a teenager?"

"I don't know when you are going to get married, but take my word on this. It isn't appropriate, okay?"

She slightly pulls away from being so close to me, and I realize I spoke my last words with a little more force that I had intended.

"Sorry. I didn't mean to sound harsh." This protective nature that comes out in regard to Phoebe is foreign to me.

"It's okay." Once again her voice is soft and small like she is.

"No, it's not. I'm sorry. We'll leave Princess Bea in her music room with all the drama for now."

Maybe when she goes to school, I'll write down the rest of the story, so I'm not totally working on the fly every time.

It's the day of the photo shoot.

It's like the words are whispered and pass by me. How Phoebe was able to make me forget about the most important day of my new life is a mystery to me.

For the second time that morning a loud knock sounds on my door. "Jenny. Wake up. Phoebe isn't in her room."

Stephen sounds frantic.

Phoebe's eyes grow wide. "I'm in here, Mr. Stephen."

Nothing.

Silence greets us.

"Stephen?" I call out. "Did you hear her? Phoebe is in here. We'll be right out."

"Oh, okay. Sorry to bother you."

The footsteps I didn't hear approach, retreat quickly, leaving Phoebe and me alone again. A hazy gray replaces the darkness outside the windows. The leaves sway slightly showing off the ever present breeze.

Doesn't Stephen know he could never be a bother?

BESTOWED

"ARE YOU NERVOUS?" Stephen asks.

"Very."

"It'll be good. I know it."

Ann will be here any minute. We agreed on ten a.m. and according to my phone it will be ten a.m.in one minute. "I wish I had as much confidence in me as you do."

"You've been around this for the last ten years. You know more of what you're doing than you think you do."

The doorbell rings.

"I'll get it." He taps my nose with his finger. "Try and relax. And stay put."

Easy for him to say. "Thank you."

By put, he means at the kitchen island where all things seem to go down in the house of Stephen. Conversations take place around this island, food is prepared on this island, meals are eaten at this island.

Even wounds have been healed while sitting at the island. I think back to Stephen gently touching my legs, wiping the blood from them. Luckily there are no scars and I can't even tell where the little cuts had been.

"Here's Ann," Stephen announces.

My mind reels in from thinking about Stephen's touch and shifts to the journey I'm about to embark on. One that I can't imagine being successful.

But Stephen seems to have a measure of faith in me.

It must be the churchy part of him.

"Hi." I stand and greet Ann.

"Hi. Are you sure you still want me to do this?" Her tone is hesitant.

I try to calm my heart as I digest her words. I can't fathom what I would do if she were to back out. "Of course I am. The clothes are in my room, the second room on the right. Everything is laid out on the bed. Whatever you want to wear first, that's what we'll go with."

"I wasn't sure what you wanted to do about my hair and makeup, so I didn't do anything. I have my half sister on call." She smiles as she talks about her sister.

I hadn't even thought about her hair and makeup. I'm not a whiz at it. With so many people doing mine over the last few years, the thing I'm best at is sitting in the chair sipping something cool and preferably bubbly while it's being done.

"Is she far?" I ask.

"She's next door. I didn't want to bring her if you wanted to do it, you know. I didn't want this to be more awkward than it already is."

I'm not sure how to take her comment. I don't take it as an insult. But I'm not sure it's a compliment either. "Great. Call her. If she's up for staying, maybe we could switch the hair up for different shots or outfits."

"Trust me, she'd like nothing more. In fact, when you see her, I'm sure you are going to want to ditch me and use her for the shoot."

"No. I promise that's not going to happen, but I would love her assistance with the hair and makeup."

"Two seconds, then," Ann says as she puts her phone to her ear and walks toward the front door.

"Another save by Ann." Stephen walks toward me.

"Stephen, I so don't know what I'm doing."

I try not to focus on that fact, but I feel like such an impostor. Pretending I know how to design, to photograph. At least I didn't pretend I knew how to do hair and makeup.

"If it will make you feel better, Cheetah, I don't mind sticking around."

My skin warms at his words. "As long as you don't call me that crazy name around them."

"Promise."

He steps closer to me, and in what seems like a thing he's forever doing, he places my hair behind my ear.

"Stephen—"

"Ssh." His voice is whisper-soft before he leans over and places his lips on mine, pressing slightly. His kiss doesn't last long enough. He kisses the tip of my nose then backs up a step. "Don't ever hide anything about yourself."

"But I'm more comfortable with my hair untucked." My lips still tingle at the kiss he bestowed on me with such tenderness.

A tenderness I could become used to if I let myself.

I won't let myself.

I can't let myself.

"Excuse us."

Ann's voice breaks through our kiss-filled air.

"Come on in." I step even further away from Stephen.

Ann walks into the kitchen followed by one of the most beautiful women I've ever seen in my life. She favors Ann in so many ways, yet while Ann has the classic girl-next-door beauty, the brunette has an exotic look that captivates.

Looking over at Stephen, I'm surprised to find him fiddling with his computer, not paying the least bit of attention to Ann and her sister.

He, who admires beauty, should certainly pay attention to this gorgeous creation. While Ann has put together a simple white pullover T, a pair of casual jeans and a pair of black ballet slippers, her half sister is dressed in a flowy, flowery dress, heels and jewelry to match.

Ann introduces her sister. "Jenny, Stephen, this is Anastasia, my half sister. I'm sure you're wondering where the half even comes in." She laughs after she speaks.

I'm watching as Stephen turns around, I'm sure in an attempt to be polite, but his eyes widen somewhat as he takes in our guests.

"I prefer to be called Stace. Ann and my mother are the only people who call me Anastasia. I'm pleased to meet you both."

"Stace. I like it." I try to ignore how her gaze quickly sweeps from my face but lingers on Stephen's.

"Hi." Stephen, ever the gentleman, walks to the sisters. He politely offers his hand to Stace.

She shakes his hand. I'm surprised at how carefully I watch their interaction.

146

Her eyes narrow as her smile widens. "I hear congratulations are in order. So congratulations."

"Thank you."

I'm momentarily confused. Oh, the engagement. And they did catch us kissing. They have no idea we are pretending.

Except, I'm not sure how that last kiss happened because we weren't in front of anybody, and there was no need to pretend at all.

If I were engaged to Stephen I would want those kind of exchanges all the time.

If.

I have to quit living in the if.

The real world is unfolding before my eyes. I have to make what I can of it. "Well, like I told Ann, the second room on the right is where you can set up base. The clothes are in there."

"My makeup is in a case by the front door. Ready, Ann?" Stace asks.

"As ready as I'll ever be for something like this." Ann looks directly at me. "Are you sure you haven't changed your mind?" Her gaze cuts over toward the exotic one.

"Positive. Now scoot. We don't want to lose the light."

"Okay." She shrugs as she and Stace disappear around the corner.

"Lose the light?" Stephen asks, walking to me.

I smile. "It sounds like something a photographer would say, doesn't it?"

He laughs. "It does."

"Her sister is beautiful, isn't she?" Part of me hopes he throws out a lie, while the other part of me prepares for the honest truth. The fact that I don't even know how I'll react to his reaction of the exotic beauty makes me realize my heart is different.

It's not indifferent anymore.

"The way the Lord has put her features together is crazy beautiful. But remember, there's more to a person that what we see."

Crazy beautiful? No one will ever say that about me again. My body prickles and I tap down the anger that threatens to surface at his extra-special description of Stace. Beautiful would have sufficed.

I wave him off with my hand. "I think I've got this. You can go and do whatever photographers do when they're not working."

Aware that I've compromised my own fate because of my jealousy, I want to take the words back. But doing so would show Stephen more of me than I want him to see.

I do need him.

In the short time I've been around him, I've come to appreciate who he is and what he has to say. He's opened up a world that I've probably been around but never paid attention to.

Everything's changed.

He catches my hand midair, weaving his fingers through mine. His hand is strong, like it's conveying who he is and what he is about. "Nonworking photographers, at least the ones in Hampton Cove, Florida, are mesmerized by crazy beautiful blondes."

Not letting go of my hand, he pulls me close to him. "You've totally captivated me, Cheetah."

Releasing my hand, he gently grabs my shoulders, his hands slowly moving up until he's cradling both sides of my neck. Heat explodes off every part of my body that he touches.

His gaze never leaves mine, and it's a struggle to not close my eyes, to remove the vision of my face from my mind's eye of how he sees me.

How can he see beauty?

"You are crazy beautiful inside and out. Don't ever doubt it."

"I can't help but doubt it. I don't see things like you do."

"See this."

His lips claim mine. Shots of wanting and perfection arrow through me, shattering the vision of my scar, replacing it with bright stars of wonder and a beauty I never thought I'd see again.

I kiss him with abandonment, thankful for his constant reminder of who he sees when he looks at me.

Our kiss slows.

A tender rendition of white-hot passion at its finest.

He ends our kiss, then moves his lips softly along my jaw line. He stops when he's close to my ear.

"Do you still want me to leave?" he asks.

Leave? Oh. Yeah. I have a job to do. The job that my whole existence depends on.

This photo shoot that will make me or break me has completely been replaced by the photographer's amazing kisses.

I'm that weak.

And undisciplined.

And crazy.

Focus!

Releasing my grip on his body, I back up, still dazed from his mouth on mine, his hands caressing my neck, his grand view of who I am.

I am nobody.

A nobody who is filled with the desire to be somebody again.

Like I used to be.

He runs his finger down my arm. "Or, I could stay. I would like to stay."

"If you would, please." I need any help he can give me, and I'm possessed with enough desperation to warrant begging if I have to.

"I would. You feeling comfy with Millie?" He nods towards his camera which sits on the island.

"As comfortable as I can feel at this point. I'm not overly confidant if that's what you mean."

"No. Just making sure you're feeling all right about it all."

I grab Millie and drape her over my neck. "I'm not feeling all right about anything, honestly. I've never been more scared, unsure and generally frightened in my life than I am right now."

"Maybe this will make you feel better."

Stephen and I turn at the sound of Stace's voice. I can't believe the exotic beauty heard me voice all of my insecurities.

She stands in the kitchen alone but waves her fingers toward the doorway, like she's urging somebody to come into the kitchen.

That somebody would be Ann.

Ann steps into the room. Gone is the simple girl-next-door. In her place is the I-wish-you-lived-next door-to-me girl. While she doesn't appear different, everything about her is different.

"Amazing." I wonder how Stace could capture the look I wanted without us even having a conversation about it.

The swirly skirt and blousy top look fabulous on Ann. She's barefoot, yet gorgeous, elegant, yet casual. An odd combination, I realize, but my brain is still trying to process Stephen. The man of contrasts.

Stace turns to Ann. "I told you it was all good."

Ann shakes her head. "I'm still not sure of this."

"Ditch that attitude quickly. We have pictures to take." Unable to contain my excitement, I decide I need to heed my own advice.

"Actually, a little of that attitude can add a lot to your pictures." Stephen nods toward Ann.

I cut him a look, not believing he's contradicting me, but then I remember he's the photographer, not me. Then I remember he doesn't photograph humans.

Now I'm confused. "Explain?"

"Uncertainty mixed with passion will be a great combination."

I look at him. "What?"

"You're both raw. You're raw with passion, she's raw with nervousness and uncertainty. It's bound to create great chemistry."

I shrug my shoulders, smart enough to know I'm too ignorant to argue with his reasoning. "Let's go, then."

Walking to the sliding doors, I motion for Ann to follow. Stace and Stephen are right behind, all four of us looking like quite the awkward group as we stand on the patio.

"Where to start?" I ask out loud, hoping to sound rhetorical, yet hoping Stephen will answer.

He doesn't.

I scan the pool area, all the little nuances he's told me over the last few days disappearing from my brain.

Probably run out by his kisses.

Taking a deep breath, I try to pull it all together. Everything I've been hoping for since the botched surgery has come down to this. My clothes, the perfect woman wearing them, a gal with an amazing knack for makeup and hairstyles waiting in the wings, and a gorgeous photographer, who doesn't photograph humans but has an eye for what makes an award-winning photo.

And I'm stalled.

BRILLIANT

SPOTTING THE POTTED plant sitting halfway on the stone tile and halfway on the wooden deck brought back part of a conversation Stephen and I had regarding contrasts.

I start walking toward the plant. "Ann, follow me. Please."

Stace and Stephen look with interest as Ann and I walk to the other side of the pool. I try to ignore them as I start with Ann.

"Stand next to the plant."

Ann does.

I shake my head. "No. Move left a little so you are partially in front of the plant."

She takes a couple of steps left. "Here?"

Tilting my head left, then right, I purse my lips. "Um, maybe it's the way you are standing. You're really straight, paralleling the palm. Can you put some curve into your body? Like maybe your neck can be really straight, your chin up, while you're, I don't know, doing something else?"

Ann is looking at me like I'm crazy, and I feel crazy. Those words made no sense to me, so I have no idea how I think she is going to be able to do something with them. "Okay. Forget everything I just said. I know it didn't make any sense. It's probably easier if I showed you."

With precious Millie hanging around my neck, I walk over to where Ann is standing, her expression indicating she wants to bolt. While I don't blame her, I'm not going to let her.

Her gaze cuts over to Stace and Stephen.

"Are they making you nervous?" I ask.

She swallows and nods. "I'm already nervous enough around you,

151

but…"

"I know. Be right back."

Stephen meets me halfway and speaks before I can. "We'll scoot. I'll be in the kitchen if you need anything."

The man can read my mind?

I hope he can't because it's filled with how he'll be hanging in the kitchen with the exotic Stace. Who has no ring on her finger.

At least she thinks Stephen is spoken for.

Why is this important to me?

My future is riding on the brink of a missionary turned model-for-a-morning and my focus is Stephen Day. Not good.

"Thanks." My truth is Stephen's leaving makes me nervous. As much as I don't want him around, I want him around.

"You can do it." He winks at me. "Get your shot."

After giving me a thumbs up, he turns and walks into the house. It doesn't escape my notice that Stace waited for Stephen before going into the house.

Future.

Focus.

As I approach Ann I see she is sweating a little around her hair line. It's not that warm right now. I'm sure she's putting a lot of pressure on herself. I wish I could assure her that's not necessary. The pressure is on me.

"Okay, they're gone. I didn't even have to say anything. Stephen just knew."

Ann laughs softly. "Brett and I are like that, too. Often, we know what each other is thinking. It's crazy how when you're in love with someone things like that happen, huh?"

These things I say don't register in my mind that they might be construed as they are. While I found it amazing that he knew what I wanted, Ann thinks it's natural for two people in love.

Except that we aren't in love.

Not even close.

Shaking her words out of my mind I try to gain control of this situation. "Okay, so now we are alone. Nobody is watching. Let's trade places for a minute."

When I stand where Ann was, I picture my designs on me instead of Ann. Closing my eyes, I see myself playing out the scenario of showing off the clothes.

"Watch." I strike a pose. Bending my arm, I hold onto the palm tree, throw my head back a little, pivot on my right foot.

"That looks..." Ann starts.

"Weird. I know. I'm trying to find the mood. The feel of things."

Ann stands there while I walk around the palm, stopping a couple of times as a vision enters my mind. After a minute or so I say, "Okay. Here goes."

In a matter of thirty seconds I pose in ways I've done thousands of times. I watch the transformation on her face, and she starts shaking her head.

"Okay. Yeah. I can't do that."

I dampen the energy the switching of roles has brought me. The life I feel inside at this outward display. "Right. You can't. I'm not expecting you to do what I did. Bring yourself to the table. Just you."

"I'm pretty boring."

I sigh, trying not to lose hope. "None of that. Now come on back over here. Do your thing."

"It would be nice if I knew what my thing was."

It's like I'm walking on air as I switch places with Ann. That amazing feeling of the camera focused on me, waiting for me to bring whatever it is I'm wearing to life is great, but there's a greater rush stepping behind the camera.

Taking the shot. Not being the shot.

I glance over my shoulder before turning around to take my stand as photographer. Blood surges through my body as I see Ann.

Ann, who isn't doing anything special because she doesn't think I'm ready. I'm supposed to be walking a few more feet at least.

But I stop and turn. She still has no idea I'm focusing the camera. The light is perfect.

She's perfect.

I push the button and magic starts to happen. The shutter clicks rapidly and I snap several shots before she realizes what I'm doing. Then I catch her look of surprise when she does, and I know that shot will be worth looking at again.

"Keep it up." I wave to her, urging her on.

"Keep what up?" Her puzzled expression has ruined at least five shots.

"Don't talk. Just do. Think of Brett. Think of your wedding. Go to your happy place."

Instead of arguing, she smiles. I snap a few shots, but they're just pictures on a camera. Nothing radiates. Stands out as special.

I think capturing her unaware was my best shot with this set of props.

"Let's move." I point to the right. "Over there."

Millie weighs heavy on my chest as we walk to the other side of the pool. That sunflower that Stephen was talking up has been pushed next to one of the red-cushioned chairs. I look through the viewfinder. Luscious green trees provide an amazing back-drop for the colorful chair and sunflower.

"Hang out right here." I point Ann to the chair.

She looks confused.

"Do something natural," I continue.

"The only thing natural to me right now is to run."

The wind picks up, blowing her skirt around her legs. The clothes do look perfect on her. And she has the perfect look for the clothes. But unfortunately it's not connecting for the camera.

"Cheetah."

My body warms at the sound of his voice. My heart saddens at his observance of my failure. I don't want to admit to him I can't connect all the dots here.

But then again, I'm sure I don't have to tell him. I'm sure he can tell. It doesn't take a rocket scientist to figure out not much is happening right now.

"Hi." I'll let him make the first move.

"What are you trying to capture?" He cocks his head toward Ann.

I follow with my gaze and take in only the area of what I would see through the viewfinder. "I thought the combination of the colors and shapes could pull together for a nice shot."

He nods. "I can see that. But what is the essence of what you're saying in this scenario?"

"Essence?" I wasn't aware I needed essence.

"Yes. Simplicity? Fun? Innocence? What word are you wanting to emote?"

"My first thought would be to say fun. But in looking at the items and place I'm not sure where the fun would come in."

"Fun probably isn't the best word for this scenario, I agree. What are your clothes saying to you?"

Now my clothes are supposed to talk to me? The mentality of this photographer is not my mentality. "Right now they're saying, 'take my picture because I'm on a deadline to get these pictures to Dominick.'"

Stephen shakes his head. "It shows. Your objective has to have soul, not greed as the driving force."

I'm aware that Ann can hear our conversation, but I don't care. I push down my frustration at his use of the word greedy. I'm not greedy. I need to survive. "I have soul. Plenty of soul. I'm sorry you can't see it. And the will to survive can't be classified as greedy."

Ann looks away, her feet shifting uncomfortably.

"Do me a favor." His voice is caring, even after my speech.

"What?" My response is curt. I can see my new career tanking before my eyes.

"Hand me Millie, then go stand where Ann is." He looks at Ann. "Do you mind stepping back here with me for a minute?"

"No." She walks toward Stephen. "Be glad to."

It's hard to step lightly when my heart is heavy, so after handing Millie off to Stephen, I trudge to the chair, knowing Stephen is going to make me pose.

"Sit in the chair. Please." He smiles as he adds the please.

I sit in the chair in an auto-pose. I've done this so many times it's simply the natural thing to do when a camera is pointing at me. Although I do notice Millie is still laying against Stephen's chest. He hasn't touched her yet.

"Talk to me." Stephen's tone is insistent.

"Talk?" He wants me to chat now?

"Yes. Tell Ann how you feel. Explain to her what you see playing out right now."

How do you explain something that comes natural? It's not like Millie, who is technical and has buttons and settings. Modeling doesn't have a menu. "It's hard to explain. It's something that just happens."

Ann crosses her arms. "Or it doesn't. And it's not happening with me."

I jump up out of the chair. "I was able to snap some great pictures when you didn't even know I was looking. Come on over here. Sit in the chair."

"I don't know what the point is." She speaks as she talks, but she does make her way over and sits in the red chair.

Stephen hands me Millie, then nods toward Ann. I tell her to relax and ask her about the wedding.

She smiles and visibly relaxes.

"We are so excited. My mom will be here tomorrow. Oh, and my Aunt Venus's boyfriend Trevor is coming with her. Even with all these weddings we can't convince them to tie the knot. They've been dating over twenty years."

She tells me about her mother's recent marriage, but I'm only half-listening. The other half of me catches Stephen's attention who quickly follows my lead by keeping the conversation going.

Naturally pretty, Ann's smile is amazing.

She turns in the chair, places her elbow on her thigh and cups her chin in her palm. Auburn waves flow around her face like a lazy stream of water.

"Brilliant shot." Stephen points to her.

Millie is clicking away and I know Ann knows I'm taking her picture.

But she seems to be in some sort of groove with it. She stands and acts like she's smelling the fake sunflower.

"Good, good," Stephen says, encouraging her.

Encouraging me.

"You're pretty into this for someone who doesn't shoot people," I say.

"Just trying to help you out. We all have our part to play. You're the teacher, she's the pupil and I'm helping out where I can."

A teacher? I guess I can see it. Even though Ann is somewhat relaxed now, I don't think I've done a very good job of instructing.

The sound of the sliding glass door opening breaks our little photo-spell. A woman runs out the door. She's smiling, totally unaware she's interrupting my future.

"Stephen!" she says, arms ready to embrace him.

"Mom?"

BURNT

MOM?

I look to the sliding glass door to see a man walking out along with Stace. The man must be Stephen's father. He looks like he belongs to the woman. Same age, grayish hair, Stephen's handsome look.

Stephen's mom's face is out of view as she is hugging Stephen. I can see his expression, which bears a look of confusion.

His mom steps back and places her palms on either side of his face. "If I didn't love you so much, I'd be very mad at you right now. Engaged! To your sister's best friend and you don't even tell your mother?"

Heat permeates inside me. What started out as a desperate attempt to secure my future, and help Stephen out, has turned into a disaster like I could have never imagined.

"Mom, Dad," he says while giving his father a hug. "It's a long story. I'd like you to meet Jenny."

Stephen walks to me. He pushes my hair behind my ear. "Time to meet the in-laws," he whispers, smiling, confusing me.

Why is he calm and playing along so well? This has now been upped to a dangerous level of deceit. And he's the one who was so adamant about not lying.

We all say hello, and introduce Ann and Stace. Stephen briefly explains what is going on with the photos.

"Honey," Liza Day, says. "You don't know how long we've waited to hear you have found your wife."

She grasps my hands in hers. "We are so blessed to have you in our lives. In Stephen's life. I know you've been Katherine's best friend for a

158

while now. I'm glad we finally have this opportunity to meet."

Liza hugs me with a grip that's like an exclamation point for her words.

It's like my heart is being squeezed as well. Shutting my eyes, images flash through my mind. Ann wearing the clothes I've designed, Stephen acting like he doesn't want to help but stepping in, Gary and Alice giving us that nice ornament.

It's really all too much, and the whole situation, everything, has spiraled so out of control, my heart and brain can't take it anymore. I wiggle out of Liza's embrace. "I, we, have something to tell you. It's all been a big misunderstanding. Stephen and I—"

"We wanted to tell you from the beginning," Stephen interrupts, and I'm glad he's going to take over. They're his parents. He'll be able to word my catastrophe in a way they'll understand and hopefully not be too mad.

Or disappointed.

"But a situation arose where we had to tell Gary and Alice. Then Gary, Gary must have called you. You called Uncle Roger, didn't you?"

"My only son is engaged. I called everybody."

I swallow hard. Stephen has got to make this right with his parents.

"I'm sure you did." He shoves his hands in his pockets. "It's been really busy here. My housekeeper, Teresa, had an emergency in Mexico, so we are taking care of her daughter, Phoebe, then with Jenny's deadline on getting these photos taken, we've been nonstop for days."

And?

I'm waiting for the part where he tells them the engagement isn't real. Maybe he's trying to figure out how to word it best.

"Of course we understand," Liza says. "This is going to be a Christmas we won't forget. We've checked into The Cove. With this change of plans we have to celebrate together."

"Stephen," I nudge, "Isn't there something else you want to tell your parents?"

He smiles, not looking stressed at all. "I guess there is. The big confession. Mom, Dad, don't hold it against me that Jenny doesn't have a ring, yet. I haven't found the right one for her, and I didn't want to settle for anything less than perfect."

He embraces me and gives me a kiss on the top of my head. My arms instinctively wrap around him. At this point they are probably the only thing holding me up.

What is he doing?

STEPHEN'S PARENTS leave with a promise of getting together for dinner. He squelches my questions with a look and we resume taking photos of Ann. Photos which were the reason I had been existing up to this point.

Ann has donned the wedding dress and she's rocking it. Now I'm watching the photo shoot unfold with a new outlook. An outlook of I'm not sure what's real and fake right now.

"We need to go to the boardwalk," Stephen says. "Pack it up, ladies, and let's go."

All three of us look at him like he's lost his mind.

"What?" I ask.

"Cheetah, grab the clothes, Stace, grab that makeup case, and everybody pile into the Landcruiser. We're headed for the boardwalk."

We all do as he says, and at this point I'm wondering how my whole life has gotten so far out of my control. As we drive the short distance to the boardwalk I realize everything I envisioned when I left New York is nonexistent now.

"The light is perfect," Stephen says as we pile out of his ride. "Not too sunny, not too cloudy."

We walk toward the boardwalk and Stephen places Millie around my neck.

"This will make for great shots," he says. "Ann, love the wedding dress. Act natural. Walk around like the happy bride-to-be that you are. Don't worry about Jenny and the camera, okay?"

"I'm going to photograph her here?" I ask. "In the wedding dress?"

"You are. Ann, when we're done with the dress, there's a ladies room, over there," he points, "where you can change clothes. I'll take the dress back to the car. Stace, work your magic with the hair and touch up her makeup if it needs it. Don't worry about Jenny and me. Got it?"

"Yes," they answer.

"I'm going to touch up your hair," Stace says to Ann. "Stay still.."

As they focus on Ann's hair I turn to Stephen. "What—"

"We'll talk about it later. When there's more time."

I switch from fiancée mode to photographer mode. "Yeah. I guess. Although I'm a little confused right now. About a lot of things."

"You need to focus. This is your big chance, remember?"

"I would add the clichéd, 'how could I forget' saying, but seriously, other things have happened so that forgetting this isn't out of the realm of possibility right now. And that's scary."

"Focus on your future, Cheetah. Focus."

We receive a lot of stares as we walk the boardwalk, stalking Ann who, for the first few minutes, is wearing the wedding dress. Then she switches into the shorts and same lacy top that she wore with the skirt at the beginning of the shoot.

After about ten minutes, Stephen stops us. "How are you feeling?" His question is directed at me.

"I don't know. I'm not feeling anything."

He takes the camera and looks at the pictures. "These, uh, these are okay." He turns to me. "They're missing something."

His words aren't meant to be cold, just realistic. Honest. I try to warm my heart with those thoughts.

"I think too much has happened today."

"Ann, Stace," he says, "let's call it a day."

"I'm not doing well, am I?" Ann asks.

"You're great," I say. "It's me. I'm not capturing the essence. I can't figure it out."

Ann looks to Stephen. "You can't help your fiancée out?" She smiles, like she's making light of the situation, but I detect a hint of realness in her voice.

"I can't guess at the 'essence' she's trying to capture. We'll regroup later."

"My schedule is pretty full between now and the wedding," she says.

I try not to let panic take over. Hopelessness attempts to seep into my heart, but stubborn will pushes it away. We may be through for now, but we still have a day and a half before the wedding. And a couple of days after, before Christmas.

The fact that Stephen's parents are here tries to dampen my spirits as well. Right now I want to crawl in the bed, under the covers and cry. But I won't. "It'll work out somehow." I wish I could believe my own words.

Dejection fills the ride back to Stephen's house.

"I didn't fulfill my end of the bargain." Ann hops out of the Landcruiser.

"What?" I walk around Stephen's monster SUV.

"My part. In exchange for modeling the clothes you were going to let me wear the dress in my wedding."

"Oh, Ann. I'd still love for you to wear the dress."

Stace, already out of the car, grabs her makeup bag. "Ann, after seeing your dress, you need to take Jenny up on her offer. I can't believe with all the money you have at your disposal, you could buy such an ugly dress."

Ann puts her hands on her hips. "It's not ugly, it's unique. But I'll admit, it wasn't one of my wisest choices. I was trying to stand out, be a little different on my wedding day."

"Jenny's dress will let you do that, in a *good* way." Stace shakes her head.

After Ann changes her clothes, she and Stace leave, Ann carrying the dress with her.

I watch part of SunKissed! disappear and wondered if it's a vision of what lies ahead for me.

Disappearing Jenny.

Of course it's hard to totally disappear with this scar. It's not like people won't notice me. I tried to pretend all the looks on the boardwalk were directed at Stephen and his handsomeness, but I know they were looking at my face and wondering what happened.

If only I could take it all back. The longing for a little more beauty. The desire to be just a little prettier than I was, than other girls.

Than Katherine, if I am honest.

She had started landing some jobs I thought I'd land. Her name was being talked up more than mine.

I'd felt a little stale, like my childhood was coming back to haunt me. In my opinion I had to be the best or I wasn't anything at all. I mean, that's how things had been in the past.

And now I'm here, in her brother's house, playing her brother's fiancée in a world that has gone totally crazy and unreal.

I rub my arms to ward off the chill that threatens to set in, and in doing so I feel pain.

Pain?

I feel my gaze widen as reality sinks in.

I'm burnt.

MY SHOWER STINGS as I get ready for dinner with Stephen's parents. We are taking Phoebe with us and going to a restaurant near the hotel where they are staying.

I lather lotion on my body, rubbing the lavender scented liquid into my arms like it will undo the sunburn.

Giving me a headache is more like what is happening.

A headache brought on not only by the scent, but also by the frustration at the fact that I haven't been able to talk to Stephen about why he seemed so eager to have his parents think we are engaged.

Cringing as I carefully put on a white spaghetti-strapped camisole, I then don a loose-fitting, long-sleeved see-through white gauzy shirt with bell sleeves. After I button what seems like a hundred buttons, I pull on a pair of black leggings. My cheetah pumps dress up my outfit and I'm ready to take on the evening.

"Hi, Miss Jenny," Phoebe says as I walk into the kitchen. She's sitting at the island, sipping a glass of milk. Cookie crumbs are scattered in front of her, and a half-eaten snowman cookie is clutched in her hand, his head missing.

"Hi, Pheebes. You *are* going to be hungry for dinner, I hope?"

"I am."

"Good. Did Mr. Stephen tell you we were going out?"

She bites the cookie. "He did. With his mommy and daddy."

I barely make out what she says. "Hey, what would your mom say about talking with your mouth full?"

She closes her mouth and chews.

"That's what I thought."

Phoebe swallows hard, then gulps her milk. She wipes her mouth with her arm. "But you asked me a question right when I was taking a bite."

"I did. I also saw you take the bite, and I would have been patient while you chewed."

"Okay," she says.

"Here's my two girls." Stephen walks in. He dresses up very nice. I wouldn't have believed he could look more handsome, but I swear he does.

"Did you decide to let Phoebe have her dessert before dinner?" I ask.

"She's a kid. They have appetites. Besides you eat lunch at ten-thirty or something ridiculous like that, don't you, Phoebe?" He takes a bite of a cookie, too.

"Yeah. We eat early. I was starving."

I'm still trying to figure out how I can get Stephen alone before we join up with his parents for dinner. I need to know what he is going to tell them, to know why he was so enthusiastic for them to think he was engaged. If I thought prayer would work I would pray for that minute.

But I'm not convinced.

"Do you have a minute?" he asks, nodding his head toward the patio.

Seriously? I turn my head so fast toward him that I almost become dizzy. Could God really have heard what was going on in my mind? "Sure."

"Is it adult talk time?" Phoebe asks.

"Yes," Stephen answers. "Finish your cookie. We'll be right back."

Stephen opens the door to the patio. His phone makes a chirping noise.

"Text," he says.

Glancing at his phone he guides his fingers across the keyboard, obviously replying to the text.

He shoves his phone back in its case. "That was Mom and Dad. I told them we were leaving in less than five."

He smiles. I love his smile. The best thing about it is that it's genuine. Stephen isn't the smile-because-I-have-to kind of guy.

Also, there's his gentle spirit. I've never been around someone with his demeanor.

He takes a deep breath and for a moment I'm inclined to believe he is nervous. But only for a moment. Men like Stephen aren't nervous.

He grasps my hands in his. "For all practical purposes, and according to what everyone thinks, we are engaged. Right?"

Usually I'm a smart gal, but right now I'm clueless. "Right."

"I'm thinking we keep with the plan around my parents. It's either that or break up right now."

I'm unable to put into words how my heart feels. My head feels great, as in knowing the plan and knowing the breakup was inevitable. But my heart has somehow attached itself to his heart and it's only at this moment that I can admit this.

But I certainly can't let him know.

I can't reveal to him how my heart will miss him when we part ways. When he heads off to some foreign country to take photos of creatures that have four legs for the most part.

Creatures that don't talk back.

Creatures that don't become sad when he leaves.

The picture of him and the lion pops into my mind. There's no doubt the lion was pleased to see him. But how did the lion react when he left?

Did the lion's heart drop?

I refuse to think of what mine will do. "Okay. They're your parents."

"Cheetah." He lets go of my hands and steps closer to me. His finger slides up my neck, tilting my head so my gaze can't help but stare into his.

I don't want to speak in fear of distracting him from kissing me. Because I do want him to kiss me.

Not only has my heart grown fond of Stephen, but my lips also anticipate his touch. My eyes plead with him to kiss me, but he doesn't move any closer.

I'm not sure what this exchange is as we are readying to meet with his parents. Maybe he's just preparing for a night of acting like we are a couple.

Instinctively, because I wouldn't *knowingly* do this, my tongue runs over my lower lip. When I realize what is happening, I pull my wayward tongue back into my mouth, imagining what he must be thinking.

He slowly gets down on one knee.

"Cheetah," he repeats. "Will you marry me?"

BLUE

I KNOW I HAVEN'T heard him correctly.

He fishes in his pocket and pulls out a black velvet box. "I found this at a local jewelers. Since we're pretending to be engaged, I thought we might as well make it look as real as possible. Including the kneeling thing."

Telling myself the disappointment that quickly slid over me at his use of the word pretend is really relief, I try to stop the hammering of my heart at the sight of the box.

As he opens the box, my hand covers my heart so it doesn't fly out of my chest onto the patio. The ring is gorgeous.

Beautiful.

Sparkling.

Brilliant.

How did he know I'd dreamed of my engagement ring looking like the square cut diamond he's holding right now? And just as big.

I don't dare look at him. Not yet. I'm having trouble wrapping my mind around this whole scenario. "Why are you giving me a ring?"

He stands, and I follow his movements. Lifting my gaze, I see a look pass over his eyes. Not sure what kind of look, but it isn't intense, it isn't lazy, it is somewhere in between, like he's unsure of what is taking place.

"It seems like the right thing to do. Besides, I saw my mom's disappointed look when I told her I hadn't bought you a ring. And I don't like to see my mom disappointed. Ever."

I lift my hand to rub my forehead, but he hijacks my hand and slips the ring onto the fourth finger.

The wedding finger.

My hand doesn't feel weighted like I thought it would feel if I ever accepted a proposal. No, it feels light, not burdening at all. But then again, there is no proposal. It's pretend.

So his mom won't be disappointed.

Like the Princess Bea story with Phoebe.

"I hoped you'd say yes." His voice sounds raspy. Sad?

I was hoping he would kiss me, not ask me to marry him. "You caught me off guard." He's forever catching me off guard.

"Will you wear it?" He holds onto my hand, his warmth coursing into my palm and up my arm.

Nothing pretend about that. "Stephen, using the word pretend doesn't change reality."

A soft wind rustles the tree tops, their protest mirroring the stirring of my heart as Stephen's gaze lingers on me. His eyes search mine, and I want them to find an anchor inside me.

"No harm in pretending just a little while longer, is there?" he asks.

My heart soars. "No harm."

I stand on my tiptoes, my hands on either side of his face, pulling him toward me. Our lips meet in that anticipated kiss.

After our kiss ends, I rest my head on his shoulder and marvel at the fact that he thought he could drop all this on me in less than five minutes. This guy is gorgeous. He's nice. He seems to like kids. Why wouldn't I want to marry a guy like this? A deep sense of loss at the thought of us breaking up consumes me.

That feeling can't be misconstrued as love.

Can it?

Facts are facts. Just because I'm going to miss him when we break up doesn't mean I'm in love with him.

"If we were really going to be engaged," he says, "it's the ring I would pick for you."

His statement is bold. Has he thought of asking me to marry him?

There is something I do love about Stephen. I do love to kiss him. That should count for something.

I can't bring myself to think about the possibilities of what could be with someone in my life who isn't bothered by what makes me insecure, but instead encourages me to hope for a better life.

Leaving the safety of his arms, I step back. "If you were to really ask me to marry you, I can't see myself turning down a beautiful ring like this." The words burst forth without much thought on my part. But they're out. And I can't take them back.

Looking at him expectantly I notice his gorgeous smile that I love so much isn't gracing his face. Yet, he brings my hand to his lips, yes, the hand with the ring, and brushes a kiss across my skin. A kiss that I might have missed had the heat from his lips not warmed my hand.

"Let's go. Your future in-laws are waiting for us."

I MUST ADMIT WE do look like a family as we walk to the table at the restaurant. I'm holding Phoebe's hand, Stephen is walking behind us like a protective father and husband.

Gazes linger on us, but instead of bothering me, they fuel me.

Stephen's parents arrived before us, of course, and stand to greet us as we reach the table. It only takes moments for everyone to settle into their seats. The waiter immediately comes over with a glass of water for Phoebe and pours red wine for me and Stephen. His parents had chosen a bottle and insisted on sharing with us. Celebration wine they said.

I have a feeling it's going to be a long evening. We have to remember Phoebe has school in the morning.

The menu has no prices, and I wonder who's paying. Phoebe and I have a conversation about the food selection on the menu, and she makes a decision. I feel at home in this swanky place. It reminds me of my life in New York. A life I thought I'd left behind.

Stephen's family obviously has money. The house he lives in is pricy. I know he must make a great living doing what he does, but everything about his parents, including their restaurant choice, screams money.

I reach for my wine glass, but before I can grab hold of it, Stephen's mom grabs my hand.

"Oh, my. Look at this ring! William," she turns to her husband, "look. Isn't this gorgeous? Stephen, I always knew you had good taste. This is exquisite. Simply exquisite."

"Thank you." I better get used to this. It is a beautiful ring. There will be comments no matter where I go.

"I learned from the best." Stephen nudges his father.

"Miss Jenny has a ring?" Phoebe asks. "Can I feel it?"

"Sure." I place my hand by hers, and she proceeds to run her fingers across my ring.

"It's big."

We all laugh.

"Yes, it is," Stephen answers.

The waiter arrives and takes our orders. We make small talk while waiting for our food, then continue as the food arrives. We decide we must not ignore the famous desserts, so we order and split them amongst ourselves.

Phoebe shoves the last spoonful of brownie fudge sundae into her mouth. "I'm—"

"Phoebe?" I interrupt.

She covers her mouth with her hand and chews fast.

"It's okay," I say to her. "We can wait until you are done."

She swallows hard. "Sorry. I was going to say I was full."

We laugh. "I am too," I say.

Stephen's father raises his wine glass. "Here's to the engagement of my son and his bride-to-be. Stephen, we couldn't be happier that you are marrying Jenny."

Then I guess they'll be less than happy when we break up.

"Here, here," Liza says. "We are thrilled for you two. Now, when is this wedding?"

Stephen looks at me before he speaks. "We haven't chosen a date yet."

Liza waves her hand in front of her face. "Of course. We understand. But you are talking sooner rather than later, aren't you?"

I'm leaving the talking to Stephen. These are his parents.

My lie, but his parents.

"Mom, I know you all too well. What's on your mind?"

Liza and William laugh, and William reaches out to brush his wife's arm. A gesture so gentle and loving. I see where Stephen gets his touching trait from. "He's got you pegged, honey," William says.

Liza smiles at her husband before turning her attention toward Stephen. Her eyes are brimming with tears, and I sense a moment between mother and son coming with her next words.

And I feel a sense of gloom. Sadness. His parents, his boss, his church friends. This is out of control. I don't know who else we can meet that this false engagement is going to affect. Thank goodness Katherine is out of town. Although if she had been in town, we wouldn't be in this mess to begin with.

Liza uses her heavy white napkin to dab the corners of her eyes. "I'm sorry to get so emotional," she starts.

William takes her free hand in his. "It's okay, doll. It's not every day your only son becomes engaged."

Or unengaged.

"I know, I know," she mutters.

Phoebe leans to me. "Is everything okay?" she whispers.

"Yes," I answer. Phoebe's heart is big, and she always wants everyone to be happy.

"Good," she says.

"I have a story to tell," Liza says, but now I notice her attention is not focused on Stephen anymore, it's focused on me.

Liza looks in her purse and pulls out a small box. Bigger than a ring box, but not by much.

A sense of doom starts to swirl around that sense of gloom. I know without a doubt what Stephen's mother has in the box, paired with whatever words she is going to speak, will change my life forever.

"When I was pregnant," she begins, "The doctors knew that Stephen was a boy. But I didn't want to know. I wanted to be surprised. We had a girl's name and a boy's name picked out, so we were prepared. Remember that day, William? The day I went into labor?"

"How can I forget? Even if I wanted to, you remind me of it almost every year on his birthday."

William laughs as he finishes talking. Stephen and Liza chuckle as well, which I guess causes Phoebe to chuckle. The contagious laugh stops at me.

I don't laugh.

I prepare.

Because at this moment I realize I don't even know when his birthday is.

"Actually, it all worked out well, as if I had planned my day. I slept well, got up in the morning and went into labor. I knew it before I had eaten my breakfast. So William called the office and we settled in to wait until the contractions were five minutes apart."

"You wanted to leave when they were eight minutes, but I told you to hold on."

"I don't think so, but, anyway, that's not important. When we walked out of the house, I saw it. A blue butterfly." Liza's eyes sparkle, shimmering with tears. Her expression is one of love. Pure love. And it's directed at me.

A blue butterfly? A feeling of being drenched waves over me as I think of that day I sat in the gazebo, watching the blue butterfly.

Thinking of Stephen.

"We arrive at the hospital and after that sign God graced our path with that morning, I knew I was having a boy. Things started moving quickly. Five hours later a nurse put this beautiful boy in my arms, wrapped in a soft baby-blue blanket. With tears streaming down my face, I looked into the bluest eyes I had ever seen. Just like that butterfly."

This cannot be happening. Is this how God works? In amazing ways that have no earthly explanation?

"I said to William right then and there, 'we need to start praying right away for the woman God has chosen to be his wife.' And we did. We said a prayer right there and have been praying for you every day."

I have no idea what to say. I'm at the point of tears, but I can't speak. What do you say to someone who tells you they've been praying for you your whole life?

"This is where I step in," William says. "I felt the Lord nudging me all along that we were going to have a boy, so I had gone and picked up a little something for Liza. I had it with me that day, and when we laid our eyes on Stephen, I couldn't believe what I was seeing. You tell her the rest, honey."

I notice I'm about on the edge of my seat now. I don't know at what point I sat up straight and leaned forward, but this is how I find myself after William speaks.

"I love this story, so far," Phoebe says. "I can't wait to hear more."

"Well," Liza continues, "Here I am, holding the most beautiful baby boy the world had ever seen and my husband dangles something in front of me. At first I had no idea what he was doing, but it only took moments for it to quit moving and I realized it was a silver necklace. And hanging from the necklace was a star sapphire."

She opens the box that sits in front of her, and scoots it towards me. The star sapphire sits on a white velvet board.

"The stone was the color of that butterfly and the color of Stephen's eyes. The star also reminded me of how God knows the names of all the stars He's created. And I knew then that He knew the name of Stephen's wife. And now we all know her name is Jenny."

I want to blurt out, "it's not Jenny," but I can't determine if that would be appropriate behavior.

Liza pulls the velvet box back toward her. I'm relieved because I thought for a moment she was going to give me the necklace, and there is no way, no how I could accept it.

Instead of closing the lid, Liza removes the necklace from the box, scoots back her chair and stands. My momentary relief is gone and I look to Stephen with eyes that I know are wild, pleading.

Liza walks behind me. "Grab your hair, darling, I don't want to get it tangled in this necklace."

I do as she says, wondering why I'm doing as she says. I guess I'm waiting for Stephen to stop the madness, but he's just sitting there, his gaze glued on me and his mom.

"Jenny," she says as she drapes the necklace on me, clasps the clasp, then comes around to face me. She takes my hands in hers. I'm sure she can feel me shaking. She has no idea the true reason behind my nervousness. "We welcome you into our family. We welcome you as Stephen's wife. It would be our honor if you would wear this as your 'something blue' as you walk down the aisle."

My heart is breaking as tears seep from the corners of my eyes.

"Liza, you've made our Jenny cry." William sounds choked up as he speaks.

I'm a total puddle if his dad cries.

I look at Stephen and softly speak. "Stephen, don't you have something to say?"

Please, please tell them the truth.

"Yes." He clears his throat. "Yes, I do. The necklace looks beautiful on you, Jenny. Simply beautiful."

BREATHE

"I BET YOUR necklace is so pretty, Miss Jenny." Phoebe sits on the counter in her bathroom as I brush her hair.

"The necklace is pretty." I cannot remove the image of Stephen's mom's joy as she asked me to wear the necklace in the wedding as my something blue.

Even the sound of their voices reveled in the good news.

It took this act of kindness and love to truly show me we have gone too far.

I took the necklace off when we arrived home. As soon as I put Phoebe to bed, I'm going to give the ring and the necklace back to Stephen. I'll make the phone calls. I'll do whatever it takes to tell the truth right now.

Tonight.

"You decided to replace me, Phoebe? Get a new hairdresser?" Stephen asks from the doorway.

Phoebe laughs. "No, Mr. Stephen. Miss Jenny was already in here so I thought I'd give you a break tonight."

Learning that Stephen brushed out Phoebe's hair each night inches him that much further into my heart, which immediately weakens my resolve to end our relationship tonight. The faux relationship I should say.

I only wish the jewelry was as fake as we are.

"Miss Jenny is going to tell me more of our story. Then I'm going to bed."

Stephen crosses his arms which serves to accentuate his muscles. "I hope it's a short addition. Dinner out has us behind schedule tonight."

Phoebe's hand covers her mouth as she yawns. "I know."

"I'll keep it short. Promise," I say. *Then we need to talk.*

He nods. "Night, Phoebe. See you in the morning."

"Good night," she replies.

She then turns to me. "Princess Bea is in the music room, remember? And the prince has to figure out what he's going to do with the letter."

My mind drifts back to our last Princess conversation. "Yes, he couldn't go back home without delivering the letter, yet he didn't really want to deliver the letter, did he?"

"No. Because he decided he liked Princess Bea a lot. I think he should give her some jewelry. Like Mr. Stephen gave you a ring. Does that mean you are getting married?"

The lie started out fun, but now causes a feeling of dread to run through me every time it's brought up. Maybe she won't notice if I don't answer her question about me and Stephen. "What kind of jewelry should the prince give to Princess Bea?"

"How about a pretty necklace."

I think about the necklace Stephen's mother gave me. The beautiful blue necklace is in its box, on the dresser. "Okay. Is he going to give it to her right away?"

She laughs. "Not in front of all the people. But why would he bring the necklace with him? He didn't even know about Princess Bea until he heard her playing the music."

"Maybe the necklace was for someone else."

"Yeah, like Princess Bea's mean sister." She kicks her feet and claps her hands. The drama of a seven-year-old.

"Overdone. Think of something else."

Now she's sporting a really big smile. She must have thought of something really good.

"I know, I know. It's the necklace that is going to break the curse."

A smidgen of happy enters my heart at her excitement. I have no idea how this is going to work out, but we can go with it. "Okay. Good job. Now we have to figure out how it all comes together." I set the brush down. "We're done. It's late."

"I'm going to be thinking about Princess Bea all night," Phoebe announces as we leave the bathroom. "I think I'm going to dream about her."

Phoebe makes me want to scoop her up, hug her and never let her go. But she's too old, a little heavy, and would no doubt think I'm crazy. "Sweet dreams," I say to her as we reach the study.

"You, too, Miss Jenny." She crawls into bed.

Her little fists grab her blanket before she snuggles under the covers. I so want to snuggle with her. Somehow being around Phoebe makes the rest of the world seem unimportant.

I turn off the light. "Goodnight."

"Night," she replies.

The Christmas tree lights sparkle and blink in the keeping room. Stephen must have plugged them in, but I don't see him. It's late for Phoebe but early for us.

Maybe he's dodging me. He probably doesn't want to talk about what happened tonight. How I accepted his mom's gift with tears slipping down my cheeks.

They plan to spend Christmas here with us. Celebrating the birth of Jesus and our engagement.

We used my shoot, Ann and Brett's wedding, and Phoebe's caroling party as excuses not to get together for the next couple of days. They said they had plenty of shopping to do anyway.

Shopping. Christmas.

I've been so focused on my miserable state that I haven't thought of what time of the season it is. Unless I've been forced to.

Nothing seems to be working out. Nothing seems to be coming together. Everything I touch falls apart.

Grabbing the throw blanket, I sit on the couch. I tuck the blanket around me as I find a comfortable position. The festive lights dance around the tree, their tune unnamed.

A stillness that should be healing lingers in the air. My soul should be soothed at the quietness, the time it has to bask alone.

While I came here to be alone, my time has been occupied by a sweet little girl and a guy I can't shake out of my mind.

My SunKissed! line has been nothing but rain-kissed at the moment. RainKissed?

Slickers, umbrellas, rain boots of all colors and styles flash into my mind. That's it.

My break.

Kissed!

I'll brand myself with Kissed! and all the clothes will belong to a specific line. SunKissed! RainKissed! RomanceKissed! SportKissed!

I fling the blanket off and race to my room, grab my sketch pad and pencils, and sit on the bed.

Flipping to an empty page I write the word RainKissed! The bold, blue letters instantly remind me of the necklace Stephen's mom gave me.

Will I ever look at anything without having some part of Stephen and who he is invade my thought process?

Grabbing the gray pencil, I place a star on top of the "i" in the rain part of the word RainKissed! and shade it with my white pencil.

Beyond excited, I almost can't contain myself.

Maybe Stephen was right when he said we were supposed to be here for a reason. He and I.

Could this God thing be real? Could God orchestrate people's paths so they will cross and change the course of someone's life?

"There you are." Stephen's voice startles me.

He's standing in the doorway to my room, reminding me of the first day we met. When he was barely clothed.

He's fully clothed right now, yet no less attractive. The blue slacks and white dress shirt he wore to dinner fit him perfectly.

Looking good is something Stephen Day does naturally.

"Working?" he asks.

"Yes. I think I'm really onto something."

He steps into the room. "Do you mind if I look?"

I shrug my shoulders as he sits on the edge of the bed. "There's nothing much to see right now."

Turning the sketch pad toward him, I smile.

"That star looks familiar," he says, pointing to the dotted "i".

Embarrassed, I look away from him.

"Look at me," he whispers.

As I turn my head, he takes the sketch pad and pencil out of my hands and places them on the floor.

"I know that tonight was hard on you." His hand brushes back my hair as he speaks.

"This has become so out of control. I really never thought when I uttered those words to your boss that we would be here now. This huge ring on my finger, your mom's prized possession on my dresser waiting for our wedding day. I never envisioned this. Never."

"When I boarded that plane in Zaunesia I never imagined something like this happening. I thought I was destined to spend a quiet holiday in my house by myself."

He takes my hands into his, reminding me of his mom at the restaurant. One thing is for sure regarding Stephen. It feels natural to be around him. I don't flinch when he touches me anymore. It's like I need to be touched by him.

Dare I think, even for a moment, that I was created to be with him?

I've never been drawn this much to someone this fast. Maybe it's because I've heard of him off and on from Katherine, but my soul feels like it knows his soul. Like my soul is really only half a soul and he possesses the other half.

If I voice any of these thoughts, I know he'll think I'm way out there.

But while I don't want to throw myself at him, a part of me wants him to know that I feel a connection with him that supersedes any feeling I've ever had for a guy before.

Jeff is a distant memory. I can barely remember what he looks like in the presence of someone like Stephen.

"You're hardly by yourself at all. Between me and Phoebe and the plethora of guests that have popped in and out, the house has been full of people," I say.

"For a guy like me, who'd rather be in the wilderness surrounded by trees, being around people can become a bit overwhelming."

Looking at him I wonder if I'll ever become used to his handsome face. Not that I'm going to be around him that much longer. "After tonight you have to believe me when I say to you I'm sorry. I'm sorry for all the trouble I've caused. I'm sorry for the hurt feelings that I think are going to happen when we announce our breakup."

"We both are to blame. I could have easily told my parents tonight what was going on. In fact, the closer we got to the restaurant the more I had made up my mind to do just that."

"What happened?" I think of my thoughts in the bathroom, about giving the ring back, but I push them away. For a little while, anyway.

"I can't explain it. Watching you carry yourself with grace, nurturing Phoebe at the table. It came to my attention you are what I would want in a wife. I guess I got carried away on that dream. Every time I opened my mouth to tell my parents the truth, some other thought always took over."

While I like him saying I'm what he would want in a wife, I also realize we aren't really getting married.

My gaze catches the corner of my sketch pad on the floor by Stephen's feet. Stephen who has the ability to switch my focus to him, no matter the situation.

"Just two more days," I say. "Then we can have the biggest breakup in the history of breakups."

He taps me on the nose. "You're certainly a mean girl breaking up with me right before Christmas. Heartless."

"I think you're the heartless one, teasing me with this ring. Introducing me to your family. All the while knowing none of this is real."

"That's not true. Some of this is unbelievably real."

"Like what?"

His fingers caress my hair. "Your soft hair. And your even softer lips."

Giving me no time to respond, his lips touch mine in what starts out as a soft kiss. This attention Stephen gives me fuels my belief that I'm beautiful again in some way.

I stop our kiss but hold onto his shoulders as I scoot further back on the bed. I pull him down with me, ignoring the slight pain of my sunburned arms as I rest in the softness of the bed. His lips capture mine in a kiss that says this is more than a kiss.

Kisses like this lead to other boundaries being broken. Boundaries I thought no man would ever want to break again.

His lips have left mine but have continued to rain kisses along my jaw, down my neck. The same path his finger took the first day I met him.

"I need to be careful," he says. "I don't want to touch your sunburn."

Should I tell him that in the presence of his kisses my sunburn feels nonexistent?

"So I'll unbutton your shirt very carefully."

I have no idea if he's purposely being cheesy or if this man is this meticulous, but he slowly unbuttons every tiny button on the front of my shirt.

And there are a lot of buttons.

He helps me sit up and gently slips the shirt from my shoulders, leaving me clad in my white spaghetti-strapped top. I'm still craving the feel of his lips and start to lie back down, but stop when he takes my shirt and leaves the bed.

He drapes my shirt on the chair by the bathroom door, I lose sight of him as he enters the bathroom. But he's only gone for a moment and when he reappears, he's carrying a bottle of lotion.

Aloe lotion.

"Your job is to keep your hair in check." He squeezes lotion onto his palm.

With a touch I wouldn't have imagined being so soft, he rubs the aloe into my skin. Stephen is not only healing my burnt skin, he has no idea the mending he's doing in my heart.

"All done." I release my hair as he places the lotion bottle next to my sketch pad. I have no idea where my pencil is. I'll probably step on it tomorrow morning.

"Now, where were we?" he asks as he leans into me. I lie down, and as I feel the softness of the bed beneath me, I feel him kissing me. A long, luxurious kiss, the likes of which I never experienced before.

My fingers play in his hair, not wanting these moments to end.

Our kiss ends from need. A need to breathe. He stares at me, and I know I'll always see stars when I see his blue eyes. I'll remember what he said about God knowing the names of all the stars.

About how his mother said God knew Stephen's wife's name was Jenny.

How can we defy God?

Of course she only said those things because she thinks we're getting married. I wonder if she'll tell the same story to the woman Stephen will eventually marry?

"Cheetah." He breathes my name softly. "You drive me insane."

I laugh. "I'm not exactly cool, calm and collected, here. See how fast my heart is beating?" I place his hand over my heart, a dangerous move I realize, but I'm in a dangerous mood.

He's very careful, too careful, in keeping his hand in the center of my chest, away from the more intimate parts of my body.

I wonder at this.

We're adults. I'm sure he's been in this type of situation before. I never thought I'd be in this situation again.

"My heart is beating just as fast." His gaze never leaves mine, but his hand leaves my heart and he wraps me in his arms.

"Not fast enough, apparently."

"There are two things you need to know." He kisses me.

"When we make love, one, we'll be married." He kisses me again. "Two, it will be because you love me, not because you want to feel like you're not ugly."

His words take my breath away.

Because I want to feel his skin against mine.

Because I want to know everything I can about this man.

Because he said when, not if.

BEDLAM

IT'S THE BIG day.

The wedding day.

Ann and Brett are getting married in about one hour.

Since Stephen's declaration the other night, I've done a good job avoiding him. I feel out of sorts. I venture out in the main parts of the house when he's gone. Otherwise I stay in my room, unless Phoebe is around. She's a great buffer.

The positive result of my avoiding him is that I've come up with some great designs. My creativity seems to spark when I'm highly agitated, moved, or flat-out upset.

Which is bad for me but good for designs.

The avoiding-of-Stephen-Day is about to come to an end, though. Yes, the happily engaged Jenny and Stephen are about to attend a wedding, the wedding which will trigger our breakup.

It will be interesting to see if anything happens that can fuel my reasoning, or if we fall back on the "I'm afraid of really committing" aspect.

Since we have to take Phoebe to her caroling party tomorrow night the big breakup won't happen until Sunday.

Then I really don't know what will happen.

All I do know is that my heart is sad.

I have to admit I've fallen for Stephen.

Who hasn't fallen for me.

But, I have to act bright and shiny, like my ring, while we are around people for the next two days.

Phoebe and I haven't made any progress on the Princess Bea story. I think I've used all my creative juices sketching clothing and accessories onto paper. Phoebe has been understanding, and I promised her we would add to the story tonight. Though we need to finish it up in the next couple of days, because her mom is coming home. I know Phoebe will be in the wedding kind of mood after tonight's festivities.

Stephen is pretty sure Teresa is coming home Tuesday, Christmas Eve. After Phoebe leaves, there'll be no reason for me to stay.

So, I'll leave.

I've already made reservations at a hotel not far from here. I'll stay there for only couple of days because dipping into the design budget isn't smart. Hopefully I can regroup once again, then move on.

Back to New York after the holidays.

Back to the cold.

Back to life without Stephen.

But hopefully a life with a new career. Although that's not looking too promising.

My sunburn is gone, only lasting a day. But now my arms have a slight color to them, a contrast to the rest of my body. I feel like nothing about me is in sync right now. Everything is off kilter.

And I don't like it. At all.

I've worked so hard to be at the place I am in life. And to have it taken from me without warning has created havoc like I never imagined.

Stephen can upload and send me the photos we have of Ann, but since we didn't have an opportunity to take any more, I'm not sure I'll have more than a couple of photos to send to Dominick.

And I need a better chance than that.

At least I had the chance to photograph Ann in the dress.

And now I will watch her marry her love in the dress.

I slip my earrings in my ear, spray my hair a final time and decide this is good as it's going to get.

Ever.

Imperfect face.

Hurt heart.

Jenny Harris.

A knock on my door pulls me out of wallowing in self-pity. I promised to help Phoebe as soon as I got ready, so I open the door and look down, expecting to see a little girl.

Instead, I'm looking at a very expensive pair of dress shoes, which are being worn by Stephen.

As I pull my gaze up I have to rely on what inner strength I have to act cool and nonchalant. Every woman at this wedding will be shooting me looks because they think he's mine.

If only they knew.

Stephen reaches out, taking my left hand in his. "Still wearing the ring?" he asks.

"I am." Does the man think I would ditch the gorgeous diamond one minute before I have to?

"Good. Are you ready to be the happy couple once again?"

We've crossed so many lines in this lie I don't have a choice but to be ready. "I am. I have to help Phoebe with her hair."

"All right. Roger and Celine popped in to say hello, but I told them you were still getting ready. I'll meet you in the kitchen in a few minutes, and we'll head out."

I did forget we would be seeing more of his family today. I'm surprised his mom and dad haven't shown up here these last couple of days. "Okay."

I turn and pick up my clutch off the bed. It's a good thing I brought a couple of just-in-case outfits. I thought I might have some networking opportunities and wanted to have something on hand. I never thought I'd be attending a wedding in my party attire.

After insisting to Phoebe that I'm wearing my hair down, so she can too, I maneuver my way out of doing an updo.

"Would Princess Bea be wearing her hair down at a wedding?" she asks.

"Yes, actually she would. Back in those days the girls weren't allowed to wear their hair up unless they were married. So, since you aren't married, you are perfectly fine."

She laughs. "Miss Jenny. I'm too little to get married."

"I know, silly girl."

"So is that why you are wearing your hair down? Because you and Mr. Stephen aren't married yet?"

"Yes, that's why." I try not to laugh at the complicated mess that

Stephen and I are.

"Can I have some hairspray on my hair? Just a little? Please?"

Unable to say no to this child, I tell her to stay put. I go to my bathroom and grab my hairspray.

I lightly dust some hairspray on her hair. "That smells good."

"It does have a good fruity smell, doesn't it?" I ask.

"Now I can smell like you." She gives me a hug, which consists of her wrapping her arms around my legs.

"You're sweet." I bend down so I can hug her. Not an easy feat in these shoes.

"I wanna be just like you when I grow up," she says.

I stiffen and I hope she doesn't notice. "You need to be just like yourself. There's nobody like you. Don't you forget it."

"But I can tell you're glamorous. Like Princess Bea is glamorous. I wanna be glamorous, too."

I tilt her chin up. "You've got so much Phoebe glam. Why do you think that girl invited you to her caroling party tomorrow night?"

Now she stiffens and I do notice. "I don't know."

I feel bad at bringing up the party. She had seemed so excited about it, but in the last couple of days, her excitement had been waning. "Well, tonight we have another party. See, you are quite the party girl. Very glamorous."

She smiles at my remark. I stand and hold her hand. This time she doesn't protest or let go.

We meet Stephen in the kitchen.

"Wow," he says. "You ladies are looking great. Phoebe, nice dress."

"Thank you, Mr. Stephen."

"Let's go." He motions for us to go before him, and we all walk to the front door. With all the finesse of the gentleman that he is, he scoots around me and opens the front door for us.

Phoebe and I are still holding hands and continue to do so down the driveway. The December air is warm, and I have to keep reminding myself it's only a few days before Christmas. Somehow, after all the years spent north, Christmas never seems right in these warmer temperatures.

But since this is an outdoor wedding I am thankful for the warm weather.

A small crowd is gathering in the cul de sac. White chairs are set up, and I spot a flutist playing music.

"So," I ask Stephen, "How many people do you know here?"

"Only Roger, Celine, Ann and Brett. Unless there are some more people from the church, but I'm not sure if they invited everyone with this being such a small space."

We step off the driveway into the street, Phoebe grasping my hand like she'll never let go, Stephen very close to me on my right side.

"There's Barb and Randy from church," Stephen says.

Oh goody, people he knows. Now that feeling of being alone in the crowd hovers at the edge of my precipice. But I do have Phoebe. She didn't bring her cane, so she needs to stick with me.

I'm thrilled to be her guide.

I refuse to admit it is a bit of a comfort knowing I won't be left alone here, even if my constant companion is only seven years old.

My other bright spot for the evening is seeing Ann in my dress. I know she is going to look gorgeous, and I'm thrilled that she thought the dress I designed would be perfect for her special day.

We make small talk, acting like we are a normal happy couple. A few remarks about our wedding have been made by the people that were at church, and we are very noncommittal in responding.

Everyone starts sitting, and we find a spot about halfway back on the groom's side. There are only about thirty people or so in attendance. This is so different from the lavish weddings I've attended in New York. Some of my friends spent tens of thousands of dollars on their weddings. Dollars they'll never recoup.

I'm starting to see the benefit of the small ceremony. This setting is nice, the weather is cooperative and the whole event has an intimate feel to it, even though I'm not connected to it in that way.

The flutist's music is a bit louder now that everyone has sat down and stopped their conversation. After Roger, Brett and a guy who must be the best man, although he looks really young, stand under the arbor, Celine stands next to the flutist. She sings a song I've never heard, her voice a beautiful sound for this warm, winter evening.

When Celine finishes, she sits in a seat on the front row, and the flutist switches songs. Stace slowly walks up the aisle in a tea length red dress that hugs her in all the right places. She's so beautiful, but I know Ann will be even more so.

As the melody of the wedding march floats through the air, a woman, whom I'm assuming is the mother of the bride, stands, then we all follow suit. Ann walks down the aisle, escorted by a man who I know isn't her father, because he's no longer living. Probably her step-father. No doubt I will meet all these people at the reception.

My dress looks like it was made for Ann. It floats. It shimmers. It shows off her great body. I hear a couple of soft comments about the beautiful dress.

As the gentleman kisses Ann on the cheek and gives her to Brett a scream pierces through the air.

Then another.

As I look to the left, in the direction of the scream, I see a little girl, probably a couple of years older than Phoebe, running in the cul-de-sac. Seconds later, another little girl, who looks a lot like the first girl, is running behind her. When the second girl catches up, she grabs the first girl's long dark hair, which mirrors her own, and pulls.

Another high-pitched scream escapes the first girl. Then she pushes the second girl down, which leads to a loud yell and threats of telling dad.

One of the ladies I recognize from the church, I think it's Barb, runs out to the girls. Barb has her index finger over her lips in the universal be quiet sign, but the girls don't seem to care.

"What's going on?" Phoebe whispers.

I lean over to whisper back. "A couple of girls, I think they're twins, are having an argument in the cul-de-sac."

"They are loud," Phoebe says.

"Yes. Someone has gone out there to try and rein them in."

"Excuse me." Stephen passes in front of Phoebe and me.

Everyone's attention is now on the cul-de-sac.

After a moment, I see why Stephen left his seat. A dark-haired man, wearing dress clothes is sauntering down his driveway. Must be Stephen's neighbor. The guy whose wife died.

He doesn't seem to be in a hurry. Of course, he probably doesn't know there is a wedding going on.

Way to run interference, Stephen. Nice.

Barb is trying her best to calm the girls, but they are in a total cat fight. Bedlam ensues as they continually grab for each other, their voices shouting and screaming.

I can tell the second Stephen's explanation registers with the man, who I'm assuming is their father. He quickly shakes Stephen's hand, before rescuing Barb. The man quietly talks to the girls, who with tear-streaked faces look at the crowd. They are hiccupping and wiping their eyes as Barb and Stephen return to their seats. The man takes their hands and the three of them walk to their house.

I can see from here the matted mess both the girl's hair has become as a result of their fighting. Dad is going to have a hard time brushing that out tonight.

While the girls look to be a little older than Phoebe, their disposition appears to be younger.

Of course Phoebe doesn't have anyone to fight with at our house.

"Mr. Stephen's back," Phoebe whispers. "Are the girls gone?"

"Yes," I answer.

"That was a bit of excitement to start your wedding, wasn't it?" Roger says to Ann and Brett.

Everyone laughs.

Roger tells us all we can be seated.

As I sit I can't stop thinking about the girls and how out-of-control they were.

Maybe because it's a reminder of my life right now.

BOMBSHELL

THE REST OF the wedding continues without any screaming interruptions. No more kids running in the cul-de-sac.

How ironic that they picked this time to have a fight.

Thinking of the incident keeps my mind from focusing too much on the wedding itself. A part of me wants to imagine Stephen and I exchanging vows. The other part of me, the one that knows that won't happen, saddens. When Brett jumps the gun on kissing the bride, I can see Stephen doing the same.

And I wouldn't care at all.

The few of us that aren't family and aren't a part of the bridal party head to the reception which is being held in the house Ann inherited. I guess it's Ann and Brett's house now.

The house is beautiful and has a great view of the bay. A view that Stephen's house doesn't have. There is a path to the water, though. I wonder why he doesn't clear some trees in exchange for a view?

Phoebe, Stephen and I give off the perfect little family vibe as we meet and chat with people. The huge living area has several doors that open to a veranda. All the doors are opened, a nice breeze is blowing as dusk starts its descent, and the flutist has now moved in here. She's joined by a couple of other musicians, and the music is festive.

Poinsettias give a punch of color to the room.

This house is much bigger than Stephen's. But I like Stephen's house. I like it's comfy, cozy feeling I've learned to appreciate.

I'm surprised that I like that, but I do.

Two women carrying trays offer the guests hors d'ouevres and champagne. Neither of which Phoebe will want or can have.

Stephen, Phoebe and I have separated ourselves slightly from the crowd in a corner of the veranda.

"Here." Stephen guides Phoebe to a chair.

She sits and he hands her a glass of punch which he procured from one of the tray carrying women.

"Thank you," she says.

"You're welcome."

A quiet hum of voices carry on the wind from the living area. The night hasn't cooled down yet, and I'm enjoying these warm temperatures. "At some point tonight one of us needs to go back to the house and bring over our gift and cards," I say, spotting the gift table.

"I'll go in a little while," Stephen says. "Are you sure you don't want a glass of champagne or something to drink? I can get you some punch."

"No, thanks, though. So, what did you say to the guy who lives next door to you when you met him in the cul-de-sac? I guess he was clueless about the wedding taking place."

"Yeah. He had no idea. When I told him he apologized. He told me to make sure I tell the bride and groom he was sorry. I told him he could tell them himself at church on Sunday."

I raise my eyebrows. "Really? Do you think he'll come?"

Stephen shrugs. "He didn't commit if that's what you mean. I think he mumbled the word maybe. He might have been too concerned about breaking up his girls so the wedding could continue."

"Somebody needs to take control of those kids. Didn't you say his wife died?" I touch the tip of one of the red roses in the centerpiece.

"Yes. He looked tired. Worn out. His name is Court Treyhune."

"Treyhune? That sounds familiar."

"Racing family. His father is Cal Treyhune."

"Okay. I know that name. He does a lot of commercials."

"I guess. Not too many televisions in the wilderness."

I laugh. "Probably not."

We sit in silence for a few minutes, the sounds of music and conversation filling the air.

I notice a few of the family members arriving. Then the musicians stop playing. Momentarily, Ann and Brett are announced.

The party has begun.

As soon as the bride and groom enter the room, the musicians start up a little louder than before and a lot more festive. I don't see a dance floor, but the music creates a nice atmosphere.

"I wish I could play with those little girls. Maybe they wouldn't fight," Phoebe says. "It would be more fun than sitting here."

I'm surprised by Phoebe's complaint. I haven't seen this side of her. Although I know where she's coming from. It must be pretty boring when you're the only kid at the wedding. She can't even see and appreciate the pretty dresses and decorations like I can to distract myself from the awkward feeling of wondering why you are even here.

Her little legs kick at the air as she sits in her chair.

"We won't stay long, Pheebes," I assure her.

"We're going to say hello to Ann and Brett," Stephen says to her. "Do you want to come along?"

"No," Phoebe says. "I wanna sit here and drink my punch."

I want to stay here with Phoebe, but apparently I don't have a choice. Stephen takes my hand in a couple-like gesture, and we make our way to the bride and groom.

As we approach, Ann sees us. She smiles and motions to a woman standing close to her. "Mom, here she is, Jenny Harris. She designed this dress. Jenny, this is my mom, Trixie Diaz."

A beautiful woman with short red hair clasps my hands with hers. "The dress is absolutely stunning. The perfect dress for Ann. I was blown away when I saw her today. You have quite a gift for design, dear."

The whole time she's speaking, her gaze is glued to my face, unfaltering. I see no pity reflected in her gaze. "Thank you." I'm unable to look away from her boldness.

"I'd like you to meet my husband, Luis."

She lets go of my hands, her attention now on her husband.

"Nice to meet you," I say. "And this is Stephen."

"Jenny and Stephen are engaged," Ann says.

The guys shake hands.

"Congratulations. I love seeing all these young couples starting their lives together. And like my Ann and her Brett, you two are going to make pretty babies."

"Mom." Ann rolls her eyes. "Really? I already told you, you aren't going to be a grandmother anytime soon."

"It was a beautiful wedding." This statement is my attempt at changing the subject. I don't really want to talk about weddings, but it's certainly a safer subject than babies.

"Besides," Ann continues, "After watching those two kids scrap it out in the cul-de-sac, I'm not sure I want to sign up for that."

"I'm with you." I nod my head.

I'm not considering kids in any way, shape or form.

I don't even have a potential groom.

Looking around at the group, I catch my breath.

What would these people think if they knew our engagement was false? The magnitude of the number of people we've pulled into our story has grown magnificently. They all have feelings, and they all, in one form or another, care for one of us.

An unexpected sense of grief filters through my body, hitting me hard amid the festive atmosphere of this wedding. I'm not sure I can handle this charade anymore. Stephen looks so amazing, he's kind, he's everything I would want in a guy, but he's not mine.

Stace approaches our group. She introduces a very beautiful older woman as her mother, Lovey.

I smile at the name. Lovey's dark hair and olive complexion are the exact opposite of Trixie's fair skin and red hair. Ann and Stace's father didn't pass down too many genes to his daughters as they both resembled their mothers. Funny how that happens sometimes.

"Isn't this an elegant wedding and reception?" Lovey asks to no one in particular.

"It is, Mama," Stace responds. "It's so small and quaint. Perfect for our Ann."

"And so not for you," Ann says with a smile on her face. The half sisters are equally beautiful, yet very different in every other way.

I see Stace eyeing Stephen. I don't blame her. At all.

"So" Stace looks at Stephen and then me. "When is your big day? Soon?"

Her gaze, like Trixie's a few minutes ago boldly stares at me. But I sense a more calculating brain working behind Stace's calm exterior.

Probably trying to figure out how close we are to the wedding to see if there is enough time to try and steal Stephen from me.

In looking at the two of them standing so close to each other, I can see compatibility. They are both beautiful, proud, and would be perfect for each other.

Yet here I am, stealing any opportunity he might have to be with someone who would really complement him.

"We haven't set a date yet." Stephen grabs onto my hand.

The music seems to have gotten louder.

The buzz of the conversation now tries to compete with the music.

The combination suffocates me.

In this moment, wanting to be who I'm pretending to be overwhelms me. I know that it will never be. And my selfishness is possibly holding Stephen back from finding happiness with someone else.

"Actually, there is no wedding date because there is no wedding."

My statement silences the small crowd around us, including Ann and Brett. Shame at dropping this bombshell at their wedding engulfs me, but so does a sense of relief.

"Cheetah," Stephen says softly.

"This is my fault," I continue. "I needed a place to stay and Stephen's boss needed to think he was in a relationship, so I lied. It felt more like helping out than lying but now it's gone too far."

Letting go of Stephen's hand I take off the ring and set it in his palm, then fold his fingers around it. "You are really a great guy. Now you need to go out and find the woman who you are truly meant to be with."

Cutting a look toward Stace, I smile. As in you have my permission to flirt with him.

That permission hurts my heart, but I'm through thinking about myself and what is good for me. I've caused too much hurt with that mentality.

I start walking over to Phoebe, to retrieve my little shadow and go back to the Stephen's house.

"Cheetah."

Stephen's voice calls my name. I know the music is still playing and people are still chatting, but I can only hear Stephen.

I turn around to find him walking toward me.

Memories of his kisses cause my face to flush. He's all masculinity standing in front of me. Protector. Any woman will be lucky to call him hers.

"Jenny. I'm not good with words. But I've got to say that the thought of you walking out that door is destroying me. We may have come into this house, literally, in a false engagement, but I want to leave this house in a real engagement."

Trying to process his words makes me overthink in so many ways. Is he just doing this to perpetuate the false engagement? Is he being sincere? I'm not at all sure what is happening here at this moment.

Because he can't be seriously wanting to marry me.

"Stephen, you don't have to do this."

My voice is a whisper, in hopes that others won't hear.

"I'm not doing anything I don't want to. It's come to my attention that you are a woman with class, integrity and a drive to succeed. I've fallen in love with your spirit of caring, loving and determination."

He kneels on one knee and holds out the ring. "Cheetah, will you marry me?"

I feel a tug on my dress. Phoebe is looking at me, smiling.

"Miss Jenny, now is when you say yes."

BOLD

"I AGREE WITH Phoebe," Stephen says. "Say yes."

This man wants to spend his life with me? I've realized now for a couple of days that I am in love with Stephen. But is he truly in love with me?

My brain can't fathom it, but my heart doesn't want to live without him.

"You're serious?" My gaze clings to his, hoping.

"I'm extremely serious. I love you."

Am I dreaming? I pray I'm not. "I love you. Yes. I say yes."

I'll never tire of his gorgeous smile. Phoebe claps, and he slips the ring back onto the finger it left just a few minutes ago.

The ring sparkles and feels weightless as people around us start to clap. Brett and Ann are by our side in a moment, congratulating us and giving us hugs.

"I really don't know what just happened," Ann says, "But as long as there is a wedding involved, it's all good."

"I'm sorry about doing this at your reception. I feel awful, but I couldn't keep deceiving everyone." I look at Stephen, still not believing he and I are really engaged.

"We'll just say our happy reception influenced you." Ann takes a sip of champagne.

Roger and Celine are next in line to give us congratulations.

"Like Ann said, I'm not sure what's going on, but I do believe you are really getting married, right?" Roger's expression screams confusion. Celine looks perplexed as well.

"Rog," Stephen says. "It's a long story, one I'll tell you later, but yes, Jenny and I are engaged. Really engaged."

"As opposed to a staged engagement? Why would you stage an engagement?" Roger asks.

Time to rescue Stephen from the preacher, even if it is his uncle. "It's my fault, and I apologize. I was trying to help Stephen out of a mess with his boss, and it escalated into this crazy scenario I never in a million years envisioned."

Celine, breathtaking in a coral-colored dress, gives me a hug. "Maybe you're a prophet. Welcome. You'll love being a part of this family."

I can't believe tears are threatening. I blink and swallow trying to keep them at bay. This lie has been emotionally draining.

Who knew the truth would be so wonderful.

The girl who has been playing the flute announces the buffet dinner is now ready.

Stephen grabs Phoebe's hand. "You hungry?"

She's all smiles as she answers. "Yes."

Ann and Brett go through the line first, and Stephen and I, along with Phoebe, take a place in line. People are congratulating us and I feel truly happy. I still am having a hard time taking the real engagement in. I keep looking at the ring. It hasn't been on my finger long, but I've done my share of gawking at it these last few days.

I see it now in a whole different light.

I don't even see it as mine.

I see it as ours, a beginning of a life I thought I would never have. Stephen doesn't care about my scar, he doesn't care that I'm not a model anymore.

"I love seeing that smile on your face," he says. "Just makes you that much more beautiful."

I'm not beautiful anymore.

That's what I think. That's not what Stephen thinks.

But he sees beauty in a different way than I do. I love how he loves life, how he embraces all things. How he wants to protect what needs protecting.

He has a real sense of duty.

A sense of love.

A sense of how to kiss amazingly.

I can't wait for more of his kisses. I almost hyperventilate thinking what comes after those kisses.

Think about the food. The delicious looking food that is right in front of me.

Stephen hands me a plate and fixes one for Phoebe, although this wedding food isn't her usual fare. I tell her the items, and she says yes or no.

We take a seat at a table on the veranda, the cool air perfect for my hot thoughts. I barely taste the food I'm eating. A shame because I'm sure it's expensive and very tasty.

Phoebe's mood has lightened since Stephen's proposal.

I'm still in a daze and seriously can't keep my eyes away from the ring. I think it's drawing me in because I can't be drawn in by Stephen right now. I want to kiss him, tell him how happy I am and kiss him again.

When I do look his way, I catch him looking at me.

These looks we are exchanging have me wishing we weren't around a lot of people. They also have me looking forward to our alone time tonight.

I KICK OFF MY pumps as I tuck the covers around Phoebe. Although I have been relishing our story time, tonight I want to see how my own real-life story is going to play out.

But, I squelch my enthusiasm and sit with Phoebe. We still haven't told her that her mom is coming home on Christmas Eve day. Stephen says until he receives the final word, he refuses to bring her hopes up.

Again, Stephen the protector.

I wiggle my toes, free of my shoes.

"I think you're smiling a lot, Miss Jenny," Phoebe says.

"I am."

"Mr. Stephen makes you happy, doesn't he?"

My heart goes to its happy place just thinking about him. "He does."

"I'm glad. Prince Jonah is going to make Princess Bea happy, isn't he?"

Okay, time to switch from Stephen mode to princess mode. "He is. But he has some things to take care of first, doesn't he?"

"Yes. But he has the necklace that is going to break the curse," Phoebe reminds me.

"He does." I tuck her hair behind her ears. "I think Prince Jonah is going to follow Princess Bea's father when he leaves the music room. He's going to show him the necklace he wants to give to Princess Bea."

Phoebe claps. "Is the king going to let the prince give it to her?"

"The king is going to see that the necklace is worth a lot of money, which makes the king very interested as to why the prince is there."

"Why doesn't Prince Jonah tell the king he wants to marry Princess Bea?"

I tap her on the nose. "The letter?"

"Oh, yeah. I forgot. So does he show the king the letter?"

"He is about to pull the letter out of his pocket when Princess Bea comes into the room."

"She does? Why?" Phoebe's voice is breathy, showing her excitement.

"She came to tell her father about the prince because she thought he left."

Hugging her blanket, Phoebe yawns. "What was she going to tell her father?"

"She was going to ask her father if he knew Prince Jonah."

"And he was there. She's busted!"

I laugh at her exuberance. "She was busted."

"So what does she do?"

"We'll figure that out tomorrow night."

"Okay. I'm really tired. The wedding ended up being fun."

The wedding ended up being amazing.

Glancing down at my engagement ring I realize what an incredible turn my life has taken. We haven't even discussed the simplest of things, like where we are going to live. From what I know he's traveling most of the time. I wouldn't mind traveling some, but I want to see SunKissed! come to life. I know my designs are good. Ann proved that today.

I give Phoebe a kiss on her forehead. "Good night. Sleep well. We have a big day tomorrow."

"I'm still going to the caroling party?" she asks.

"Of course." I wonder why she doesn't seem to want to go to the party she was so excited about when she received the invitation.

It's probably her nerves, I decide as I pick up my pumps. I know how she feels. As much as I can't wait to see Stephen, I feel the butterflies in my stomach come to life.

Like the one that landed on the gazebo that day.

Like the one that Stephen's mother saw.

I bet the ones in my stomach are blue, too.

TENTATIVELY I WALK from the study to the kitchen, anticipation bubbling to the surface at seeing my fiancé. When I boarded the plane that cold, dark December night, I had no clue what was in store for me when I walked out of the airport, hailed the cab and walked up the driveway of this seemingly sleepy house in Hampton Cove, Florida.

Life has been a whirlwind of the best kind since I stepped through that door.

It hasn't always felt like the best kind, but it is.

As I step into the kitchen from the back hall, Stephen steps into the kitchen from the front hall. We both stop, our gazes connect. Heat spreads through my body.

I drop my shoes, the sound of them hitting the floor muffled by the beating of my heart.

He's in front of me in an instant, my arms wrap around him in a second, and our lips touch for eternity.

Because I will never forget the wonder of his lips on mine.

Whatever happens on this crazy journey of ours, his kisses will never fade from my memory.

As my arms are wrapped around his waist, his hands cup the sides of my face, his fingers digging into my hair.

As amazing as his kisses are, I want more.

Letting go of his waist, I run my palms up his chest, his shirt a soft barrier. My fingers fumble momentarily, but finally connect to the top button. Within a matter of seconds I have two buttons undone. Button number three pops loose when his kisses stop.

"Cheetah," he rasps, grabbing my hands.

Desire tumbles through my body. He can't possibly know how much I need his touch. I weave my fingers through his.

I kiss him gently on the lips.

The kiss ends quickly.

"I not only love you, I love kissing you." He wraps his arms around me.

I love the feeling. It's a safe, sexy place I never want to leave. I'm not sure if he's being coy or he's nervous, but he seems hesitant to leave this brightly lit kitchen. "You were kidding when you said we wouldn't be together until we're married, weren't you?"

His sudden intake of breath doesn't escape my notice, and I'm not sure if my words or my lightly brushed kisses on his shoulder are the cause.

Slowly, he takes a couple of steps back, his deep blue eyes conveying a confused look.

Or maybe tortured is a more appropriate word.

Either way, I'm left feeling like a panting deer looking for the nearest stream to quench its thirst.

"I was serious. I think we need to revisit our boundaries talk."

I search his face for the coming smile because I know he's joking. He can't be serious. The same stern expression remains.

"But we're engaged now." I smile at him.

He leans back against the counter, shoving his hands in his pockets. "All the more reason to set boundaries. Until the wedding, that is."

Now his amazing smile graces his face, which leaves me perplexed. "Is it because of God? Because I think God understands that we are in love."

Downcast eyes and a straight-line grimace make me wonder what's going on inside his mind. I've never been met with such resistance.

And he says he loves me?

As if I will it, his gaze rises, connecting with mine. My soul blossoms with the knowledge that this man is mine. That he's declared his love for me in a way that's bold and true.

The moment intensifies and when he does speak I know it's not fly-off-the-handle type of talk.

It's from knowing who he is and what he wants.

"God fully understands that we are in love. But showing our love for one another has perfect timing where God is concerned. After we say our vows in front of God, we'll be together in all things, with Him and through Him."

Trying to process his declaration of love, and postponing the act of love has my head reeling. My body, too. "This is so foreign to me. I mean, I know right and wrong, and sure we all try, but I've never met anyone who has tried this hard to do the right thing, if you know what I mean. The Godly thing."

He breaches the distance between us, placing his hands on my shoulders. There is still a physical connection between us, but instead of it being like lightning bolts slashing around us at full speed, it's now more like a slow electric current, with a lot of spark, but a destination in mind.

My body still buzzes with his presence. His nearness.

But I no longer feel in attack mode.

I think he's safe with me.

For a little while, anyway.

"Before you go thinking I'm something I'm not, I need to add to my explanation."

I'm not sure how much more my brain can handle, but I need to try. "Go ahead. Explain."

"Jesus is the only reason I have any self control. Let me set that part straight right away. But I have to admit there is another reason I'm determined to wait until we're married."

His serious tone intensifies the already tense situation. He lowers his head, I'm thinking for a kiss.

"Because if we're married you can't leave," he says before tenderly kissing my earlobe.

BLOSSOM

NOW IT'S MY turn to tense and step back. "Leave? Why would I leave?"

I can't imagine what he is talking about. Does *he* have some hideous scar he's hiding and he thinks it might scare me away? He's too good of a kisser to be that bad at anything else physical.

He frowns. "I can't believe I'm spending the evening I become engaged talking about my past."

"I want to know everything about you. Why you are the way you are. Why you think the way you think. This is important to you, and it's only natural that I would want to know why."

"Let's sit on the couch." He takes my hand.

After he plugs in the Christmas tree lights, we settle on the couch, sitting close to each other, hands clasped. I've draped my legs over his and I know I'll never tire of being this close to him.

The colored lights on the tree blink into the otherwise dark room that surrounds us.

"There was a girl once. Her name was Leah."

Arrows shoot through my chest proving I was unprepared for his statement. Leah.

"So I've heard."

"It's not a long story or detailed. Pretty simple, actually. We talked about forever, Leah and I. I hadn't given her a ring or asked her to marry me, but it was understood. At least I thought it was. After many battles with my mind knowing what I should do, and my body knowing what it wanted to do, I lost the battle of my mind and we were together."

Okay, so it never entered my mind that he hadn't been with other girls, but knowing that he has and apparently only one, I'm speechless at the jealousy running rampant through me. Why so much control around me and not around her?

"And it was bad?" I know that question is lame, but something obviously happened.

"No. Not bad. But let's just say when the going got tough, she left."

"How tough?"

He leans his head against the back of the couch, and closes his eyes for a moment. When they open, he leans over and kisses me on the nose. "Tough enough for her to want to leave. I'll never have back what I gave to her. That's not happening again. You and I?" He kisses me again on the nose. "Are forever."

"I like that."

"Remember the first day you came here? When you asked me to take that mirror out of the guest room?" His thumb caresses the top of my hand.

"Yes." I remember his body beautiful. And his muscles.

"It was that day, in that room, at that time, that I knew I was going to marry you."

My mind rolls back to everything that has happened since then. "How could you know that?"

He shakes his head. "I wish I could tell you, but the feeling was strong. Strong and clear. I felt like it could only come from God."

I faintly remember that crazy feeling that came over me that morning. But I had no idea I was going to marry Stephen.

I'm going to crack open that Bible in the room I'm staying in and see what about it has captured his heart.

Because, although some would say it's too good to be true, I want what he has. What makes him strong.

What makes him the man I love.

PHOEBE AND I are both in an apprehensive mood as Saturday afternoon rolls around.

Sleep evaded me last night.

After cuddling in Stephen's arms for what seemed like an instant but was really a couple of hours, we parted ways, much to my dismay and confusion.

I hit the bed with determination and the Bible. I flipped pages and read some verses. I remember one of my mom's friends saying once if you wanted to read the Bible you should start with the book of John. Which I did.

But as I read the words, some of them didn't make any sense to me. Parts of it actually caused me more confusion than comfort. I would nod off, then try to sleep.

I dozed fitfully at best, and at six o'clock this morning I made a cup of coffee and went back at it.

Jesus was definitely a good guy.

The woman at the well story triggered memories of vacation Bible school. But reading as an adult gave it a new perspective, one that settled in my heart. I felt strangely compelled to quit reading there. A somewhat pensive, thought-provoking mood overtook me. Almost brought me to tears.

Now I'm apprehensive as to what that is all about. Maybe I'll share it with Stephen later tonight.

I'm not sure.

Right now we are in the car on the way to Phoebe's caroling party. A party which seems to have just recently caused Phoebe some concern.

But she won't say why.

Stephen and I are looking forward to the caroling, something neither one of us has done in a long time.

"We're here, Phoebe." I open my door.

The three of us walk to the door, Phoebe carrying the small hostess gift we brought for Raney.

I ring the doorbell of the huge, pretentious house. Massive wooden double doors wait to be opened.

"These doors remind me of the doors of the palace Princess Bea lives in," I say. "They are big and wooden."

"So this house is like a palace?" she asks.

"Not quite, but close. But we'll keep that information to ourselves."

Stephen squeezes my hand.

"In other words, don't say anything to anybody," Phoebe says.

Just like when I went to church, I'm wearing my hair pulled back in a ponytail, leaving my scar front and center for all to see. I don't care if the world disses me because of it. I have Stephen and a new sense of confidence that comes with knowing I am loved by this man.

One of the big doors is opened by a butler. I grab Phoebe's hand. When we are inside the butler offers to take Phoebe's sweater. She shrugs it off as I take in all the decorations in the foyer. There's a Christmas tree that must be nine feet tall, decorated all in blues and silvers. Greenery lined with soft blue blinking bulbs twists its way up the curved staircase.

"Follow me." The butler leads us down a hall into an even more elaborately decorated living room.

Ornate and exquisite are the only words I can use to describe the interior of this home. With the beautiful Christmas decorations gracing every available surface, I almost expect snow to start falling and Santa Claus to pop out of the huge fireplace.

They must start decorating in July.

More than likely they hire a crew who comes in and takes care of it in a couple of days.

Half the fun of Christmas is the decorating. I guess they are missing out.

Most of the people have stopped talking as we stand there. I'm aware that I'm staring, but I don't care. The decorations were put out to be looked at.

At least that's what I think.

Once again all eyes are on me. I know they are.

Two girls Phoebe's age start walking toward us, followed by a man and a woman.

"Hi Phoebe, it's Raney. Claire is with me."

Raney's tone isn't very friendly, and I'm instantly put on guard.

"Hi," Phoebe says. "Here's a gift we brought for you."

A smile creeps at the corners of Raney's mouth but doesn't fully develop. Still, she thanks Phoebe and tears open the package.

Raney holds up a pink scarf. "Thank you," she says. "Pink is my favorite color. Oh, and it's so soft."

"That's why I picked it out." Phoebe scoots closer to me. "Miss Jenny told me it was pink, and I could feel it was very soft."

Claire is almost in a full-fledge scowl as Raney keeps talking about the scarf.

The atmosphere here is strange.

The couple walks up to us. "Hi. We're Raney's parents. Amanda and Tony. That was very nice of Phoebe to bring a gift."

The couple offers their hands, and Stephen and I return their greeting.

"I'm Jenny, and this is Stephen. Phoebe is staying at Stephen's house until her mother returns."

"Well, we're delighted Phoebe could come to Raney's caroling party. As soon as Lydia arrives, we'll depart. We are going to carol in this neighborhood, then we'll come back and have dinner. We have a bonfire with marshmallows to roast after we eat. Raney saw that in a movie recently and has been badgering me ever since to do it here."

"Sounds like a fun time," I say.

"Why don't you plan on coming back for the marshmallow roasting?" Amanda asks.

I look at Stephen and I see the same look on his face that I'm sure I have on mine. We need to stay with Phoebe.

I latch on to Stephen's hand. "We were wondering if we could stay around for the caroling. Phoebe's mother left her in our care, and oh, wow, this is terribly awkward."

Amanda and Tony nod. "I understand," Amanda says. "No problem. You can carol with us and have dinner. It's a simple menu. Kids, you know? Or maybe you don't if you don't have any."

"We don't have any," I say, "but we do understand. You probably have mac and cheese on the menu, right?"

Amanda stares blankly at me. "No. Actually we don't. I think Raney has tried it once, hasn't she, dear? That dish with the lobster in it she had while we were on vacation?"

"Maybe." Tony speaks although he's clearly checked out of the realm of what food his daughter eats.

"Come on in." Amanda points to the other adults. "Can we get you something to drink? I'm drinking Scotch."

Stephen and I both opt for water, with ice, which is brought to us by the bartender-butler whose name is James.

Moments later another little girl runs into the room, obviously having been here before, and joins Phoebe and the other girls.

Glancing over now and then, I notice Phoebe always seems to be standing on the edge of the girls. She's not fully engaged. The other three girls are clearly good friends, and I'm beginning to understand Phoebe's hesitation at coming to the party.

Amanda gathers us all, and after James returns everyone's jackets or sweaters, we head out. Raney has offered to hold Phoebe's hand and be her guide, but Phoebe insists on using her cane. The girls started out walking together, but it soon becomes apparent Phoebe is left to catch up to them.

"Phoebe, hurry!" Raney shouts as she, Claire and Lydia wait by a door. Amanda gave the girls specific instructions not to knock on the door until they were all there and ready.

Phoebe reaches them, and Raney knocks on the door.

The homeowners are delighted and smiling, and the girls sing "Jingle Bells" for them. Then we sing "We Wish You a Merry Christmas," before making our way to the next house.

By the time we reach the fourth house, I'm fed up with the behavior of the three girls.

Stephen and I stay on the sidewalk and let Amanda and Tony walk up to the house with the girls. "There's something clearly wrong here," I say.

"I've noticed. It's like the girls don't care whether Phoebe is here or not."

"Which doesn't make sense, because Raney invited her. Why would she invite her if she didn't want her here?"

"I don't understand females, let alone seven-year-old ones. No clue." Stephen keeps his voice low.

"I'm going to keep watching, and if things don't improve, I'm going to say something."

"Truly a cheetah," he says, smiling.

We make our way to three more houses. A lot of the yards have big blow-up Santas and reindeers. One has a nativity scene.

We've about circled around to the Lee's home when I hear Claire say, "She's too slow, just knock, already."

"That's it." I pull my hand from Stephen's. "I've had enough."

"I wouldn't knock just yet." My voice carries to the girls as I make my way to the front door right behind Phoebe. "What's going on here? You girls act like you don't want Phoebe around, yet you invited her to your 'exclusive' party. What gives?"

Claire and Lydia and Raney all have the decency to bow their heads.

Stephen bends down and gathers Phoebe in his arms, and even though I didn't think it was possible, I fall even more in love with him.

"She made me invite her." Raney lifts her gaze to her mother.

Amanda looks embarrassed while her husband continues to look clueless. And totally uninterested in our conversation, which makes me appreciate Stephen all the more.

"Raney's teacher called a couple of weeks ago about an incident at school involving Phoebe." Amanda has a confessional expression about her.

"What incident?" I ask.

Amanda shoves her hands in the pockets of her red sweater. "Phoebe's mother knows all about it. There was a little scuffle between Raney and Phoebe on the playground. I told Raney to make it up to Phoebe she should invite her to her caroling party."

Memories of the pity invite shower over me. The only invites I ever received were those type.

How dare they? Phoebe is a beautiful girl with a lot to offer, but just like when I was in school, no one cares to look past the outside to get to know someone.

Some things never change.

But things are going to change now.

"I think it's time we leave." I push my shoulders back. "Phoebe is a fabulous girl who doesn't need to be around kids who are forced to be with her."

Now Claire and Lydia scoot closer to Raney, like they are joining forces. Well, they can join forces all they want. Phoebe is too good for them. All three of them put together.

Stephen is folding up her cane and I take her hand. "Come on, Pheebes."

"Pheebes?" Raney asks. "You call her Pheebes?"

If that kid decides to make a smart remark about the nickname, I'm going to probably say not very nice things to her mother. "Sometimes."

"That's a cool name," Raney says.

About to take my first step away from this insincere crowd, I stop. I don't say anything, but I stop.

"I don't want Phoebe to leave." Raney's voice is soft, like maybe she doesn't want to admit that in front of her friends.

I turn around. Her eyes are sad, but hopeful.

"You don't?" I ask.

"No. I like her. I like the pink, soft scarf she brought me, too. None of my other *friends* brought me a gift."

"Raney, apologize to Claire and Lydia right now for that statement." Amanda now has an embarrassed look on her face.

"I'm sorry."

Amanda looks at me. "Please come back to the house and have dinner. I know things haven't gone well so far, but I know Raney does want to be friends with Phoebe."

"I'm leaving this up to Phoebe. It's her choice."

Stephen stands close to me. We both look at Phoebe who of course doesn't know we are looking at her. "Pheebes?"

"If Raney really wants me to stay, I would like to."

The child part of me gets it, the adult part doesn't. I would hightail it out of here as fast as I could if it was my choice. But I know back then, when I was little and not well liked, I would have stayed given the opportunity.

I hope Raney has good intentions.

I know I'll know if she doesn't.

DINNER WENT WELL. Claire ended up going home complaining of a stomach ache, but I think it was more of a jealous ache. Being a kid is tough.

Making it through is the toughest of all.

Amanda made really good conversation while Tony didn't say a whole lot. Often we were interrupted by the sounds of the girls laughing, which brought tears to my eyes more than once.

Now, we are sitting around a bonfire in the backyard. An elaborate amount of stonework has been done, including the pit that holds the bonfire.

Raney is helping Phoebe put the marshmallow in her wooden stick. Amanda said Raney had rejected the store-bought skewers and had insisted on finding tree branches to use, because that's what they did in the movie.

I think Raney has a lot of power in this house.

But that's Amanda and Tony's problem.

Well, truthfully, probably Amanda's.

I think Tony's here because he makes the cash that lets them live in this huge beautiful house.

"Sure, we can eat one without roasting it," Raney says. She hands the white puffy marshmallow to Phoebe who shoves it in her mouth.

Raney follow suit, Lydia moments behind.

"We have to stand right here." Raney holds her hand in front of Phoebe. "We can't get too close to the fire."

"What color are the marshmallows," Phoebe asks.

"They're white," Raney answers.

"White is fluffy." Phoebe's statement causes us all to pause.

"Fluffy?" Raney asks. "Sometimes. Sometimes white is cold, like this." She grabs Phoebe's hand and places it on the wrought iron frame of the chair Amanda is sitting in.

"Oh, cold." Phoebe takes her hand away from the chair. "What about red? What does red feel like?"

"Like getting too close to the fire." Raney's voice is full of excitement.

"I like this game," Lydia chimes in.

"Me, too." Raney looks around. "What other colors do you want to know about?"

"Yellow," Phoebe says. "What about yellow."

Raney looks around, the porch light only illuminating a small area.

"Yellow might be hard." Raney looks at her mom. "Mom? Do you know what something yellow feels like?"

Amanda glances around for a moment before pointing to my hair.

"Oh." Raney grabs Phoebe's hand. "Here, this is what yellow is like, Pheebes."

As the girls stand close, Phoebe's hand brushes over my hair. A measure of contentment fills me. This could be my life one day. Stephen, friends, children, games.

To someday watch my children blossom like Phoebe is right now would be a dream I never thought I'd live out. My children will always feel confident in themselves.

Always.

I look at Stephen and smile at the man who is going to father my children.

He smiles back having no idea what is going on in my mind right now.

The fire cracks and the girls go back to their marshmallows. Amanda continues to talk about nothing of real importance, and I sit, next to Stephen, glad we brought Phoebe to this party.

This has been a special night for her. She's made some real friends, ones that will have her back and not let anyone make fun of her.

This night is a special night for me, too, as it has brought me to a very important realization.

The realization that I don't want to be engaged.

No, I want to be married.

BLISS

I DON'T EVER remember having a sense of excitement about going to church like I have today.

Maybe it's because I read more of the Bible last night. Maybe it's because we heard from Teresa that she is coming home on Christmas Eve. Maybe it's because Stephen's parents are coming to church this morning.

All I know is, I've painstakingly made sure I look my absolute best today.

I have a man who loves me as I am. All my flaws, inside and out. So I'm relishing it. I'm surprised at the relief I feel, the worry that has left me. The freedom I'm experiencing.

The atmosphere is very different from last Sunday. I know it's my perception of it all, but I feel more comfortable, and I actually know people and can talk to them.

Phoebe is excited to hang out with the older girls, and I hear her telling them about her marshmallow roasting last night. She's had a smile on her face ever since we left the party. She didn't even mention Princess Bea last night.

We sing a couple of Christmas songs this morning. Then the girls go up and light the Advent candle. They've asked Phoebe to come up, and they guide her hand as she lights the fourth Advent candle.

I listen intently as Roger talks about Jesus being the gift. The gift of love that God sent for us. Emotion rages through me as I grasp what God really did for us.

The world had waited four hundred years, according to Roger, for God to speak. He sent Jesus as his voice to us, to declare his love and give us hope. Hope for eternal life.

I look at Stephen as tears fall down my cheeks. I see now what he has that makes him special. He's got that hope, that assurance.

And I can have it, too.

Because God sent Jesus for me, just like He sent Him for everyone.

Stephen smiles at me and with his thumbs brushes my tears away. I'm glad I didn't overdo the makeup. What I did put on is probably streaking down my face.

I never cry in public.

But that was the Jenny who came here without any hope. The Jenny that sits in this chair now has hope.

Hope for a wonderful marriage.

Hope for a career in design.

And assurance for an eternity with Jesus Christ.

THE AFTERNOON AND the next day speed by. I managed to slip out, borrow Stephens's SUV and shop for a gift for Phoebe.

And Stephen.

His family is coming over for Christmas Eve dinner. Teresa will be here in time to eat, so Stephen asked her to stay as well.

We kept it simple, buying an already cooked ham. His mom said she would come over and help make some mashed potatoes, some vegetables, and I offered to make macaroni and cheese out of the box.

My new specialty.

Phoebe is a fan.

Phoebe comes into my room as I'm finishing up my makeup. We have about an hour until Stephen's mom arrives.

"I'm going home tonight," she says.

"I know. And I know you are excited," I reply.

"I am. But we need to finish our Princess Bea story."

"Want some lipstick?" I ask. "It's clear. I don't think your mom will mind."

"Sure," she says.

I hand her a small tube. "It will make your lips look shiny."

"Thank you."

She opens the lid and slides the tube across her lips. "Like this?"

"Perfect." I sit on the bed with her. "So, Princess Bea is with her father and Prince Jonah."

"Yes. He was about to pull out the letter."

"But when he sees Princess Bea, he stops. Instead of pulling out the letter, he pulls out the necklace."

Phoebe claps her hands. "Does she gasp because it's so pretty?"

I laugh. "She does. And she tells him it's beautiful. He tells her it's a peace offering. That his father sent him to take the lands, but he knows that's not right. The necklace will unite their families if Princess Bea agrees to marry him."

Phoebe covers her mouth with her hand momentarily. "Marries him? But what about the potion? The curse? She has to keep playing her beautiful music."

"There was never any power in the potion or the curse, Pheebes. The ladies only thought there was. And sometimes, when you think something is true, you believe it whether it is or not."

A realness settles in me as I speak the words.

"So the potion couldn't make anybody fall in love?" Her voice sounds a little sad.

"No. It couldn't. But Prince Jonah didn't need any potion. He takes the necklace and opens the gold circle that hangs from the chain. There are initials inscribed, one on each side. On the left is a J and on the right is a B."

"One for Prince Jonah and one for Princess Bea."

"Exactly. Prince Jonah explains how it has been destined for many years that he and Princess Bea are to be married, and when the kings have passed on they are to rule the lands together."

"But, wait. Right now there are two kings. Prince Jonah's father and Princess Bea's father."

"Yes, but do you know what their names are?"

"No?"

"King Bertrand and King...Jarvis." Stephen will never know I used his real life king for a made-up story with Phoebe. "The king agrees he is to reign together with Prince Jonah's father." Wouldn't that be great if in real life a simple solution would solve everyone's problems?

"And Princess Bea and Prince Jonah have a big kingdom wedding."

"They do."

"I'd like to have a big wedding someday," Phoebe says.

She looks so cute in her Christmas dress. Festive. But much too young to even be thinking about a wedding. "One day."

"Do you think I'll meet a Prince Jonah? Because I would like to be a princess. Like Bea."

Her little feet with her shiny black patent leather shoes kick back and forth against the bedspread. "Phoebe." Like a light shining through the darkness, my heart jolts with revelation. "Phoebe. Phoe-be. Bea. You named the princess after yourself, didn't you?"

She shrugs. "I wanted to feel special, like a princess does. A princess is glamorous and pretty."

And with those words my life is summed up. This little girl's honesty brings to the surface what I've been fighting since I was her age. It all comes together now. We all want to feel special, but feeling special has nothing to do with how we look or what we have.

Feeling special has to do with who you are on the inside.

"Last night I felt like a princess. I want to feel like that all the time. And I want to meet a prince. Like Mr. Stephen."

"I'm glad you had a good time last night." I can barely speak as my throat chokes with tears. "And one day, you'll meet the guy who will be your prince. I'm going to pray for him every day."

My makeup will have to be redone as I freely let the tears fall down my face, the culmination of years of searching for what was inside me all along and thinking about how Stephen's mother and father were praying for me every day.

She hugs me tightly. "I love you, Miss Jenny."

"I love you, too, Pheebes."

Each day I learn more and more about this gift of love God has given us. And with the power of that love comes the hope that I've needed to believe in.

THIS DAY HAS been pure bliss.

Stephen and I hung the ornament Gary and Alice gave us on the tree.

Our very first together gift.

We'll never forget it.

Stephen's mother and I have worked side-by-side in the kitchen. She's given me the easy duties, but I don't mind. I'm too thrilled with life to retain much of what she is saying right now.

I'm living in my Stephen-dream world.

He's been hanging out with his dad, talking plants and outdoorsy things. Phoebe has gone back and forth between us, waiting anxiously for her mother.

The front door opens, and Teresa comes into the kitchen.

"There's my girl." She races to her daughter.

"Mommy!"

Teresa grabs her off the bar stool and they hug, tears streaming down Teresa's face.

"I've missed you," Teresa says, not letting go of Phoebe.

"I missed you too, Mommy. But I've had fun with Miss Jenny and Mr. Stephen. They are getting married!"

Teresa looks at me. "Married?"

"Yes." I show her my ring.

"So happy for you two. I knew you were meant to be together. I just knew it."

"Thank you," I say. "You've met Stephen's mother, Liza, haven't you?"

"I have." Teresa smiles at Liza. "Nice to see you again."

"You too, dear. So glad you could get back in time for Christmas with your daughter."

Teresa sets Phoebe back on the bar stool. "I am, too. My parents are settled in their nursing home. I'll have to make more visits down there, but for now, I need to be here."

"When you go, can I stay with Miss Jenny and Mr. Stephen?"

Teresa raises her eyebrows at me. "You are living here?"

Liza is looking at me as well. "I've been staying here in one of the guest rooms while Phoebe has been here. But I'm leaving tonight. I have a hotel reservation for a couple of days, then I'll figure out where to stay until the wedding. It's all come about so fast."

Liza's eyes tear up. "Jenny, you *are* the perfect girl for Stephen."

"Thank you. I'm beginning to think so, too. Is everything ready? Can we start taking the food to the table?"

An air of nervousness comes over Liza. I'm not sure why. The dinner is done, Teresa is here.

The doorbell rings and Liza's eyes light up. "Jenny, will you get the door please while I start taking the food to the table?"

"Sure." I wipe my hands on the dish towel and go to the front door. Maybe she's having something delivered for Stephen.

I open the front door and freeze.

"Jenny!"

Katherine, her boyfriend Joe and another couple I don't know are standing outside the door. I'm so excited to see her and so happy in life, I forget for a moment that she ditched me in my time of need. Now she's here hugging me.

"Hi," she says. "You're still here."

"I am. What happened to your trip? Is everything okay?"

I don't know who the other couple is, but it's rude having all of them stand out front. "Come on in." I hold the door open.

"Katherine?" Stephen's voice sounds from behind me and in an instant he's hugging Katherine.

"Stephen?" Her gaze darts around the room like she's looking for something. Someone. "Where's Mom?"

I'm caught up watching Katherine, but then I see Stephen's face harden, turn a little pale even. His brows raise, and he pushes back from Katherine.

"Leah?"

"Hi, Stephen."

BROKEN

STEPHEN SEEMS AS perplexed as I am. "Katherine, what's going on?"

"Katherine." Liza comes into the foyer from the dining room. She stops short of hugging Katherine, probably because she spots Leah.

Leah.

The only girl Stephen has ever been with.

I breathe deeply, trying to remain in control.

Trying to remain calm.

Trying to keep from asking her to leave.

The silence is awkward. I back up, hands in the air. "Don't let me stop anybody from having a reunion."

Before I can leave the room, Stephen takes my hand. "Don't leave."

"Katherine, honey," Liza says. "What's going on?"

She sounds nervous and tense.

"You know, I'm not sure. You call me and tell me I have to come to Florida by Christmas Day. So Joe and I packed up and jumped on the first plane out. Do you know how hard it is to get off a cruise ship? You tell me what's going on."

"Oh dear," Liza says. "Leah. It's good to see you. I don't believe I know this other gentleman."

"It's good to see you, too, Liza. This is Patrick. My husband."

A smidgen of tension leaves me. I notice Stephen's hand relaxes in mine a little.

"Why are you two holding hands." Katherine is staring at Stephen and me.

Stephen's dad, Teresa and Phoebe, Roger and Celine have all come to the foyer, everyone obviously aware of the tense atmosphere as hellos and Merry Christmases are silenced for the moment.

Liza's eye light up and she smiles. "That's why I called you home, darling. I wanted to surprise you with the news. Stephen and Jenny are engaged."

Katherine takes a step back before flying into my arms, hugging me. "Engaged! To my brother! I love this."

She lets go of me and embraces Stephen. "I didn't even know you were here. You weren't supposed to be here, right?"

"I wasn't. But God had other plans, right, Jenny?"

His smooth voice has a way of calming my insides. For a moment I even forget Leah is standing a few feet away.

In all honesty, she probably feels just as awkward as I do.

It only takes a few seconds after our announcement for the tension to return.

"Obviously I didn't know Stephen was here," Katherine says. "I ran into Leah and Patrick at the airport and thought you would want to say hello," she says to her mom. "I wasn't sure why we were gathering here at Stephen's, but since her parents live so close, I asked her to come by."

I start to feel okay about this. I mean we're all adults, Leah is married now. Stephen is mine.

So they had a past. I have one, too. Mine isn't standing in the foyer of this house on Christmas Eve day, but it exists.

"We were about ready to sit down for dinner," Liza says, looking at me.

I nod my head, giving her permission to do what all good hostesses do. Invite the unexpected guests to stay for the meal.

She looks at Leah and Patrick. "There's plenty of food if you would like to stay."

"No. We appreciate the invite," Leah says. "But my folks are waiting for us at the Marriott. I just wanted to say hello and Merry Christmas. It's been a while, and it felt like old times running into Katherine. It was like we hadn't missed a beat all these years. And I wanted to let everyone know I am doing really well."

I have no idea what that last sentence means. Was her breakup with

Stephen so rough she wasn't doing well for a while?

"So, you have full use of your leg now?" Liza asks.

"Yes." Leah smiles. "I do. I've had a couple more surgeries, but that was a couple of years ago. Patrick didn't even notice I limped when I first met him, did you?"

"No. I was distracted by everything else about you."

Facts are facts. Leah is beautiful. She has one of those faces girls dream about having. Great complexion, high cheek bones. Straight teeth, pretty smile.

The more attributes of hers I list, the more uneasy I become.

She has a limp.

Although it's barely noticeable now, she says.

Leah turns her attention toward Stephen. "Congratulations. I'm really happy for you two," she says looking at me.

"Thank you. I'm glad to hear you are doing well. And that you're married. You look very happy." Stephen's voice takes on that tense tone.

"I am," she says, answering Stephen but her gaze is locked on me. "So what happened?" She brushes her hand along her cheek.

I step back at her abrupt question.

"Leah, really?" Stephen squeezes my hand tighter.

She laughs. "Hanging with you in the wilds got me attacked by a tiger, so I just assumed. I don't mean anything rude by it. I am genuinely curious."

A tiger attacked her? When she was with Stephen?

I start breathing hard as it all starts to come together. His ability to go into protector mode quickly. His need to assure. His insistence that my scar wasn't something that should hold me back.

He was making up for what happened to Leah.

No, he couldn't get back what he gave her physically, but he could try and ease his conscience by taking care of me.

Was that tiger on his computer screen a reminder of what had happened? Of what he couldn't change?

All it takes is one look in his eyes, those deep blue pools that I love, and I see the truth. I see his past all over his face.

It doesn't make it any less gorgeous, it just makes it less mine.

I wriggle my hand away from his.

"Jenny," he says.

I look at his family. All staring at me like I have two heads. Or one big head with an ugly scar.

Nothing.

Ever.

Changes.

I walk quickly to my room. Luckily everything is packed. Before I change my mind, I slip the ring off my finger and set it on the dresser. It looks lonely and elegant all at the same time. It's then I notice those two red roses I had brought in here the first day. They lay on the dresser top, dried, faded.

The brittle petals mirror my heart. One by one I pick them off the rose, leaving their crushed brokenness next to the ring.

Might as well be my heart.

Finding my phone in my purse, I call the cab company.

As I open the bedroom door Stephen is standing there. "Don't," I say.

"But Jenny…"

"Oh, it's Jenny now? What happened to Cheetah? Or did you call Leah Cheetah, too? Never mind. I don't want to know."

He blocks the door, just like he did the day I arrived. "I wouldn't do that."

"Excuse me." I sweep past him. The two of us have come so far, yet we're further apart than when we didn't know each other.

I walk into the midst of the awkward silence that is his family. Katherine doesn't even have anything to say. Of course she's probably reliving inviting Stephen's ex to his house.

Bad move.

Phoebe, holding her mother's hand, meets me at the door.

"Are you leaving, Miss Jenny? We haven't had our Christmas dinner."

I bend down and hug her. "Yes, I have to go. I left a present for you under the tree. Don't forget to take it home so you can open it tomorrow morning."

She wraps her arms around me, and I hold back my tears not wanting to upset her.

"Okay," she says.

"And I'll stay in touch. I have your phone number. We'll get together soon, okay?"

She nods her head.

The doorbell rings. My cab is here. "I have to go now. Merry Christmas, Phoebe."

"Merry Christmas, Miss Jenny."

I straighten up and open the door. The familiar face of Malcolm greets me, and I think I see a hint of a smile on his face. He's still wearing his Santa hat.

"Could you grab my bags, please?" I ask before blowing past him.

As I walk down the driveway I hear footsteps behind me. I know they aren't Malcolm's. They're Stephen's.

"Jenny," he calls.

I stop and turn around. "It's okay, Stephen. Really. I'll be fine."

"I don't understand why you're leaving," he says.

"I know. That's why I'm leaving. Merry Christmas, Stephen."

Malcolm has caught up to me, and I follow him to the cab. I know Stephen isn't following me, which is okay.

This isn't the first time I've picked up the broken pieces of my heart and started over.

But it will be the last.

BETHROTHED

IT'S EIGHT O'CLOCK in the morning.

Christmas morning.

I can't say I awoke early because I never went to sleep.

Oh, and my eyes are puffy, too. Crying will do that to a girl. And I'm not one of those pretty criers.

I spent part of the night trying to figure out why I didn't see through Stephen. Even though I kept thinking he was too good to be true, I just turned my mind off where that was concerned and continued to believe he really loved me and wanted to marry me.

That he needed to absolve himself from his past hadn't entered my mind.

I spent another part of the night immersed in the Bible kept in the drawer of the hotel nightstand. This is when I cried the most. I keep remembering what Roger said Sunday morning. God had sent us a gift.

Jesus.

Any hope I have at this moment comes through the strength of Jesus.

The Son of God.

My room phone rings. "Hello?"

"Merry Christmas, Ms. Harris. We have a package here at the front desk for you."

Package?

My heart immediately thinks of Stephen. He probably bought me a Christmas present, feels guilty, and still wants me to have it. One way to find out. "I thought the delivery services would have Christmas Day off."

"Maybe they do. A gentleman brought this package."

Just as I thought. I know it's not good for me, but I can't help being on edge, in a good way, thinking Stephen might be downstairs. "Is the gentleman still here?"

"No. He left after he dropped the package off. I'll have it sent right up."

My resolve steels. "Actually I was almost asleep. I'll call you later when I wake up."

"As you wish, Ms. Harris."

I haul myself out of the bed, place the "do not disturb" sign on the door and climb back into the bed that the hotel swears is sent from heaven.

AT FOUR O'CLOCK I head downstairs, slightly refreshed.

And starving.

I missed Christmas Eve dinner last night and slept the day away today. I need nourishment.

Exiting the elevator I don't look left toward the front desk. Where the package is. I don't want to think about the package right now.

I don't want to think about Stephen right now.

But as I walk toward the restaurant I see him sitting on one of the couches in the atrium of the hotel. Has he been here since this morning? My heart races, but I turn around and head back toward the elevator, praying he doesn't see me.

After I take a couple of steps, several people come from that direction, laughing and making a lot of noise.

Knowing they will attract attention, and not close enough to slip into their crowd, I dart out the door that leads to a large veranda. The fresh air actually feels good, and I'm glad I have a moment to try and determine Stephen's agenda.

I was somewhat settled with the way everything had turned out. Or I thought I was. Seeing Stephen sitting in the lobby brought my mind and heart to a place I don't want them to inhabit.

Walking to the railing I let the wind blow my hair, caress my skin. The ocean waves rush to the shore, only to quickly retreat, taking bits of sand with them.

I shake my head realizing the parallel between the sand and my heart.

Stephen was my ocean, and he has taken bits of me with him.

Bits I'm not sure I'll ever retrieve.

Even with my back turned, I know he's on the veranda. His presence is as strong as the wind. Knowing he's there causes me to want to fall back into his arms, to the safe place he'd become for me.

But I'd never been his safe place. I was his redemption. His cure. His Leah remedy.

"I had to come." His voice cuts through the breeze. "I know what you think. And I'm sorry."

I can tell things are different. His apology settles into my heart. But the facts are still the same. Christmas music plays above us, the music a festive addition to this otherwise somber occasion.

He places his hands on the railing, his left pinky almost touching my right. I'm glad it isn't. His touch is hard to resist. I need all the help I can get.

Preparing my heart, I look to my right. Sighing inwardly at his deep blue eyes, I can't help but feel the connection between us. Like my eyes were meant to meet his and form a bond that can't be broken.

But it has been.

I won't be pitied anymore.

"So you admit I was right?" I ask.

His pinky brushes mine.

I feel it in my knees.

"I will only admit to one thing. Loving you. Nothing else."

Deciding against abruptly pulling my pinky away, I settle mine against his. "You couldn't protect Leah, and you can't protect me. I can't be the person who can absolve your past. I can't."

He shakes his head. "I see why you think that way. But I don't think that way. Yes, Leah was hurt on my watch, yes I tried to make it up to her by caring for her, but she wouldn't let me. She left."

I once again look into his eyes, praying that he's going to understand what I'm about to say. His hair lifts with the wind, showing off his angled, beautiful face. Still, I speak the words I must. "You said you can't have back what you gave Leah. I'm sorry she left you. But I need to be loved for me, not so you can prove you're able to protect and care for somebody. Somebody wounded."

He turns and leans against the railing, leaving me missing his small touch. "You need to love somebody because you believe they love you. Not because you need somebody to make you feel beautiful. And I'm that guy. I love you for you."

Oh, how I want to believe him, but questions still linger. "How do I know I'm not like a wounded bird you feel bound to care for?"

"Because you're not a wounded bird. You're strong. Talented. You were right. Leah wouldn't let me take care of her. There was a time I took responsibility for that situation. But I also learned from it. Only God can heal the wounded soul. Once I put Leah in His hands, I let it go. I promise you, I let it go."

I feel his truth in the air. It covers me with an assurance that we'll have tomorrow.

And the next day.

And the day after that.

He smiles. "Stay here. Don't move."

Pushing off the railing, he walks into the hotel. I breathe in, gathering my composure as best as I can. I nearly have enough gathered when he returns.

He has a package wrapped in pretty silver Christmas paper tied with a big red bow. "Merry Christmas and I love you."

I stare at the package, the rather large package, and wish I was in the mood to open Christmas presents. Spending all day sleeping trying to forget about Stephen and the fact that it is Christmas apparently was to no avail.

"Have you been here since this morning?" I ask.

"Open your package," he replies, which answers my question.

I tear the paper which threatens to fly away in the breeze, but Stephen catches it and crumbles it in his hands, the crumbled paper reflective of my Stephen-heart.

A black portfolio is my gift. I can't help but be a little disappointed. It's a very necessary item that I needed to buy, but it is very impersonal for the conversation we were having.

Maybe he just doesn't get it.

At all.

"Open it." One of my favorite things, his smile, warms my heart.

I do and gasp.

A beautiful picture of Ann wearing the wedding dress at her wedding graces the page. "How, where did you get this?" I ask.

"Turn the page."

The next two pages have the pictures I took of Ann at the pool wearing the dress.

I flip the page again and immediately recognize a picture I took of Ann wearing the shorts and top and carrying the beach bag on the boardwalk. I swallow hard, not believing what I'm seeing.

"I managed to squeeze in some time to put this together," he says. "This is a great designer with a great future."

I keep flipping the pages, amazed at how my designs look in print.

"Ann and Brett's wedding photographer was in on this and took a few pictures of her at the wedding for me. People will be impressed when they see the dress was already worn in a wedding. And wait until you get to the end."

Unable to absorb the generosity of this gift, I flip to the back. A big logo SunKissed! is creatively put into an ad format.

"Do you like it?" he asks.

I run the tips of my fingers over the logo. "I love it."

He folds the portfolio shut, sets it on a nearby table and tosses the paper into a trash can.

It seems like he's walking to me in slow motion, but I know it's only the filter of how I'm seeing him. Like my heart is again slowly becoming used to the idea of Stephen as an occupant.

He reaches for me. "You look very beautiful and classy."

"I do?" I smile at his words.

"Yes. Like royalty, like a princess."

My heart warms. "My father isn't a king."

"Yes He is. He is the King of Kings. And you will never feel less than the princess you are." He takes me in his arms, and I know he's going to kiss me. His lips capture mine but only for a moment because the next thing I know, he's on his knee with that gorgeous ring at the ready.

For the third time.

"Cheetah, will you marry me?"

"Yes." He slips the ring on my finger. "This is the third time we've been betrothed, you know."

"And it's the last." He stands, taking my hands in his. "Jenny, I don't know what I'd ever do without you, and now I know I'll never have to."

Our lips meet once again, filled with passion, love and truth, and I savor every second of our promise of tomorrow. When we part, I look at him, my handsome fiancé.

"I have your Christmas present in my room." I don't take my eyes off him.

"I already have my gift. Your promise to be my wife."

I brush his hair out of his eyes. "Merry Christmas, Stephen."

"Merry Christmas, Cheetah."

We meet again in a kiss that says forever.

BRIDE

WE PURPOSEFULLY arrive late to our engagement party. We have an agenda.

I'm wearing a dress I designed. Different from the one Ann wore, but beautiful and elegant nonetheless.

I scan the crowd and spot Katherine in the blue dress I picked out for her. Katherine who, after a Christmas Day engagement, now has a wedding date in June of next year. Looking further I see Phoebe in her cream-colored dress.

Perfect.

"Jenny!"

That voice can only belong to my mother. "Ready to meet your soon-to-be in-laws?" I ask Stephen.

"I am. Oh, and I forgot to tell you, the new bedroom suite is being delivered while we are on our honeymoon. No more sleeping in guest rooms."

I love this man who is about to become my husband. "New furniture for a new start."

I barely get the words out before my mom reaches me. I hug my mom and my dad extra long. It's been over a month since I've seen them. They cut their trip back a week to be here tonight. They wouldn't miss their only daughter's wedding.

Stephen receives the nod of approval from my dad, and I'm glad.

There's no turning back now.

Liza and William greet us. "Oh, Jenny, you're wearing the necklace I gave you. It's absolutely stunning on you."

I touch the beautiful blue necklace. "Thank you. I think we're about ready."

"Wait. I have a surprise for you, Cheetah."

Stephen grabs my hand and squeezes it. With his free hand he motions, like he's calling somebody over.

Dominick Redding walks out of the crowd.

"Stephen?" I look at him.

Before Stephen can answer Dominick hugs me. "Jenny. How beautiful you are tonight. Absolutely glowing! I have never seen you more radiant. Like your designs, which are magnificent." He points to my dress. "Your design as well?"

"It is. I can't believe you're here for my special day." Katherine must have told Dominick about the wedding.

Dominick smiles. "I'm happy to be here. You and I will talk when you come back from your honeymoon. Until then, ciao, my darling Jenny."

He hugs me again then shakes Stephen's hand. "Thank you, Stephen, for the invitation."

Stephen invited Dominick?

As Dominick walks away I turn to Stephen. "How—"

Cutting off my question, he brushes a kiss across my lips. "He was going to call you anyway. The invitation seemed like the natural thing to do."

I cannot wait for this man to become my husband.

We motion for Roger and Celine to come over as well as Katherine and Teresa, who will bring Phoebe.

"Ready for me to make the announcement?" Gary asks.

Stephen looks at me and I smile at him. "I'm so ready," I say.

"Let's do this thing, Cheetah."

"Wait," Gary says. "I have a surprise for you. Look."

He steps out from in front of a table. A computer sits on the table and a picture of a man is on the screen. The picture moves and I realize it's real.

"Your highness," Steven says, walking toward the table.

The king? King Jarvis?

"Stephen. I was informed of your upcoming nuptials and wanted to see them for myself."

Stephen laughs. "Not trusting word of mouth, huh? I don't blame you."

"I see in your face that you are very happy. I'm very glad. I wish you many happy years with your beautiful bride. You are welcome in Zaunesia anytime. Understand?"

"I understand."

"Good. You'll be receiving an invitation soon. My wayward Arabella has found her husband. I know now she was using you to try and make the lad jealous. It worked. She will be married in a few months. You and your bride will be our guests?"

Stephen looks at me. I shrug my shoulders and nod.

"Sure. We'll be there."

"Good. Good. Now go. Make that beautiful woman your bride."

"I will. Later, your highness."

Stephen walks over to me, and I truly feel beautiful.

"All right, Gare."

He kisses me, then I grab Phoebe's hand. Katherine, Phoebe, my father and I walk over to the entrance.

Gary silences the crowd. "Okay, folks. We thank everyone for coming to Stephen and Jenny's engagement party. But I'm afraid I have some news. It's not an engagement party."

A despaired groan murmurs through the crowd. Gary silences them again. "No, no engagement party. But it is a wedding. And you're all invited. If we could all clear to one side or another, we'll make an aisle Jenny can walk down."

The crowd cheers and separates, and I see Stephen at the other end of the room.

My love.

I watch Phoebe and Katherine walk hand in hand toward him. I hold on tight to my father.

"Ready?" he asks.

"I am."

We start walking and my gaze never leaves Stephen's.

I may be broke, but I'm rich in hope for my life with Stephen, with God, and knowing this man will think I'm beautiful for the rest of my life.

THE END

COMING NEXT

Rich in Faith

Book THREE of the *Richness in Faith* Trilogy

"And why do you worry about clothes? See how the lilies of the field grow.
They do not labor or spin."
Matthew 6:28
NKJV

MISTAKE

AS I STAND ON Peachtree Street in downtown Atlanta waiting for a cab to take me to the airport, I'm reminded of the night I lost my faith. At least that's what Mama would have called my lapse in judgment.

Losing my faith.

A muggy haze hangs over the evening, reminiscent of that long ago night. Paul Wentworth had been my boyfriend for awhile. He was also the richest guy in school, and when I envisioned our first time together, I thought it would happen in a grand place, like his parent's weekend lake house.

Or maybe an elegant hotel, like the Ritz at Lenox.

So imagine my disappointment when he pulled up to a motel on the outskirts of nowhere important.

More than ten years have passed, but it seems like nothing has changed.

My wealthy, attractive fiancé has dumped me for the heiress of a clothing company claiming he's finally found true love. Simply a coincidence that his break-up came shortly after dinner at my parent's house.

Trailer.

House trailer.

Now I, Shelby Madison, am left on the outskirts of nowhere important once again.

Alone.

Alone and more determined than ever not to let anyone in. Because it's too hard when they tell you they want out.

233

"WHAT DO YOU MEAN the position is filled? There must be a mistake. Barb Simmons said she had arranged everything." Unable to calm my racing heart, I stand in the foyer of the Hampton Cove mansion, my two suitcases flanking either side of me. My backpack straps cut into my shoulder while my overly large purse is about to break my forearm.

"I believe Ms. Simmons was misinformed regarding the position of housekeeper." The older, sturdy woman isn't mean. No, adamant is more like it. "I'm the housekeeper. And I intend to keep my position."

My purse slips off my forearm and plummets to the rug. "Ms.. . ?"

"*Mrs.* Stratton."

"*Mrs.* Stratton. Are you sure there hasn't been a mistake? Do you know Barb? Why would she let me sublet my Atlanta apartment for the summer if you had no intention of leaving your job?"

Mrs. Stratton shoves her hands inside the pockets of her gray, knee-length uniform. "The name Simmons sounds familiar. I believe Mr. and Mrs. Simmons are friends of Mr. Treyhune. But I haven't any idea why she would arrange for your trip here. Why don't you call and ask her?"

The events of the last couple of weeks have really worn on my brain. Of course I need to call Barb. "I'll will."

Before I can rummage through my purse which still sits on the rug, a scream fills the air. Startled, I look at Mrs. Stratton who simply rolls her eyes.

Then two flashes of small bodies with very long black hair rush across what appears to be a formal living room.

Another girl, this one in her twenties, enters the living room from the same direction the small girls did. But she doesn't follow their path. No, she walks towards Mrs. Stratton and me.

She has a purse slung over her shoulder and a frown on her face. She holds a key out toward Mrs. Stratton. "Here. Tell Mr. Treyhune I'm done. I can't work out my notice. It's not worth the money. That's how done I am."

Mrs. Stratton doesn't say anything, but she does take the key.

The girl who couldn't work her notice stares at me momentarily before taking in my luggage. She shakes her head. "If you're the new nanny, good luck is all I can say."

With those words, she passes by me, her sweet smelling perfume moving along with her.

After the door clicks shut I look at Mrs. Stratton. "The new nanny?"

She shakes her head. "The previous nanny left almost a month ago. Tracy was filling in until Mr. Treyhune could hire someone else. Maybe Mrs. Simmons arranged *that* position for you."

I shudder. "I doubt it. I don't have any experience taking care of a child. Let alone two."

"And they're a pair, all right."

As if they'd been summoned the girls fly back across the living room in the direction from which they had come a couple of minutes ago. They are still screaming.

Covering my ears I kind of hunch down. "Does that go on a lot?"

"Depends."

"On what?"

"On lots of things. If you want to stay I'll show you your room."

I uncover my ears then run my hand through my hair. "No. I don't want to stay. Can I talk to Mr. Treyhune?"

Mrs. Stratton chuckles. "You may. You can pull up a couch until he arrives home from work about nine o'clock this evening."

"Nine? That's late." Memories of my long days as CFO at Brady Engineering fill my mind. There were times I considered leaving at nine o'clock leaving early. Of course a lot of those times I was working closely with Dale. Dale Brady had started the company, hired me as the CFO and together we had built a nice business.

And a nice relationship. The fourth finger on my left hand is now void of the engagement ring he gave me.

Then took back.

I wonder if he'll give his new girlfriend a ring someday and if so, will it be the same ring?

I need a distraction from these thoughts that keep assailing me. Will Dale ever leave my brain? "I could go to Mr. Treyhune's office if you give me the address."

"He has several offices. One at each dealership. Treyhune Chevrolet, Treyhune Ford, Treyhune Dodge. Take your pick. Maybe you'll get lucky."

I steady my hand on my luggage handle. "Mr. Treyhune is *that*

Treyhune?"

Mrs. Stratton looks at me like I've grown two heads. "What do you mean by *that* Treyhune?"

"Please don't tell me he's the racing Treyhune. The one that won all the championships way back."

She shakes her head. "He's not that Treyhune."

My nerves steady. "Okay. Good."

"He's his son. Court."

I stand stunned. My dad would have a heart attack if he had an inkling his daughter was standing in the home of Court Treyhune. The fact that he couldn't ever live up to his father's racing greatness made him no less important in the eyes of the racing fans.

They still loved him.

According to the media what Court lacked in his inability to drive, he made up for in his looks and charitable doings. Great. "Court Treyhune. And these are his daughters?"

"They are. Bristol and Darling."

I laugh at the irony. "Race tracks." I point to myself. "I'm named after a car, myself. Shelby. Shelby Madison."

Mrs. Stratton cracks a smile for the first time in our conversation. "Nice to meet you, Shelby."

"His wife died a couple of years ago, didn't she?"

"Yes. I only knew her a short time before she passed away. I started working here when they moved in, but she didn't live long after the move. She was very sick."

I'm not telling Mrs. Stratton I feel like I know the Treyhunes. My dad is a huge fan, and I probably know way more about them than any sane person should. And half the stuff my dad told me, I tuned out. Like maybe the fact that Court Treyhune lived in Hampton Cove, Florida. "I'm sorry to hear that. I'm sure the girls miss their mother."

"They do. And now it looks like I'm not only the housekeeper but the nanny for the rest of the day."

I rummage through my purse and find my phone. Two o'clock. I could go and try to catch Court Treyhune at one of his offices. Or I could stay here until he comes home.

I hold my phone up. "I'm going to call my friend Barb and see what is going on."

"That sounds like a good idea." Mrs. Stratton's expression matches my thoughts.

I turn away as my phone connects to Barbs and starts ringing. It rings several times and I leave a message for her to call me back. As soon as I hang up, the two girls, who's screams had been silent for the last few minutes, come flying from the right once again. But this time they head straight for Mrs. Stratton.

Mrs. Stratton who almost falls as each girl grabs onto one leg. I reach out and steady the older lady. I notice the girl's faces are tear-streaked and they are identical. They're both sobbing, then one of them starts hitting the other one on the arm.

"Stop hitting me." The girl being hit pushes off of Mrs. Stratton and plops on the floor.

"You stop pulling my hair. Tracy left because of you." The other girl makes no move, continuing to cling tightly to the housekeeper.

The housekeeper who was obviously right about being the nanny for the rest of the day.

"She did not," the other girl counters. "She left 'cause you have a big mouth and won't be quiet."

I wonder which one is Darling. Although it really doesn't matter. They both seem 'too tough to tame,' the nickname for Darlington Motor Speedway.

And racing at Bristol Motor Speedway is like driving around inside a fishbowl, cars always wrecking. Are their names premonitions of their lives?

Crazy.

I know too much about a sport I dislike.

Silence hovers, and in looking down at the crumpled girls, I decide they've run out of steam. At least for a minute.

Maybe Mrs. Stratton will have a reprieve.

My phone vibrates and I see that it is Barb calling. I answer quickly.

"Barb. It's Shelby, hi. I'm at the Treyhune home, but there's some sort of mistake. I'm standing here with Mrs. Stratton. The housekeeper. Who has no intention of leaving her job. So, I'm confused as to why I'm here."

"Shell, sweets. So glad you made it. While I've got you on the phone I must tell you Rhea, the gal who sublet your place, loves it. She's thrilled with it. Okay, I'm at my desk, I know the information is here somewhere, bear with me a moment, sweets."

I can hear ruffling and shuffling going on as my body relaxes that knowing momentarily this mix-up will be solved. "I'm bearing."

"Ah. Here it is. I wrote it all down while I was talking to Court. Such a precious man. Single, too."

"Barb, please. I need a distraction from the male population."

"He'll distract you, all right. Sweets, here's all the info. Nanny needed for the summer. Gal gave two week notice. Come as soon as you can."

My relieved feeling swiftly tenses. "Barb. You told me housekeeper." I lower my voice to whisper status and move as far away from Mrs. Stratton and the twins as possible. "Remember? I needed to get away and do something totally different for a couple of months. Cleaning houses I can do. It's in my blood. Kids? No."

"Housekeeper, nanny. All the same. Domestic help, right?"

I'm surprised the phone doesn't shatter in my hand at the tight grip I have on it. "No, Barb. Not the same at all."

"Shells. You're a whiz at whatever you do. And you wanted a change of pace. I'm sure you can handle any position Court has for you. Need to run. Love."

"Love." My tone is flat as the phone is now silent.

I drop my phone in my purse and slowly turn. Mrs. Stratton is staring at me.

So are the two girls.

"Are you our new nanny?" The one who asks scoots closer to the other girl, like they are a team and a force to be reckoned with.

Even at their young age they know this.

I don't know if I am the one who can reckon with Team Twin.

But it appears I'm the one hired to do just that.

DISCUSSION QUESTIONS

1. Jenny thought improving her looks would give her security. Is there some tangible thing you have done that gave you security? Did you feel secure? Why or why not.

2. Jenny's heart is captured by a seven-year old girl. Is there a child or some person that has instantly captured your heart?

3. At the beginning of the story Jenny and Stephen see beauty differently. How do you think Jenny and Stephen learned from each other what true beauty is?

4. Stephen offers his home to the church to use for services. Have you ever attended a house church? If so, what did you like about it? If not, do you think you would like to try it sometime?

5. The lie Jenny told kept getting bigger and involving more people. Can you recall a time where you have been involved in a situation like that?

6. What would you do if you couldn't do the job you loved anymore?

7. Christmas is a season of hope. Can you recall a special Christmas memory?

8. Ann and Brett from Rich in Love are married in this book around Christmas. What do you think of Christmas weddings and Christmas birthdays?

9. Jenny realizes she is a princess in the eyes of God. Do you recall w you felt when you realized this?

10. What is your favorite scene and why?

Dear Reader,

What a blessing to be able to tell a story about the hope we have in Christ. I had fun writing this story with the backdrop of Christmas. God showed up in a way I could never put on paper. All I can say is, if you work with me, and remember those 3 days I spent crying at any given moment, those were the 3 days after I finished the book and realized how much God cares. He cares about every little thing in our lives. Don't ever forget it.

I'd like to say thank you to a few people. Hernando Nicholas, thank you for the info regarding schools in Florida. You are one special guy, whose smile and laughter brighten my day. Susan Norris, thank you for the insight of your teaching days and your story about colors. So inspiring-like you! Bekah Bratton, a huge thanks for meeting with me and showing me your designs and inspiring that part of Jenny's story. You are an amazing designer! Cathy West, your insight in everything writing is always helpful in every way.

A big thanks goes to Emily Sewell for editing this book. Your suggestions made the book stronger.

Critique partners Missy Tippens and Ciara Knight rock! You ladies keep me sane and guide me through all the crazy waters that come with this joy of writing. From quick turnaround read throughs to "help me" questions, I can't thank either of you enough. Ever. Just know I love and appreciate you.

Thanks to my mom, Jill Vaughan, for reading everything I write and giving your opinion. I love you!

My family is always supporting and amazing. Brenna, Chris, Alex, Sarah, Melanie, Jason, Ally B, Tyler, Lisa and Brian. You are my life! And we are getting ready to welcome baby Caleb. Another blessing!

To my husband, Lenny. I love life with you. I love you more every day. You show me true love at its finest.

Jesus Christ—my savior, my strength, my sustainer, my all in all. You give me love and hope and life.

ABOUT THE AUTHOR

Award winning and USA Today featured author Lindi Peterson lives in the foothills of the Blue Ridge Mountains with her husband, 1 dog, 3 cats and 3 birds. Lindi loves sharing life with her family and friends. Her passion for reading led her to writing. When God spoke words of love into her heart her life was forever changed. You can find Lindi at:

Lindipeterson.com
@lindipeterson
Thefaithgirls.com

Made in the USA
San Bernardino, CA
20 April 2017